## Harriet bounced from one bookshelf to the next, exclaiming in delight.

"What do you like to read, Harriet?" Brookes asked.

"Classics—like the fall of Troy in Homer's work. It's so heroic and romantic."

Brookes gazed deeply into her dark eyes. "Not all wars are heroic or romantic."

She colored under his gaze, staring at the floor. "I suppose that's true."

He had gone too far, lecturing like a stern schoolmaster. "I'm sorry." He studied her a bit longer, mesmerized by the pretty flush warming her cheeks. He attempted a lighter tone. "After being in battle, one realizes there is very little romance in war."

She looked up at him. "Someone should write a realistic novel about war."

Drowning in those eyes, he had to tear himself away. "I doubt anyone would read it." He cast a rueful grin her way.

After Harriet was gone, Brookes stood at the window. He was not easily flustered by anything, especially a pretty face. Rarely did anyone cause him to change his purpose or his mind.

But what if he had chosen the wrong sister?

## *LILY GEORGE*

Growing up in a small town in Texas, Lily George spent her summers devouring the books in her mother's Christian bookstore. She still counts Grace Livingston Hill, Janette Oke and L. M. Montgomery among her favorite authors. Lily has a BA in history from Southwestern University and uses her training as a historian to research her historical inspirational romance novels. She has published one nonfiction book and produced one documentary, and is in production on a second film; all of these projects reflect her love for old movies and jazz and blues music. Lily lives in the Dallas area with her husband, daughter and menagerie of animals.

# LILY GEORGE

# Captain of Her Heart

Love Inspired

Recycling programs for this product may not exist in your area.

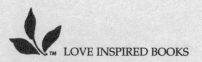

™ LOVE INSPIRED BOOKS

ISBN-13: 978-0-373-82906-4

CAPTAIN OF HER HEART
Copyright © 2012 by Sarah Baker

A FATHER'S SINS
Copyright © 2005 by Harlequin Books S.A.

www.LoveInspiredBooks.com

**Printed in U.S.A.**

Dear Reader,

In 2012, Love Inspired Books is proudly celebrating fifteen years of heartwarming inspirational romance! Love Inspired launched in September 1997 and successfully brought inspiration to series romance. From heartwarming contemporary romance to heart-stopping romantic suspense to adventurous historical romance, Love Inspired Books offers a variety of inspirational stories for every preference. And we deliver uplifting, wholesome and emotional romances that every generation can enjoy.

We're marking our fifteenth anniversary with a special theme month in Love Inspired Historical: *Family Ties*. Whether ready-made families or families in the making, these touching stories celebrate the ties that bind and prove why family matters. Because sometimes it takes a family to open one's heart to the possibility of love. With wonderful stories by favorite authors Linda Ford and Ruth Axtell Morren, an exciting new miniseries from Regina Scott and a tender tale by debut author Lily George, this month full of family-themed reads will warm your heart.

I hope you enjoy each and every story—and then come back next month for more of the most powerful, engaging stories of romance, adventure and faith set in times past. From rugged handsome cowboys of the West to proper English gentlemen in Regency England, let Love Inspired Historical sweep you away to a place where love is timeless.

Sincerely,

Tina James
Senior Editor

I'd like to thank my wonderful agent,
Mary Sue Seymour, who talked me down
off the proverbial ledge when all hope failed me.

To my critique group, who kindly and patiently
pointed out my many writing foibles and helped me
to become a stronger writer in the process.

To Melissa Endlich, my editor,
who brought me so much joy and hope.

To my pastor, who encouraged my writing, and
never forgot to check my progress every Sunday.

To my husband, who made sure I had time to write
and always encouraged me.

To my daughter, who is the reason I chose to write
inspirational books.

\* \* \*

I can do all things through Christ
who strengthens me.
—*Philippians* 4:13

# Chapter One

*Tansley Cottage*
*Tansley Village, Derbyshire*
*July 1816—the year without summer*

"What does the letter say, Mama?" Harriet ducked as her mother cast the missive aside, scattering sheets of paper around her bedroom. Alarm bells clanged in Harriet's mind. If it were good news, Mama wouldn't carry on so. Harriet gathered the foolscap sheets into a bundle, scrutinizing the bold handwriting scrawled across each page.

"They refuse to help us. Your father's own family. And what are we to do? What is left to us? I vow I am a prisoner in this dreadful cottage." Mama burst into angry tears.

How many times had Mama cried over the past year since Papa died? Harriet had long ago lost count. Their lives had gone from easy pleasantness to perpetual sorrow in just a few short months. Now—well, they had all poured their last hopes into assistance from Papa's family, and Mama's hysteria was frightening. 'Twas time to grasp control of the situation, and steady her mother's nerves.

With the expert precision borne of months of practice, Harriet flicked open the bottle of smelling salts on Mama's bedside table. The acrid smell filled the little chamber, causing her eyes and nose to burn.

"Here, Mama," Harriet murmured gently, trying to hold the vial under her nose. But Mama knocked it aside with a brusque gesture. Goodness, was it broken? Harriet scrambled after the bottle. No, but it had spilled. That was a waste they couldn't afford. Harriet sponged the solution with her handkerchief, wringing the cloth against the lip of the jar. She had to salvage as much of it as she could.

"Rose," she called to the family's faithful remaining servant, "could you please bring Mama some chamomile tea?" Sometimes the chamomile worked when the smelling salts didn't.

"Of course, dearie," Rose called back, banging the kettle in the kitchen below.

"Mama." Harriet placed the bottle back on the dressing table and sank onto the foot of her mother's creaky mahogany bed. "Even if the Handleys won't help us, I know Captain Brookes will. You know he has inherited the estate after his brother's death. He's a wealthy man now, and when Sophie marries him, I am sure he will see to our welfare."

"This whole situation is absurd." Mama lay back on her pillows, tears streaming down her cheeks. "I am Lady Handley, after all. I am no longer Cecile Varnay. I should need no one's assistance. I should have to depend on no one's sense of duty. Your father was wealthy beyond measure."

"Papa died bankrupt." The harsh words fell before Harriet thought them through, and she scrambled to lighten her tone. "Thanks to his vast library, I am an educated woman. But you know as well as I do, Mama, that we spent it all. On books or on jewels, it makes no difference now."

Mama turned on her side, away from Harriet. A brief knock on the door announced Rose's arrival with the tea tray.

"Here you go, my lady."

"I don't want it. Take it away." Mama buried her face in a lumpy pillow.

Harriet sighed. Usually the smelling salts or the chamomile tea did the trick, but this hysteria wouldn't back down. There was one last resort. She shrank from using it, because it cost so much, but there was nothing else that could be done. "Rose, if you please, go fetch Dr. Wallace. He can be here quickly if he's not out on another call."

"That's a good idea, dearie." Rose patted Harriet's shoulder and ran downstairs.

The floorboards squeaked in protest as Harriet paced the length of Mama's bedroom, seeking the solution to their problems. Mama's sobs had eased until she fell asleep, and that suited Harriet just fine. As she slept, Harriet racked her brain for a way out of their situation. They had to have money. Some other means of security than her sister's possible marriage. All of their possessions were gone. What was left? Harriet's head began to pound. There had to be a way they could survive. Harriet caught a glimpse of her reflection in the cracked mirror over Mama's vanity. Her face, drawn and pale, contrasted sharply with her eyes, which had darkened to an inky blue. Distracted, she tried to tuck a few of her dark brown locks back into their pins. She looked as disastrous as the situation she now faced.

A commotion sounded in the front entry. Relief washed over Harriet as she recognized a gruff, masculine voice that must belong to Dr. Wallace. She hurried down the stairs to meet him.

He strode into the tiny vestibule, dumping his black leather bag on the rickety bench at the foot of the stairs. Harriet steadied the bench and glanced at his wrinkled but kindly visage. "Oh, Doctor, thank you for coming. We don't know what to do with my mother—she took ill and finally cried herself to sleep."

He didn't spare her a glance, or any common courtesies. "Well, I'll have to awaken her to do a proper examination. What caused *this* outburst of hysteria?" he grumbled as he dug through his case, bringing forth a small vial.

"She received a letter that made her most upset." Hopefully that was enough explanation to satisfy him. She refrained from revealing the entire sordid tale.

With a curt nod, he hurried up the stairs.

Rose embraced Harriet, holding her as tenderly as a mother. "Come into the kitchen, dearie. We'll have a nice cup of tea." Drinking in Rose's steadfast strength, Harriet leaned on her, allowing the old servant to lead her away.

After an agonizing half hour, Dr. Wallace entered the kitchen, wiping his hands on his handkerchief. Harriet leaped from her chair. "Is…is she all right?"

He leaned against the doorframe and gave her a curt nod. "Sit down, Miss Handley. You look a bit peaked yourself."

Harriet complied, but grasped her teacup, hoping the movement would steady her hands.

The doctor peered at her from under his grizzled eyebrows. "I'll come straight to the point. Your mother is suffering from a bout of nervous hysteria." A deep frown creased the corners of his mouth. "Rest is the best thing for her at the moment. I've given her laudanum and I want you to administer more whenever the hysteria returns."

"Yes, Dr. Wallace. Is there anything else I can do?"

"If there could be a change in your mother's situation, it would be best. Something more like the style of living she knew. Are there any relatives who would take her in?" He folded his handkerchief and stuffed it back into his pocket.

"None that speak to us, sir."

The doctor was already turning to leave. "Too bad. It's her best chance. Work on that, my girl. And keep giving her the laudanum." He wagged a warning finger at her.

Harriet swallowed. She must improve Mama's situation. The Handleys wouldn't lift a hand to help, so 'twas up to her to make things right. Squaring her shoulders, she pronounced, "I shall persevere, Dr. Wallace."

Rose pushed Harriet out the door. "Go for a breath of fresh air, dearie. The doctor was right—you *do* look peaked. Ramble over to the millpond and back, there's a good girl."

She breathed deeply of the damp afternoon grasses, which smelled sweet as they dried in the pale afternoon sun. She meandered up the hill toward the pond, a large, flat oval that glinted in the sunshine. The moor grass tugged at her skirts, catching her hem, slowing her progress. Gazing out over the scrubby trees, Harriet paused for a moment, bowing her head in prayer.

*Dear Father, please show me the way. I don't know what to do. Help me find the answers.*

As a woman, her options were limited, but still, there had to be a way she could prevail. At one time, she thought she would become an authoress, but that idea died along with her father. He encouraged her writing, but Mama called it a dreadful waste of time. Could some sort of position be the answer to her prayers?

The bright jingle of a bridle pierced her reverie as a horse and rider approached. Harriet glanced over at the pair, as they crossed the field by the millpond, the black horse stamping easily through the tall grass. She frowned, her mind fixated upon her troubles. She was in no mood for politesse.

But wait—that man was familiar. He wore an army uniform with the same careless assurance that a dandy might wear an outrageous cravat. Her pulse skittered. Something was not right about his leg, though. His muscles didn't flex with the movements of his mount, yet his hands grasped the reins easily, as though he were born to the saddle.

She smoothed her hands over her wrinkled attire. Why hadn't she put on something more attractive than her lavender gown? Too many washdays had left the once-pretty dress worn and limp with age. She was perfectly attired for housekeeping, not for social graces.

The soldier reined in the horse and gazed down at her, a brief smile touching his lips. A faint scar zigzagged across his chin. She was gawping at his handsome yet rugged visage. Where were her manners? She shut her mouth with a snap.

Dismounting with care, he limped toward her, extending one gloved hand. "Miss Handley?"

"Sir?" Harriet bobbed a quick curtsy as she clasped his hand. Who was he?

"Don't you remember me? I am Captain Brookes."

"Oh!" Harriet gasped. Where was the dashing young lad who swept Sophie off her feet? Standing before her was a square-jawed man with a somber expression in his gray-green eyes. He had little in common with the wild youth she remembered. She picked up the pieces of her shattered composure. "I am so happy to see you home safe, Captain. My family will want to see you again. Have you been home long?"

"I settled in Tansley yesterday. I am home to set up house in Brookes Park and to clear up my brother's business affairs, but I haven't yet had time to make social calls."

"We were very sorry to hear of his passing, Captain." She dropped her gaze, staring in fascination at the burrs clinging to her skirt.

"Thank you." He offered his arm, and she allowed him to guide her back down the hill toward the cottage. He tucked the reins into his other hand, leading his black mount along beside them. Harriet slowed her steps to match his pace. Was he always this tall? Her head didn't even reach his shoulder. And his shoulders—were they always so broad? Being in the army made a boy into a man.

His touch burned through her sleeve. She needed a distraction, anything to curb her reactions to his presence and his touch. She cleared her throat. "I'm sure you saw a lot of Belgium, sir, what did you think of the country?"

"Not too much, I confess. Most of it was spent on horseback or slogging through the rain and mud. I spent some time at a home in Brussels."

"Brussels? The dispatches never mentioned that. I thought you remained at Waterloo."

"No, the surrounding villages were too crowded to contain all of the wounded, you know. The townspeople collected many of us who were injured." His eyes darkened to gray, and his lips stretched into a taut line.

"So, you didn't stay in a hospital?" The Handley girls were never privy to what happened after he was nearly killed at Waterloo.

"No, the hospital was full. I spent much of my time recuperating in the home of a Belgian merchant. I…I did not see much of the city, though…" His jaw tightened and he fell silent.

His brief tale had carried her away. Her fingers itched to write it all down. What a fascinating book it might make. Did his injuries cause the changes she observed in him, or his entire experience in the war? But asking such a question would be beyond rude. She had to find a more well-mannered response.

"How good of them to save you and your men." A feeble response, but a polite one. She stumbled on a rock in the path, and he gripped her, steadying her until she found her footing. A tingle zipped up her arm at the pressure of his gloved hand.

"Yes." The curtness of his reply signaled the end of the interview.

They meandered on in silence, over the rolling hills leading to the village. Birds twittered and flitted through the scrubby trees, and a cool breeze ruffled the moor grass. Brookes paused, gazing out over the vista. "I've missed this."

He had a wonderful voice with a dark and husky tone. But his responses were altogether too brief. Could she draw him out more? She smiled. "Beautiful, isn't it? There's nothing so pretty as a Derbyshire view. I come out here often. I feel closer to God out here."

"Closer to God?" He looked down at her, a harsh light kindled in his eyes.

"Yes. On the hilltop, it's easier to feel closer to Him, as though I can touch the sky."

He shrugged his shoulders. "I didn't know a view could inspire such reveries."

Was he mocking her? She must have sounded lonely, like an old maid with no one but seven cats to talk to. After all, Brookes certainly wasn't *her* confidant. Harriet gave herself a brisk mental shake.

They continued slowly down the hill. Harriet halted, regaining her sense of decorum as they neared the cottage door. "My sister is away from home this afternoon, Captain. She is visiting a friend in Riber. But if you would care to call tomorrow, she will be home."

"I shall be delighted to see all of your family. Until then?" He released her arm and touched his fingers to his brow in a brief salute.

"Until then, Captain." She bobbed a curtsy.

He led his horse to the mounting block in front of the cottage, levering himself into the saddle with ease. But then, she reminded herself, he had made a career in the saddle and would always ride well, wooden leg or no. He clicked his tongue and the horse sauntered off, switching its tail. Harriet gazed after him, aware that a brief niggle of jealousy was working its way down her spine. Sophie possessed beauty that caused strangers to turn and stare, and a graceful manner that inspired poets. Harriet never resented her little sister. On the contrary, Sophie's loveliness inspired pride. But now she held the heart of a man like Captain Brookes. Why, Sophie had everything—and she had nothing.

## Chapter Two

Brookes shifted in the saddle, breathing deeply of the damp grass as he headed home. The first hurdle lay behind him. The visit went much better than expected. Nervousness flowed away from him. No, indeed. In point of fact, he had enjoyed his conversation with Miss Harriet more than he'd first imagined.

Had she changed so much in the space of just a few years? Brookes remembered her as a spinster, a bluestocking, forever locked in her father's library. Sophie had captured his interest and later his heart with her bright beauty. Long golden ringlets, large blue eyes that twinkled with merriment, full rosy lips kissed with a dimple on each cheek—Sophie was the acknowledged beauty not only of the Handley family, but of Matlock Bath.

And yet…

An image of Harriet's dark blue eyes, fringed with sooty lashes, flashed across his mind. He could still smell her scent—violets, was it? And something else, purely feminine—mingled with the late summer breeze. Some women grew harder as the years passed, especially women who were forced to live in poverty. But Harriet had blossomed. Now, she was a truly lovely woman.

And she spoke intelligently, too. Hers was not the silly prattle that other young ladies might attempt, frivolous girls like—well, like Sophie. Harriet's conversation had spice to it—reminiscent of the gingerbread cookies that Cook used to make when he was a boy. When you devoured one, the ginger burned your tongue and made your eyes water a bit, but you couldn't resist eating another, and then another. Refreshing, that's what Harriet was.

He cleared his throat, which caused Talos to prick up his ears. It didn't matter a whit what Harriet had become in his absence. His thoughts lingered on her and he still discerned her violet scent simply because he had been away from women so long. That was all there was to it. He should concentrate solely on pretty Sophie, his intended. If his visit with Harriet foretold anything, it was that Sophie was as beautiful as ever. That was all he needed to focus on. He would see her tomorrow, and within a year, they would be wed.

Suddenly tomorrow couldn't come fast enough. Brookes kicked Talos into a canter, speeding toward the elaborate gates that marked his estate. He might ask Cook if she still had the family gingerbread recipe, and if she would bake a few. For old times' sake.

The next day, rain streamed from a leaden sky. Sophie, still clad in her chemise while dithering between two gowns, pounced on Harriet for the millionth time that morning.

"He'll never make it. Not in this weather. Oh, Harriet!"

"Stop, Sophie. A little rain won't deter a man like Brookes. He slogged through the mud at Waterloo, you know. A sprinkle won't keep him from you."

"Is Brookes still handsome? Did he say he missed me?"

"Silly goose, he couldn't have said that to me. But yes,

he is handsome. More so, I think. The war made him…"
Harriet cast about for the right word. "Distinguished."

"And…his leg?"

"He limps a little, but I did not discern any real change in
him. He still rides better than anyone in the county. If anything, Sophie dear, the war has improved him. He's not so
rowdy or childish anymore. He is a man now." Heat flamed
in her cheeks. She sounded too approving, betraying her
careful study of his character.

Sophie's eyes sparkled with mirth. "I am not used to
hearing praise about young men from *you*."

"So few young men deserve it." Harriet pursed her lips,
assuming a spinsterly manner to cover up for her earlier
warmth. "Now, for goodness' sake, go and finish dressing.
You must be ready for his arrival. I'll go sit with Mama
in her room, and make sure she is all right." With a gentle
shove, Harriet sent her sister back down the hallway to the
room they shared, then turned toward Mama's bedchamber.

Harriet knocked softly on the door, but Mama slept. She
leaned over and kissed her mother's smooth brow. Harriet
drew a chair close beside the bed and pulled out the shawl
she was knitting for the winter. Perhaps she should change
into a prettier dress, too? No, it was Sophie's afternoon to
shine. Captain Brookes would only have eyes for Sophie.

She glimpsed a movement out the window and spotted the captain picking slowly down the hill on his black
horse. She sprang from her chair, heart hammering like a
bird beating its wings against a cage. *Compose yourself,*
she scolded silently. Tiptoeing across the room, she slipped
through the doorway.

"Sophie? Sophie darling, he is here." She dared not raise
her voice, for fear of waking Mama.

Her sister collided with her at the top of the stairs. "You
meet him, open the door—I can't!" Sophie whispered

fiercely. She stayed rooted on the landing, out of sight of the entry hall.

Harriet inhaled deeply to calm her nerves, but still jerked the door open with a lightning-fast motion. Captain Brookes, hand poised to knock on the door, fell back a step in astonishment. "C-Come in, Captain," Harriet stammered.

He wore a heavy greatcoat that emphasized his broad shoulders, his Hessians still polished to a gleam even after the long ride from Brookes Park. Harriet opened the door wider, casting a tentative smile his way when he crossed the threshold. He stood in the hall, raindrops rolling down in rivulets from the brim of his hat, and gazed up. Sophie stood on the landing. How beautiful Sophie was, her lovely curls tucked up and glowing like a burnished cloud of gold in the dim hallway light. But when Sophie's gaze fell on Captain Brookes, the color drained from her face. Two bright red patches glowed on her cheeks.

Why was Sophie behaving so strangely? Why did she stand so still on the landing? She must be in shock—of course, that was the only answer. To cover for Sophie, Harriet sprang into social action. "Please, Captain," she burst out, in a voice a shade too loud. "Let me have your hat and coat. I'll spread them out so they can dry by the fire."

Captain Brookes, rooted in place beside the door, started at the sound of Harriet's voice and tore his gaze away from Sophie. He allowed Harriet to guide him into the parlor, where a fire burned brightly.

"Sophie dear, tell Rose we will take some tea," she called, in that same unnatural tone. She spread his coat over a chair and laid his hat on the warm hearth to dry. "It's the shock, you understand," Harriet whispered to him urgently. "Until we received the word that you had survived, she thought you were dead. She must feel like she is seeing a ghost."

Captain Brookes graced her with a solemn expression.

She too had met him yesterday, but her reaction was very different. At the memory, her cheeks grew warm, and she dropped her gaze to the floor.

"Yes." His tone was frosty. "I am sure it is a great shock."

Harriet ushered him to one of the chairs near the fire, a spindly one included with the original cottage furnishings. He sat, his tall frame dwarfing the chair. Sophie entered with Rose and the tea service, but her face still had the stunned expression of one recently slapped. Harriet drew a table near the fire and helped Rose and Sophie with the teapot and cups. Those few rapid domestic chores jolted Sophie out of her trance. She even managed a pale smile for the captain.

The little mantel clock chimed the quarter hour, and Harriet peeked at it in startled confusion. Surely an hour had passed already? Carrying the social niceties was exhausting. For the fifteen minutes since his arrival, Sophie refused to speak to the captain. Harriet was primed to cheerfully throttle her baby sister the moment he left. She took a small sip of tea. It tasted bitter, like stewed dandelion leaves, and a wave of nausea hit her.

Despite the tense atmosphere, Brookes responded to her stilted questions and followed the social rites like any good soldier would when confronted with a changed situation. Harriet burned with shame. When the clock chimed the half hour, he rose from his chair, nodding briefly at Sophie. Harriet helped him gather his greatcoat and hat, and showed him to the door, leaving Sophie sitting like a graceful wooden statue on the settee.

"Please, Captain." She grabbed him, ignoring the tingle that ran through her fingers when she clasped his muscled forearm. "Forgive my sister. I am sure it is the shock of seeing you again that has affected her so. I beg you, please call again soon. Sophie will rally, of that I am sure."

"Please do not distress yourself, Miss Handley." He put

on his hat with careless assurance. "I had a pleasant afternoon and am most happy to see your family again. I shall be delighted to call on you soon." He closed the door behind him with a decisive click.

Harriet grasped the cool brass doorknob for a moment, her head bowed. What a bitter reception Sophie offered the captain. He deserved better. A lump formed in her throat when she pictured him riding out into the rain, returning to his lonely home. How humiliated and angry he must be. She longed to run after him, and beg his forgiveness on Sophie's behalf. She closed her eyes, praying for strength. Then she lifted her head and trudged back to the parlor. Assuming her best "elder sister" expression, she prepared to take Sophie to task.

Sophie raised her tearstained face when Harriet entered. Her beautiful curls were no longer tucked up neatly, but instead cascaded down her back, giving her the look of a Botticellian angel. She twisted her handkerchief in her hands. "Oh, Hattie," she whispered. "He's changed so much…" Her voice broke and she wept anew. "Sister, I don't love him. I don't love John Brookes."

She glanced at the spindly chair that Captain Brookes had occupied earlier. It looked so insubstantial without his tall frame pressing it into the rug.

"Oh, Hattie, he is not the man I remembered. He is so strange."

"Sophie, he went to war. He was dreadfully wounded and lost his leg. Surely you expected some change?" Harriet sat on the settee beside Sophie, drawing her sister's head down on her shoulder.

"But oh, Hattie! He used to be so wild, so dashing. And now…his hair is gray!" With that, Sophie pushed Harriet away and draped herself over the opposite end of the sofa, weeping in earnest.

Harriet laughed at her sister's dramatic display. "He has

a few gray streaks here and there, but I vow you make him sound like Father Time."

"Don't laugh at me! Of course you can feel coolly about it. He wasn't your young man." Sophie balled up her handkerchief and flung it at Harriet.

"True." Harriet looked daggers at her sister, not caring to discuss her spinsterly state.

Sophie raised her head. "True," she echoed. "But you handled him very well, didn't you? Since you are comfortable with him, you can help me. From now on, when John comes to call, you must entertain him."

"But he will be coming to see you." Harriet flushed deeply. The thought of spending hours in Brookes's company was too enticing to even consider.

"Oh, please, Hattie, be a darling. Can't you see? If you are sociable to him, no one will think anything of it, because we're sisters. And it will give me time to get used to him. Perhaps I can fall in love with him again."

Harriet winced. She would agree to help Sophie, but not out of sisterly loyalty. She dared not admit her thoughts, even to herself. But a small, insistent voice piped up, refusing to be shushed.

*You would enjoy spending more time with the captain, wouldn't you?*

# Chapter Three

*W*ounded men moaned on every side of him. He struggled to sit up and fell from weakness. His hands sank into the mire, catching his weight. Sophie's lock of hair still clung to his right palm. Brookes tried to pray but his brain refused to form any words. God wouldn't save him. No one else would, either, unless he made it through the night. Wellington himself ordered that no man be carried off the field until daybreak.

A bark of laughter filled the air. Brookes raised his head enough to see. Two soldiers—Prussians, by their uniforms—looted the dead and finished off the dying. "Kurpi! Kurpi!" whispered one urgently, while the other removed the dead soldier's boot. "Ja! Ja!" He held up a miniature portrait in triumph, flipped it in the air like a coin, and then stuffed it in his pocket.

They moved through the corpses, picking them clean like vultures after carrion, stabbing through the wounded with expert precision, then looting them as well. By the sound of their voices, they were less than two yards away. It was only a matter of time until they found him—

Brookes jerked to awareness, bathed in cold sweat. Had he screamed out loud? He grasped around under the settee until he found what he sought. There it was—the decanter of brandy and an empty glass. He poured a tall measure with shaking hands. He was grateful that Stoames agreed to return to Brookes Hall with him after the war. Stoames was the one who set up his sofa so Brookes could sleep sitting bolt upright near the fire, and thoughtfully placed the brandy decanter within close range. Good man. He deserved a raise in pay.

On cue, his batman emerged from Brookes's dressing room, where he slept on a cot. "Everything all right, Captain? Thought I heard something."

"I was pouring myself a drink. Care to join me?"

"Don't mind if I do." He ducked back into the dressing room and brought out his shaving mug. "A short one." He politely held out the cup.

They drank in silence for a moment.

"Dream?" Stoames asked shortly.

"Yes. Same one. The looters. Before you found me, and stopped them."

They drank again, staring at the fire.

Stoames sighed. "Let's talk of something else. Your visit to Miss Sophie—how did you fare? Is she as beautiful as ever?"

Brookes hesitated. He refused to think about Sophie since returning from his disastrous visit to Tansley Cottage. But now, prompted by Stoames's question, he tried to wrap his mind around her reaction. Among other soldiers, his wooden leg wasn't even worthy of comment—a sharp contrast to the blank expression of horror in Sophie's eyes. For the first time it dawned on him that a young and pretty woman might find him unattractive, repulsive even. "She is lovely as ever, but I think she found me sorely altered."

"Surely she expected some change in you. After all, you went to war."

"I don't think many people can comprehend what happened, unless they were there." Brookes swirled the brandy around in his glass. If he wanted to capture Sophie's attention again, he needed to prove the changes the war wrought were merely superficial. That meant proving himself as lively and charismatic as he had been before he left for the peninsula—but was he? Pondering this, his thoughts drifted to Harriet, and he surprised himself by adding, "Her sister was looking well." Not that it mattered, of course. Only Sophie's opinion of him counted, since she would be his wife some day.

"Miss Harriet?" The edge of Stoames's voice was sharp as a saber's edge.

"Yes. She seemed…" He paused for a moment, searching for the elusive words. "She took the changes in stride."

"Ah, well," replied Stoames. "I've only seen the two lasses on occasion, but from what I recall, Miss Harriet was a steady girl. Quiet like. Not like Miss Sophie at all."

"No." Brookes stared into his brandy. "Not like Miss Sophie at all."

Sophie and Harriet put their plan in action the next day, in the event that the captain called later in the afternoon. After luncheon, Sophie hitched the family's one faithful nag, Esther, to the gig and drove off to call on Mary in Riber. As the gig beat a squeaky retreat, Harriet took her few remaining books outside, to read until the captain came to call. One had to take advantage of the brief break in the rain for a bit of fresh air.

Harriet's mouth went dry as she watched Captain Brookes approach. With shaking hands, she picked up a book from the stack at her feet. She forced herself to gaze at the pages, even though the words blurred into a single black line. When it was polite to look up, she saw the captain dismounting with care, and striding toward her.

"Captain Brookes, so happy to see you again."

"Miss Handley." He bowed over her extended hand.

"You find me alone this afternoon, Captain. Sophie is in Riber, and my mother is resting."

"I don't wish to intrude upon your solitude," he replied stiffly, waving a hand at her stack of books.

"Oh, no, Captain, join me. It's a pleasure to have conversation. Mama says I read far too many books."

"So I see." He stooped and picked up a volume. "Homer? You read the classics?"

She smiled. "I read anything I can get my hands on. These are a few I managed to salvage from Papa's library... before we lost it all."

He looked at her sharply. "I have a library at Brookes Park. Not grand like your father's, but you are welcome to it."

Harriet leaped out of her chair. "Can we go right now?"

For the first time since his return, Harriet saw Captain Brookes smile. It changed his whole expression, causing a tingle of awareness to flash through her being. Then she grinned in entreaty. "Please, Captain?"

"Of course. Get your horse and we will ride over together."

"Oh!" Harriet's excitement deflated. "Sophie took our horse to Riber. We only have the one."

"Then we'll walk." He offered her the crook of his arm.

Harriet glanced down at his leg, then up at the grey sky. It looked like rain at any moment. She couldn't ask him to walk that distance, especially in a downpour.

She swallowed her disappointment and shook her head. "I shall claim the horse for tomorrow and ride over when the weather is fine."

"The weather is never fine. I vow I have never seen such a chilly and wet summer. I have a better idea." He smiled down again and Harriet's heart leaped with joy. "We'll ride together on Talos."

"Together? How on earth?"

"You can ride pillion. Surely you've seen it, if your father had any medieval manuscripts." Then he added, with a soldier's air of authority, "It is the most sensible solution."

Harriet nodded reluctantly. "How do we manage it?"

"I'll get on first. Then you can put your foot on mine and swing yourself up behind me."

Harriet swallowed. "All right." She made a mental apology to her mother and Sophie, who would be horrified if they ever found out. When Captain Brookes was settled, she placed her foot on his in the stirrup and he tossed her up behind the saddle. Riding astride left nothing to the imagination, she realized in embarrassment. Her skirt hitched up much too high.

"Ready?" he called over his shoulder.

"Y-yes," Harriet stammered. He wheeled Talos around and started back up the hill.

Harriet's cheeks flamed. She leaned forward a little, against the taught smoothness of his back. Though she was precariously perched on Talos, Harriet was cherished and safe, like Mama's jewels nestled in their leather boxes at Handley Hall. She closed her eyes, relishing the security that radiated from Brookes's broad shoulders. Mercifully, he could not see the expression on her face.

A light rain began falling. "Hold on tight. I'm going to speed him up so we can get out of this wretched weather," Brookes called.

Obediently, Harriet tightened her hold on his waist and squeezed her legs around Talos's flanks. Her heart fluttered wildly in her chest. She must stop any nonsense right away. Any affection she felt was simply because she had never been this close to any man. He was her sister's intended, after all. Remorse washed over her, and a heaviness settled in the pit of her stomach. Once, when she was a little girl, she had taken one of Sophie's hair ribbons without asking, and then lost it when she was riding. The mortification she felt long ago was nothing compared to her shame today. A hair ribbon could be replaced. A man such as Brookes—well, he was one of a kind.

Harriet bounced from one shelf to the next, exclaiming in delight. Brookes watched her closely, folding his arms over his chest. This room, so isolated and lonely before her arrival, now burst with vivid life. Harriet had completely ignored the sumptuous tea tray pulled near the fire. Apparently, tea meant little when she was faced with stacks upon stacks of books.

"I have never seen you so animated." Brookes chuckled.

"You have hardly seen me at all." She laughed.

As their gazes locked, a need to make her happy suffused him. Her smile intrigued him most—he wanted to see it again. "You can borrow them all, if you want." A mischievousness threaded through his voice, designed to provoke a response.

"Oh, Captain, thank you!" Unshed tears filled her eyes. "Truly, you have no idea how happy you've made me."

"Think nothing of it. Come have some tea." He unfolded himself from his deep leather chair and pulled a velvet wingback closer to the fire. "What do you like to read, Miss Handley?"

"Please call me Harriet. Miss Handley sounds ridiculously formal." She sat gracefully.

"Very well, then, Harriet. What do you like to read?"

"Anything I can," she replied. "Before Papa lost his library, I had so many to choose from. It was his weakness, you know, collecting books. It led to our downfall, I'm afraid. I gravitate toward the classics. I salvaged the few you saw today. They are my old friends."

"Homer? What do you like about his works?"

*"Wherefore I wail alike for thee and for my hapless*

*self at grief at heart, for no longer have I anyone beside in broad Troy that is gentle to me or kind, but all men shudder at me,'"* Harriet quoted promptly. "Helen, Paris, the fall of Troy—it's all so heroic and romantic."

Brookes gazed deeply into her dark eyes. "Not all wars are heroic or romantic. After all, thousands of innocent people were slaughtered because of Helen's fickleness and her beauty."

She colored under his gaze, staring at the floor. "I suppose that's true," she said quietly.

He had gone too far, blundering and lecturing like a stern schoolmaster. "I'm sorry," he muttered.

"No, I am the one who should apologize."

"Not at all." He studied her a bit longer, mesmerized by the pretty flush warming her cheeks. He attempted a lighter tone. "After being in battle, one realizes there is very little romance in war."

"I'm sure." She looked up at him, her eyes darkening to a deep, fathomless blue. "Someone should write a realistic novel about war."

Drowning in those dark eyes, he had to tear himself away. "I doubt anyone would read it." He cast a rueful grin her way. They sat together in silence, which was broken only by the chime of the mantel clock.

"I should be going. Mama will be wondering where I am." She stood and brushed off her skirts with a practical air.

"Let me order my carriage," Brookes replied, and pulled the bell pull. "It's raining in earnest. Do take a few books home." She selected a volume of John Donne, he noted. He would read the book when she returned it.

"This should keep me occupied." She smiled again, and a warm glow flowed through him.

"Come back whenever you wish." Then, remembering his manners, he added, "Bring your sister, too."

Her smile faded. She was all business and practicality again. "Of course. Thank you for a lovely afternoon."

The carriage was ready; in an instant, Harriet was gone. Brookes stood at the window, mulling over his daily obligations. His afternoon was completely wasted. He was late to see his mill manager, and he needed to speak with his steward about this spring's crops. But it was worth it. He hadn't enjoyed himself this much in years.

He prided himself on his reputation as a career soldier, not easily flustered by anything, especially a pretty face. Rarely did anyone cause him to change his purpose or his mind. But the trained tactician in him sensed a problem.

What if he had chosen the wrong sister?

## Chapter Four

Harriet stabbed her spade savagely into the dirt. She reached into the moist earth and tugged, pulling out a small potato. Shaking the dirt off the vegetable, she tossed it into the basket by her feet. She promised to help Sophie, but she found herself in dangerous territory. If only she could dig out her devotion to Brookes as easily as she dug out roots here in the family garden.

Harriet shifted from kneeling to squatting back on her heels. Falling in love with Brookes simply was not allowed. Ridiculous, too. After all, he was the first young man that she had come into close contact with. That was the reason for the attraction, and nothing more. Her visit to his library, and the warm companionship that had settled between them bespoke nothing more than a friendly acquaintanceship. So just like a spinster perilously near to the shelf, she attached too much significance to her visit. He provided her with the first challenging conversation she shared in ages—that was all.

She needed a plan. If there were some way she could keep her promise to Sophie while keeping the captain at arm's length, she could protect her own heart. A strictly platonic arrangement, one that would allow her to enjoy

Captain Brookes's companionship, but kept any romantic nonsense at bay. What could she do?

"Hattie? Where are you?" Sophie called from the kitchen window.

"Garden," Harriet hollered back. Sophie's blonde head disappeared from between the curtains. She popped around the corner of the cottage, picking her way across the muddy garden rows.

"Oh, good. You're alone. Where's Rose?"

"She's in the village, doing the marketing. Help me, I am digging potatoes. Rose thought we could boil and mash them for our supper." She handed Sophie her spade, but her sister remained standing.

"Hattie, I am worried about Mama."

Harriet sighed. She slanted her gaze up at Sophie. "I am worried about her, too. But what in particular is causing your alarm?"

"I don't think the laudanum is helping. Or rather, it's helping too well. Mama sleeps all day long, and all night, too. It can't be good for her. Perhaps she should call on old friends, or go back to Matlock Bath for a day to see home again…"

"Sophie, if Mama were to see someone else living in our home in Matlock Bath, it would kill her. And none of her old friends will see us anymore, not since Papa lost his fortune." Harriet grabbed the spade away from Sophie's useless hands and began digging again.

"Still, there must be something we can do."

"Dr. Wallace did say that a change in her situation might help. But you know none of the family will have her." Harriet sat back on her heels and tossed another potato into the basket. "I will think of something, Sophie. Don't fret. I am sure there is a way to help Mama."

"I know you'll find a way, Hattie. That's why I always

come to you." Sophie patted Harriet's shoulder. "I'll go look in on Mama."

Harriet gazed after her sister's graceful back as Sophie wove her way across the garden. She stripped off her gloves, slapping them against her knee. The damp earth smelled sweet where she had been digging, and it calmed her jangled nerves. Time to think clearly.

She had three problems now: her infatuation with Captain Brookes, her promise to Sophie and her need to help Mama. Surely she could find a way to solve all three at once. Harriet's mind flashed back to the day they lost their home. Her own copybooks were burning. Flames licked the pages, and every now and then, a single word flared up from the page while the paper was consumed. While the duns combed through Handley Hall, she fed the fire in the great hall with her manuscripts, watching every single one smolder in the hearth. Writing about nonexistent people seemed such an extravagant waste of time, when one's own world was collapsing.

But what about now? Women could write books and sell them for money, could they not? And she wouldn't have to leave home to seek work if she became an authoress, would she?

She rose, dusting the dirt from her backside.

She had the solution.

Picking up her skirts, she dashed from the garden. Her solution would only work if she had Brookes's help.

Brookes's eyes glazed over as he stared at the ledgers piled in front of him. Henry kept meticulous records, in a tiny and cramped script that left Brookes cross-eyed after hours of reading. He spent the morning studying the mill's profitability. After examining the ledgers closely, he decided to look at making adjustments to the spinning mules. A few tweaks here and there could save valuable time and labor.

He resolved to formulate a plan with the mill manager for increasing the mill's profits and saving labor. He needed to prove himself as twice the man he had been before the war, as though gaining more wealth from the mill could make up for his lost leg. Maybe it would impress Sophie, anyway.

The door to the library swung open, and his butler, Bunting, entered, his eyebrows raised to his hairline. "Miss Handley to see you, Captain."

"S-Sophie?" he stammered in bewilderment. Had she come to make amends or offer some explanation of her standoffish behavior? Her rejection stung more than he cared to admit.

"No. Miss Harriet Handley." Bunting opened the door wider, and motioned Harriet into the room. A look of astonishment was still pasted to his usually blank countenance.

A rush of pleasure suffused Brookes. An afternoon spent in Harriet's company was preferable to proving himself anew to Sophie. But his happiness faded when he spied her. No wonder Bunting was dumbfounded. She looked positively untidy, with her rumpled gown and none-too-clean apron. He rose from the desk and grabbed her hands. "Whatever's the matter?"

She dropped his hands as though they were on fire. "I have a proposition for you, Captain."

The most adorable streak of dirt bisected her cheek. Against his better judgment, he reached up to rub it with his thumb. "Proposition?" he echoed.

"Oh, sorry." She laughed ruefully, scrubbing her cheek with the corner of her apron. "Yes. Or a business deal. Whatever term you like."

A tug of his old mischievousness pulled at his insides. He liked the sound of *proposition.* "Tell me."

"I want to write with you."

His hope deflated. Well, after all, what had he expected her to say? That she wanted to court him? He motioned her to the settee, and sat down across from her. "I don't understand you. What do you mean? Do you want to write a book?"

"Yes. Remember how we spoke about the need for realistic books about the war? Well, I want to write one. And I want your help so I can do it well."

Her words cast him into unfamiliar territory, so he fell back on his soldier's training. He peered at her, trying to assess her thoughts. Did she really want to write his memoirs? The thought of sharing what he had suffered made Brookes recoil. His palms began to sweat.

"I've always wanted to be an authoress. In fact I wrote a few books before Papa died. But I want to try it again. I want to write something and sell it. For money."

He quirked the corner of his lip in amusement at her unnecessary afterthought. Then he directed his attention back to her scheme. He shook his head, attempting to clear his thoughts. "Why write anything new? Why not try to publish what you already have?"

She looked away, blushing. "I don't have it anymore."

"Why do you need me?" His words held an edge. While he liked the idea that Harriet might need him, was she merely using him for her own gain?

"I thought we could be a team. An equal partnership. I will write, and you supply the facts."

In the army, he had been carefully schooled never to show weakness. He did not forget that training now.

"I can see how I can help you. And it's not that I don't want to assist you. But if you'll forgive me—how does this help me? Aren't most partnerships mutually beneficial?"

"Um…" She bit her lip, looking at a complete loss. "It might help you to talk about the war."

That was the last thing he wanted to do. He shook his head. "I may not want to."

"You'd only have to talk about what you want, or verify

facts, I promise. And—" she stared at him beseechingly "—if we worked at Tansley Cottage, you could see Sophie more often."

Brookes turned away. Could he really talk about the war? His ghastly experiences might shock this slip of a girl. He wanted to help her, but his memories of the war still bled like open wounds. He had no desire to take off his bandages and show the gashes to Harriet.

A compromise was in order. He sighed and turned back, staring deeply into her pale face. "My answer is yes, on two conditions."

"Name them."

"First, you speak with Stoames, as well. He served as my batman and he is a walking military encyclopedia. He knows a great deal more about the war than I do. Any details beyond what Stoames can supply, I will endeavor to help."

"Agreed."

"Second, we work here at Brookes Park. I get very busy and may need to beg off at a moment's notice. There's more room to work here, too." It was safer, too. He liked the security of his own four walls, his own familiar territory.

She nodded, but a shadow of uncertainty crossed her face. "All right."

What had he done? Brookes swallowed nervously. He needed to get away from her, and get back onto sure footing. "I'll fetch Stoames, and we will explain the plan to him."

"I would love to." She dazzled him with the brightness of her smile.

He loved that smile. Remembering her weakness, he added, "Feel free to choose a book or two while I am gone."

The blood pounded in Harriet's temples. Pressing her hands together, she forced herself to stop trembling.

Now she might see him often, to keep her vow to Sophie,

but the arrangement was strictly business. And she would write a book, and possibly save her little family in the process. Harriet gulped several lungfuls of air. Her composure returned, and her hands ceased shaking. She gazed down at her lap, startled to see she still wore her dirty gardening apron.

She looked a perfect sight. No wonder he seemed so shocked by her proposal. Sophie would never visit anyone looking less than flawless. Even in poverty, Sophie still managed an elegance that Harriet could never attain. But then, she sought his advice on a business matter and did not make a social call. He was Sophie's intended and not her young man. So who cared what she looked like?

Harriet shut off her thoughts with a snap. She gazed around the library, taking in the floor to ceiling shelves crammed with volumes bound in red and brown Moroccan leather. Brookes's offer of a new book tempted her, but she was too indebted to him already. She'd stayed awake until the wee small hours of the morning reading the volume of John Donne she borrowed the day before. She wanted to reread the book, savoring Donne's words again before returning it. Still, it would do no harm to look over the vast selection, and make a mental note of which books to borrow next time. She rose from the settee and studied the shelf in front of her, arms clasped behind her back.

Footsteps echoed in the hall, and the library door swung open. A man strode into the room, followed by Brookes. He looked about a decade older than the captain, his features roughened by long exposure to the weather and hard living. But his brown eyes held a kindly twinkle that put Harriet at ease.

"Miss Handley, allow me to present Matthew Stoames, my batman. I believe you met him once or twice before the war."

"Mr. Stoames, it's been so long I hardly remember the occasion. How do you do?" Harriet bobbed a little curtsy.

"Very well, Miss. Though you may call me Stoames. Everyone else does. Don't know what I would do if someone kept calling me Mister." He swept a courtly bow in her direction.

"Miss Handley is writing a book about the war and requires our assistance. I told her that you were the best military authority she could hope for." Brookes leaned against his desk, his arms crossed over his chest.

"I'll be happy to help the young lady whenever she wishes." Stoames nodded at Harriet.

Harriet flashed a grateful smile in return. "I really must be going, but I would like to start work this week. Is that all right?" The sooner the better. After all, if she finished quickly, she might provide Mama with a comfortable living in the space of a year or so.

"Yes, but if we work on Friday, we'll have to finish quickly. The village is having the Blessing of the Wells."

Harriet had completely forgotten the village fete. "Will we have time to work, then?"

"Of course. Come over later in the morning, and we will be done in time for the well blessing and afternoon tea." Brookes cast a glance over his shoulder at the window. "The clouds are gathering again. I am sure it will rain soon. Let me call my carriage for you."

Another kindness she might never repay. "No, I am happy to walk. The cottage is only a quarter of an hour from here, and I love the exercise. Until Friday, then, gentlemen." Her voice squeaked a little, betraying her nerves. She quit the library with a speed usually reserved for one being chased by yapping hounds.

She didn't cease her sprint until she reached the crest of the hill that looked over home.

*I did it. It's over. He said yes!*

# Chapter Five

Harriet handed her precious few coins to the shopkeeper.

"Thank you, Miss. Can I get anything else for you?"

"Oh, no. This is all I need." Harriet tucked the parcel under her arm.

"Very good. Don't forget now, we're having the Blessing of the Wells later on this morning, to be followed by a cream tea at the village hall. Please come, and bring a friend."

Harriet smiled warmly in reply. "This will be my first time to attend the event. My family came here shortly after the ceremony last year. I must confess I am intrigued. Such a funny custom, don't you think?"

"Oh, it's a tradition in Tansley. We do it to give thanks to God for the many hot springs that run through our village. They bring us our good health."

Harriet glowed in the warmth of human interaction. The buzz of activity in the little country store mounted as villagers dropped by to do their weekly marketing. She thoroughly enjoyed the chance to talk to someone outside of her tight-knit family circle, but the shopkeeper was busy and had other customers to attend to. "I shall be there. I cannot wait." She turned to leave, halting when she spied a line of soldiers on horseback creating a commotion in the middle of the street.

"What on earth?" Harriet turned back to the friendly shopkeeper. "Who are those soldiers?"

"A regiment of cavalry officers. From what I hear, they will be summering near Tansley."

"I see." Harriet reached for the doorknob. "Good day."

"Good day, Miss."

Harriet left the store, inhaling the aroma of fresh paper and ink that wafted up from her paper packet. The paper smelled fresh and crisp, like newly felled trees. The ink had a sour, tangy scent. The two odors excited Harriet, reminding her of late-night sessions spent writing by candlelight, trying to get to the heart and the soul of the stories that ran constantly through her mind. Her fingers practically itched to take up the pen right then and there. Hugging the parcel a little closer to her chest, she quickened her pace. Harriet crossed past Tansley Cottage, trudging up the hill toward Brookes Park. She hastened her steps, afraid she lingered too long and ran late for her appointment with the captain.

The imposing gates of Brookes Hall loomed up ahead. Those gates enforced dignity and majesty onto the scrubby hill. Harriet swallowed her nerves as she hurried past. The meticulous and handsome nature of Brookes Hall struck her nerves, setting them on edge. The house, made of gray stone, grew darker with every passing year, lending the estate an air of weathered distinction. The counterpanes faced the courtyard squarely, needing no shutters, framed with no curtains. This house had nothing to conceal.

The pale sun rose higher in the sky. Harriet was late. Even so, she paused briefly in the courtyard, resting her package on a nearby planter. She clasped her hands together, willing composure and calm into her inner being. Unbidden, her favorite Bible verse flashed across her mind. *I can do everything through Him that gives me strength.*

Spirits lifted, hopes buoyed, Harriet stiffened her spine and crossed the courtyard to the front door.

Bunting showed Harriet into the library. A fire glowed in the fireplace, warding off the morning chill. "I'll let the captain know you are here, Miss Handley. Do you require anything to get started?"

"Is it all right if I sit at the desk? I need to spread my paper out so that I can begin writing notes." Harriet wiped her clammy hands on her skirts.

"That will be fine, Miss. Though I can bring you a table of your own if you wish to sit closer to the fire."

"Not at all, Bunting. If you don't think the captain will mind, then this will do nicely." Harriet began unpacking her parcel onto the blotter of a massive mahogany desk.

"Very good." Bunting bowed and closed the door behind him so that it almost made no sound at all.

Harriet smoothed the sheets of foolscap with shaking fingers. She breathed deeply, inhaling the masculine scents of leather-bound books and polished wood. The familiarity of the room struck her anew, causing her eyes to mist over. She brushed the back of her hand across her eyes to dry the unwanted tears. Gazing up, she spied a portrait occupying the place of honor over the mantel. The painting showed a pretty young woman with deep gray eyes who held a baby in her arms. A toddler stood proudly beside them, resting his chubby hands on his mother's arm. Harriet crossed over to the mantel and peered at the picture closely. That sweet tableau must be Brookes's mother, his older brother, Henry, and the captain as an infant. The cozy domesticity of the painting aroused feelings of panic in Harriet. She bit her lip and looked away.

A clock ticked in the corner. Each swing of its pendulum struck Harriet's nerves, like an omen or a warning. She had made a mistake in coming back, in proposing the whole ridiculous idea to begin with. Closing her eyes, she pictured her papa. He seemed so close to her in this familiar room. Papa had secrets. Her family had secrets. She did not need to go delving in Captain Brookes's personal life for the very selfish reason of writing a book. Why invade a good man's privacy to suit her ambitions? Harriet's cheeks burned with shame.

She swallowed the bile rising in her throat. It was time, long past time, for her to leave.

The door creaked open, announcing Brookes's arrival. "Good morning, Harriet." His rich, warm baritone filled the room, startling Harriet. "I apologize for taking so long to meet you."

She spun around, her pulse pounding.

Harriet looked up at him, her eyes so blue they were almost black. He had seen this expression in her eyes once before, the first day they had met on the hill. At that time, she had been speaking of her faith, but now her eyes were so dark, they reflected something else. Fear, perhaps? He surveyed Harriet as he would a battlefield, raking his gaze over her, trying to gauge strategic points and weaknesses. Her lips trembled nervously, and she bit them in an effort to hold still. This observation gentled him, and his mouth curved into an encouraging smile. "I had to approve our well dressing. The servants finished the decorations this morning."

"Well dressing? Do you have a hot spring here at Brookes Park?"

"Yes and the servants have it properly kitted out in a mass of flowers. It's impressive. When we finish here, I would be happy to take you to see it."

She blinked and nodded, giving him a little half smile. He motioned her to a chair near the hearth. "I'll ring for some tea."

"I'm afraid I will take up too much of your time, Captain."

"Not at all. Next week, when the celebrations are over, we will have more time to talk. Today, we will get started. Where do you want to begin?" He sat down across from her, stretching his good leg out toward the warming blaze.

Her brow furrowed. She reached a hand up, tentatively touching her right temple. "I don't know."

"Would it help if I asked Stoames to join us?"

"Yes!" Her quick acceptance caused Brookes to lift an eyebrow. Why would Stoames make that big of an improvement to her manuscript? She colored under his gaze.

Bunting bustled in, balancing a tray with a lavish tea set in one hand. "Bunting, will you find Stoames, and ask him to join us?"

"Of course, Captain." Bunting placed the tea tray gently on an inlaid table near the fire.

"We'll have a little refreshment and start the discussion in that manner. Perhaps we both will feel less awkward." He motioned her toward the table.

She smiled at him, the pinkness in her cheeks ebbing, busying herself with the teapot. He regarded her squarely. "What interests you about the war?"

She poured the tea. If she was still nervous, her hands did not betray her. Not a single drop spilled outside of the fragile china cups. "I want to know the truth about war. Perhaps I feel it is time to write a realistic history, so that those of us who never go to war can know what it is like."

That sounded a bit daunting, but he nodded anyway. Best not to show any reluctance. "Then where should we begin?"

"What made you decide to become a soldier?" She gingerly sipped at her steaming hot tea.

"Well, you know I was the second son. My elder brother, Henry, inherited the estate. I had to seek my fortune elsewhere." He took a careful taste.

"Well, yes, I know," Harriet replied, stirring her tea with a small silver spoon. "But why the army? Why not the navy? Why seek the service at all? You could have been a curate, or sought a career in the church."

"Army life is most appealing, especially to a young lad full of romantic notions. I love to ride. Riding is my passion, since boyhood, and I wanted to make my living at it. I sought adventure, desired to fight grand battles. And I never had much faith in God, so following the church simply never occurred to me." He attempted a laugh to soften his words, but it caught in his throat, making an odd, strangling sound.

Her mouth dropped open. "You don't have faith?"

"I had very little when I embarked on my career. I've lost it completely since Waterloo." Absentmindedly, he stroked his leg, where wood joined ravaged flesh.

"I am very sorry to hear that." She met his steady gaze. He might well have bared his wooden calf, he was so exposed. No, it was worse even, he had bared his soul to her. And judging by the expression in her eyes, Harriet did not like what she saw. Was it possible that his lack of faith was more unattractive to her than his wooden leg?

He pretended not to understand her look, and set his teacup down with a defiant clink. They needed boundaries. He would talk to Harriet about the war, but never about faith. His mind flashed back to the fields of Waterloo, where men lay dying while their brothers in arms and enemies alike stripped them of their worldly possessions. Never once did they show mercy, not even to their fellow countrymen. His lack of religion was his own affair. In fact, he had earned it. "Where on earth is Stoames?" he barked in irritation.

"Here I am, Captain." Stoames opened the library door with brusque swiftness. "My apologies for taking so long."

"Not at all," Harriet replied smoothly, and poured another cup of tea.

He accepted it with a hearty smile. "Now, what were you discussing?"

"The beginning of my hallowed career."

Stoames raised his eyebrows at the captain's biting tone. "Well, I started as the captain's valet before the war, and then I joined up as his batman. We had some terrific sport in the fields of Belgium."

"Tell me, Stoames, did you have any trepidation about joining the army?"

"No, no, can't say I did. To young men, going off to war is a vastly exciting experience. Lots of pretty ladies kissing you goodbye, the pomp of military bands—it stirs your blood, you see. The captain and I were both young and a little wild, and the idea of seeking glory on a battlefield was like something in a story."

"An epic poem," Brookes said with a snap, and looked at Harriet from beneath his lowered brows. Did she recall her silly foolishness about Homer and the romance of war?

Harriet blushed anew, and the roses in her cheeks reminded him again of the roses in the courtyard. He remembered kneeling next to his mother in the dirt, handing her pieces of string so she could tie the roses down when the wind blew too hard. His mother had tended those blooms so carefully, nurturing them while they grew, sheltering them from storms. Like most young women, Harriet must have been raised like that, too. She couldn't help her own naïveté. The anger melted away. He ran a weary hand over his face, scrubbing the last of his ill temper from his expression.

"Harriet, I must be off for a while." The abruptness of his tone startled his companions, who both looked at him with questioning eyes. "I need to finish the preparations for the Blessing of the Wells."

"Of course." Harriet jumped up from her chair. "I've taken up too much of your time." She scurried to the desk and began stuffing the paper back in a pile, spilling half of it in her haste. Brookes's eyebrows drew together. Barking at an innocent young lady was certainly an unappealing trait in a man. His defensiveness about his lack of faith made him too snappish. A twinge of guilt assailed him.

"I can show you the well, if you like," he replied with an elaborately casual air, remembering his earlier promise.

"I would love to see it, but I must return home. Sophie and I need to get ready for the Blessing service and the tea, and I must look in on Mama."

Stoames helped her, neatly tying the sheets of foolscap with a piece of red twine. He then leaned over and whispered something in Harriet's ear, which Brookes could not hear. Harriet looked up at Stoames, her features softening, and gave him a radiant smile. A terrible tenseness grabbed at Brookes, and he glowered at his batman. Stoames gazed back at him, an expression of innocence on his roughened face.

Unreasonable jealously tugged at his insides. Brookes's jaw tightened and his eyes narrowed.

*Stoames can't be in love with her. I won't allow it.*

# Chapter Six

"What was that all about?" Brookes spat out the words and turned to his batman. "What did you say to Miss Harriet?"

"I'm sure I don't know what you mean." Stoames gazed up at the ceiling, his features schooled to blankness.

"When you were helping Miss Harriet, you whispered something in her ear. Something that, judging by the beatific smile she gave you, made her excessively happy. I must know, what did you say to her?" He clenched his fists, flexing them, balling them up at his sides.

"Begging your pardon, Captain Sir, I don't want to tell you. It's a private matter and I don't wish to provoke your anger." Stoames clasped his hands behind his back but his shoulders hunched forward defensively.

"Tell me at once or I may lose my temper and plant you a facer. I may be getting older, and I may be lame, but I can still fight with the best of them." Heat flooded his face, but he refused to recognize the overpowering emotion as jealousy. There was no possible reason to be envious of Stoames's attention to Harriet. After all, Sophie was his future bride.

Stoames stared squarely at Brookes. "I told the lady not

to lose heart. I told her that you would, in time, come around to talking about the war. You may not realize it, sir, but your behavior was almost uncivil. If Miss Harriet is to write her book, she needs your assistance, and she needs you to give it willingly."

The fire inside Brookes extinguished. He slumped into the chair behind his desk, dropping his hands. Utterly defeated, he gazed at Stoames in discomfort. "I *was* uncivil, was I not?"

"I only said *almost* uncivil, Captain."

Brookes leaned forward, resting his elbows on the mahogany wood. He toyed with the blotter, creasing it with his thumbnail. The paper crackled against his skin. "Next time, I promise to be kinder."

Stoames sat in the chair across the desk, gazing at his master eye to eye. "You'll have to face it, you know. You must make up your own mind about which young lady you want. It won't do to keep taking your confusion out on Miss Harriet."

Brookes's thumb stilled, and ice replaced the fire in his veins. Had he tipped his hand? "I'm sure I don't know what you mean."

"I've seen the way you look at Miss Harriet. You're besotted. Admit it, man. Your unkindness to her this morning is nothing more than vain attempt to cover it. But I've known you for years. And I never saw you look at Miss Sophie the way you looked at Miss Harriet when she served the tea."

A suffocating tightness seized Brookes's chest. "You're mighty blunt about it, anyway."

"You know me, Captain. I speak as I find."

Turning his chair away from his batman and closer to the window, Brookes faced the watery sunlight streaming in. The soft, insipid rays did nothing to warm his chilled skin. He took a few deep breaths, ordering himself to remain calm. "I snapped at Miss Harriet because she brought the conversation around to religion, a subject I don't care to speak of." He swallowed, measuring his words with precision. "Though I find Miss Harriet's society pleasant, I am honor bound to propose to Miss Sophie."

"Balderdash."

Brookes swiveled back, regarding his batman with a critical squint. "You would have me go back on my word of honor?"

"You know I would never say that. But I believe no engagement existed between you and Miss Sophie." Stoames tapped his forefinger on the desk for emphasis. "If you don't have a formal arrangement, and if Miss Sophie finds you too altered, then why stick so stubbornly to her?"

"Our understanding was formal enough for both of us to comprehend. Neither of us sought another in the three years I fought with Wellington." The blood pounded in his temples. "I cannot, in good conscience, back out of the understanding now."

"You were at war. When would you have time to find someone else?" Stoames leaned back in his chair with a weary air.

"You and I both know more than one soldier who broke from his sweetheart as soon as they found a nice Belgian chit. But I stayed constant, and so did she. Sophie stayed here and waited for me when others could have taken my place. Even if she finds me repulsive now, I must work to win her over. To break from her now—especially with her family in desperate financial straits—would be most unfair." He crossed his arms over his chest, daring Stoames to keep needling him.

"Then how will you control your feelings for Miss Harriet?"

"I don't have feelings for Miss Harriet." He swallowed the lie neatly. "I am helping her write a book. She wants to support her family, which shows a great deal of pluck. I admire her for it. I don't think she cares for me anyhow." He broke off and stared down at his hands for a moment.

Stoames heaved a forceful sigh that seemed to originate in his boots. "Yet you all but threatened me with pistols at ten paces for whispering in her ear."

Stoames and his intuition. Brookes covered his embarrassment by shrugging nonchalantly. "I know you, you old dog. I merely tried to protect her honor." Ridiculous excuse. He remembered Harriet pouring out tea with graceful hands, meeting his barbed words with graciousness. He recalled her fine brows, the straight bridge of her nose, and the tender curve of her mouth, her profile as pure as a cameo, a little bit of ivory transformed into vibrant flesh and blood. Her hair was dark and glossy. He imagined how the strands might feel, slipping through his fingers. He shook his head, his mouth twisting into a cynical smile.

Stoames raised a hand in defeat. "Well, then, what are your plans?"

"I've found my mother's jewelry in the safe. I will propose to Miss Sophie after the dance in the village hall."

"And Miss Harriet?" A challenge, rather than a simple question.

"I'll keep helping her to write her book. I will endeavor to give her everything she needs to make a success of it." But if she brought the subject around to God again, he had every right to leave off.

Harriet trudged home, her feet heavy and her mind clouded with self-doubt. Stoames assured her to keep trying, but she couldn't fathom the bitter look on Captain Brookes's striking face. His eyes turned from stormy green to almost slate gray when she questioned him about his loss of faith. She knew he had suffered deeply. But for Brookes to endure such tragedy without faith—well, that was enough to break her heart.

Her vain ambition led her down a slippery slope, exposing his weaknesses to her watchful gaze. She had no right to interfere, no right to pry. After all, why should she question his loss of faith? True, she suffered through hardship and deprivation, and the pinch of poverty squeezed her daily. Yet she never lost faith; she relied on it to carry her through her trials and tribulations. Papa nicknamed her "The Eternal Optimist," and joked that she could find something good in every situation—even the plague. She shivered, tightening her shawl over her chest. Perhaps her hopefulness blinded her to the terrible reality of Brookes's past.

When she finally arrived at the cottage, Sophie dashed down the stairs, an expression of blank horror in her blue eyes.

"What has happened?" Harriet assumed her usual air of sisterly authority.

"Mama took on so about the Blessing of the Wells and the Ball, I felt I had to call Dr. Wallace. It was dreadful, Harriet. I know that he is expensive, but what could I do?"

Harriet patted Sophie's arm. "It will be fine, Sophie. But why was she so upset?"

"Mama says she will not take us anywhere, as she does not want others to see our reduced circumstances."

"Whatever does that matter, in a country village? Come, let's go and speak with her and the doctor." Linking arms with her sister, Harriet pulled her up the stairs.

As they entered the room, Dr. Wallace stood beside Mama's bed, pursing his mouth into a thin line. "I thought a mild dose of laudanum would help this nervous exhaustion. Whatever are we to do with you, my lady?"

Without stopping to think, Harriet tugged at Dr. Wallace's sleeve. "The laudanum—it's not too potent, is it, Dr. Wallace? I worry that Mama is taking too much."

"The laudanum is the only thing that makes life bearable," Mama snapped, offering her wrist to Dr. Wallace so he could take her pulse.

"A little laudanum never hurt anyone, Miss Handley." Dr. Wallace smiled and placed his fingers on Mama's wrist.

Harriet stood her ground. "Well, if Mama isn't so very ill, then a mild dose of laudanum might help her now. If she takes it, though, she won't be able to attend the Blessing ceremony. But she would be all right by herself for a few hours, wouldn't she, while we go? And she might try to attend the ball tonight, Doctor?"

Dr. Wallace cast a searching glance over the patient. He nodded with satisfaction and gently let go of her wrist. "I have prescribed a regimen of rest to cure your mother's nervous exhaustion." He hesitated, and then smiled gently at Harriet and Sophie. "Still, perhaps I prescribed strict bed rest in haste. A brief social outing might help, your ladyship."

Mama sank against the pillows, with the air of a sacrificial victim. Her face was pale, her lips drawn. "Very well. I am outnumbered. We will attend the ball tonight. But I must have rest up until the moment we leave."


"Hattie, you are so good with Mama. I honestly did not know what to do with her. All I did was mention the events in the village, and she became hysterical. I sent Rose to fetch Dr. Wallace. It was all I could think to do."

"You handled the situation very well, Sophie. Don't fret." They crossed the hall, entering the room they shared. "I apologize for being gone for so long. I feel guilty for not being here to help you."

"But you were helping me! You were seeing the captain, were you not? How did you fare?"

"Poorly, I am afraid. I made a blunder, and questioned him too closely about his emotions and his faith. The whole affair grew a bit disastrous." How embarrassing the entire unfortunate morning had been. Save for Stoames's kind words, she was prepared to forget the whole episode.

"Poor Hattie. I am sure it will be fine. I imagine he is unused to speaking to anyone about his feelings." Sophie splashed water from the pitcher into the basin, and began washing her hands and face.

Harriet regarded her sister's back closely. "In truth, I treaded on sacred ground. It made me rather sick."

Sophie turned to face Harriet, patting her face dry with a threadbare towel. She flicked her eyebrows quizzically. "Whatever for? I shouldn't worry. He's promised to share his memories to help you write the book. Surely he knew what that would entail."

Harriet flopped onto the bed with a sigh. "Sharing memories and sharing facts are very different things," she murmured into her pillow. Her stomach recoiled and she could talk about her awful morning no more. Looking up, she chose the one topic of conversation designed to distract her sister. "Shall we dress for the Blessing?"

"Oh, yes! What will you wear?" Sophie managed to grow both animated and serious at the same time.

Harriet grinned at her with indulgence. "I haven't any idea."

"I've made over two old muslin dresses. They look lovely. See?" Sophie pulled them out of the wardrobe, casting an approving glance over her handiwork. "Look, I put new ribbons on the bodices, and embroidered in white— I think whitework is so divine, don't you?" She gave the dresses an expert shake. "Here, Hattie, you shall wear the one trimmed in blue, and I shall wear the pink."

She traced one finger over the embroidery, and the delicate threads caught on her rough skin. A trickle of interest suffused her body. A dawning awareness of her looks, and the desire to be pretty assumed a great significance in her consciousness. There was no driving force behind this transformation, was there? Certainly not. She just wanted to look nice, that's all.

Sophie studied Harriet with a judgmental air. "Hmm. I shall dress your hair, Hattie. I've wanted to experiment with braids. My hair is too curly, but yours is so straight it will hold a braid nicely."

Harriet gazed into the looking glass over the washstand, running a hand over her dark brown locks. Her hair was tucked up into its usual severe chignon. She could never call it attractive. Would anyone else? She rather doubted it. After all, Sophie was the acknowledged beauty of the family.

"Oh Hattie, I have ideas for our ball dress tonight, too," Sophie prattled on. She gazed into the mirror, fitting her cheek against Harriet's shoulder. Reaching up, Sophie tucked a wayward curl behind one shoulder. "Do you know, Hattie," she said breathlessly, an expression of satisfaction lighting up her china-blue eyes, "I rather think I shall fall in love with the captain tonight."

Harriet's heart dropped like a stone and she suppressed the sudden flash of jealousy that flooded her being. She closed her eyes, blocking out their reflections in the glass. "Well, I should certainly hope so, Sophie."

## Chapter Seven

Brookes glanced toward the village green, where a mass of blooms obscured the well. The riotous color of the flowers and the sun sparkling on the cornets and flugelhorns made his eyes smart. He blinked to clear his vision. Opening his eyes, his gaze fell on the two Handley sisters, strolling arm in arm, toward the garishly decorated well. The bleating of the horns died out, replaced by a buzzing in his ears. Every sense he possessed trained, with military precision, on the pretty girls clad in white, their heads so close together that their bonnets touched.

Sophie's little golden curls framed her face. Brookes stared at her, running his assessing gaze over her figure. She looked like a Dresden china doll, he decided flatly. Very pretty, to be sure, but untouchable. Casting Sophie away, he focused on Harriet. Her bonnet irritated him, for it covered her glossy brown hair and cast her fathomless blue eyes in shadow. Drat the bright sun. Harriet would keep her hat on throughout the ceremony and he would miss the chance to see her pure profile in bold relief. He noted that their servant stood beside them, but not his future mother-in-law. Where was Lady Handley? Almost everyone in the clutch of nearby Derbyshire villages was in attendance, he observed, glancing over the crowd gathering on the green.

The crisp rattle of the side drum broke through Brookes's trance, sending his pulse racing. The deafening drumbeat took him right back to Quatre Bras. Brookes and his men rode in a single column up the road to Waterloo. A drummer for the Twenty-Third Foot lay dying at the crossroads. Neither he nor his men stopped to help the lad. Everyone eagerly pressed forward, ready for their share of the battle. Brookes closed his eyes, seeing the lad's face. So young, spots still covered his cheeks. His groans sometimes haunted Brookes's nightmares.

The band launched into "God Save the King," snapping Brookes back from Quatre Bras onto the village green. He tried to will the bad memories away by forcing himself to stand at attention and sing along with the crowd. His gaze focused on the two Handley girls again. Their backs were to him, giving him no chance to study their expressions. But even without gazing upon her face, he observed Harriet's serenity. Sophie's shoulders wriggled, her bonneted head twitched from side to side. Watching her drained what little energy he possessed. In contrast, Harriet stood still, her head charmingly inclined toward the band. He involuntarily relaxed, releasing a knot he hadn't realized existed between his shoulder blades. Harriet's mere presence refreshed a man—as restorative as a long drink of water from one of the streams that crossed through Brookes Park.

He gave an impatient shrug of his shoulders, the knot returning. Harriet's effect on his spirit mattered little, and there was no call to wax poetic about her features, because she was not his intended. He would simply have to get used to a life of constant movement. Restful, peaceful moments would be few and far between once he married Sophie.

The band ended with an earsplitting flourish, and Harriet applauded with the rest of the crowd. She glanced around furtively. Excellent. None of the men in front of her appeared to be Captain Brookes. A pull of awareness gripped her, causing the baby-fine hair on the nape of her neck to stand up. He must be standing behind them. Harriet forced herself to remain motionless. It would never do to turn around and gape. Besides, he must be staring at Sophie. Harriet cast a sidelong glance at her sister. She looked so lovely, the pinkness of her bonnet highlighting the porcelain planes of her face.

A brief flurry of activity disturbed the green as the members of the brass band sat down. An elderly man with slightly stooped shoulders and a thick mane of gray hair approached the well. Facing the crowd, he smiled serenely. Harriet's heart warmed, and she grinned back. This kindly old man must be the reverend of St. Mary's, over at Crich.

"Let us pray," the reverend began. Bowing her head, Harriet allowed the prayer to wash over her soul like waves caressing the shore. In the year or so since her family moved from Matlock Bath, they had not attended Sunday services. Mama had been too conscious of the family's status, and unwilling to make the eight mile journey to Crich and back every Sunday. Tansley Village was too small to have its own church, so the Handleys' spiritual guidance had gone by the wayside.

Harriet drank in the words of the blessing, allowing them to comfort her parched spirit. Even before the family moved, going to church services had offered very little solace. Now, if you were looking for a social affair, you were in luck. If only she could have been like Mama and cared more for her perfect dress than her spiritual well-being, then that church would have been perfect. But no pretty dress ever swayed Harriet, and she searched in vain for a church that promised more than a salon. Listening to the reverend's gentle voice, Harriet discovered that elusive something more.

The simple little ceremony drew to an end, and Harriet detached herself from her sister's side. Full of strength, shining with a steadfast and pure purpose, she must tell the reverend how important his words had been, how he cast a light on her shadowy soul. Why, she didn't feel at all bashful as she glided over to the reverend. He smiled as he saw her approach. "Did you enjoy the ceremony, Miss?"

She beamed up at him, her heart glowing. "I did. Your words fell upon my soul like drops of rain in a desert."

He patted her hand with a grandfatherly air. "Now, you don't look familiar, my dear. Have you attended services at St. Mary's?"

Harriet dropped her gaze, coloring a little. "I haven't been able to, Reverend. My mother is unwell and the four miles there and four miles back would be too taxing."

"Don't fret, don't fret. You don't have to be in church to worship, you know. God is everywhere. Now, tell me your name."

"Harriet Handley."

"Well, Miss Handley, I am Reverend Kirk. If you should ever wish to join our little congregation, know that you are always welcome at St. Mary's. But even if you cannot make the journey, you must remember that God is with you, and watching over you."

Harriet's heart welled and tears stung her eyes. Such warmth and compassion had expired from her life when Papa died. Her lips trembled, and her voice caught in her throat.

"Now, now, my dear, there's no need for tears. Remember, as solitary as you may feel, you are never truly alone. Promise me you will remember that." Reverend Kirk patted her hand gently.

Harriet nodded, her heart still too full for words. Blinking away her tears, she turned from the reverend. The vivid colors and brassy tone of the band pounced on her nerves. She longed to be somewhere quiet, where she could think clearly. No such luck. Sophie grabbed her arm, pulling on Harriet excitedly.

"Why did you leave me like that? To whom were you speaking?"

"Reverend Kirk, you goose. Did you not pay any attention to the ceremony?"

"Very little," replied Sophie with her customary frankness. "I wondered if my half boots look too hideous with this gown. I think I should have worn my slippers."

Harriet sighed, linking her arm through Sophie's. "Your slippers might have been spoiled with the walk. Your half boots are very attractive."

Sophie looked down at her feet, considering them closely. "I think so, too," she pronounced.

Rose tapped Sophie's shoulder. "Come along, you two chickens. Enough chatter. The cream tea starts soon, and we are nowhere near the village hall."

Brookes watched the sisters enter the bustling village hall through narrowed eyes. Seeing Harriet and Sophie together had stiffened his resolve—he needed to break free of Harriet's spell. At some point during the tea, he would make that all-important first move. His jaw hardening, he resolved to speak to Sophie alone, for the first time since he returned home.

His vision sharpened. The sisters and their servant were selecting a tea table. One of the ladies assisting with the tea brought them a fresh pot and china cups. He stretched his legs under his own table, wondering how on earth he would find Sophie without an escort. He watched Sophie's head bobble around aimlessly. Then Harriet and the servant woman stood up. Harriet leaned down to say something to Sophie, who nodded and remained at the table while the two women strolled off. Their absence offered him the perfect time to strike. Brookes stood up, his heart hammering, and found his way through the crush of villagers to her table.

"May I sit for a moment?" His voice had a catch in it. He cleared his throat.

Sophie jumped in her chair. Her face turned as crimson as the cloth spread over her table. "Of course." Her voice was unnaturally strained and breathless.

"Lovely tea."

"I haven't tried it yet." Sophie began to pour some into her cup, but her hand shook so that she spilled a little on the cloth.

"Allow me," Brookes said smoothly, whipping out his handkerchief. Sophie reached out to grasp her saucer at the same moment he began patting at the spot on the tablecloth. He knocked against the cup and sent it flying. It landed on the floor with a crash, splintering to a thousand pieces.

"Oh!" cried Sophie. She stooped down to gather the broken pieces. Brookes stooped to help but his leg gave out, lurching him forward. He collided with Sophie, knocking her soundly on the head.

Sophie sat back in her chair with a little huff, rubbing at her skull. "Ouch."

"My deepest apologies. Did I hurt you badly?"

"I'll recover," Sophie snapped.

He cleared his throat again, trying to think of a way to salvage the situation. Should he keep charging ahead? Or should he offer to look at her wound? He peered at Sophie closely. The irritated expression on her face decided it for him. Charge ahead, ignore the little incident.

"I shall look forward to seeing you at the ball tonight," he began, hoping to restore his sense of savoir faire.

"Yes."

"Will you save a dance for me?" He remembered how, before the war, they would dance together so often that it raised the eyebrows of the matrons of Matlock Bath.

"Can you dance?" Sophie asked, with a mixture of irritation and frank curiosity that shriveled his interest.

"I don't know. I haven't tried." He inhaled deeply, seeking Sophie's smell of violets and muslin. But the scent of spilled tea permeated everything.

"Well, if you can dance, then I will be happy to reserve one for you, Captain Brookes." A pat reply, one that he instantly recognized. A sop, and nothing more. He saw her turn away countless other suitors with a similar vague gesture before.

He stood up. A good soldier recognized the right moment for retreat. "Until tonight, then, Miss Handley."

"Ah, seeing the pair of you again, it was like old times." Rose clasped her hands over her bosom. "Like the war never happened. Before we had to leave Matlock Bath."

Harriet glanced over at her sister, carefully sidestepping a rut in the road. It had not looked like old times to her. She had watched the whole scene from across the room, where she and Rose had stopped to help themselves to scones and clotted cream. When she espied the captain making his way to the table, she stayed rooted to the spot, and bid Rose do the same. Watching the awkward tableau reminded her of the amateur dramatics that trouped through Derbyshire. In fact, Harriet could not bear to watch after Captain Brookes collided with Sophie. She turned away, embarrassment and tenderness for the captain overwhelming her, making her knees weak.

Sophie's rosy lips pulled into a thin line. She kicked at a pebble in the road and remained silent.

"That marked the first time you two have been alone together since he returned from the war. If it felt a little strange, perhaps it can be linked to the passage of time." Harriet took pride in her casual voice, even though her heart pounded in her ears.

"He broke my cup."

"He did not mean to."

"He bumped my head."

"Another accident," Harriet reminded her, adopting her most authoritative, sisterly tone. Sophie's pettiness vexed Harriet more than usual. Though she hated to admit it, she was irritated that she cared so much.

"I thought you two made a pretty picture," Rose broke in.

"I don't wish to speak of it. When I see him at the ball tonight, I shall endeavor to be more civil."

Harriet could only hope her sister told the truth, but she noted that Sophie's dimples had vanished, her lips compressed in a stubborn line.

Harriet cast about for another topic of conversation. "Do you know, Sophie, Reverend Kirk invited us to attend services in Crich. Wouldn't that be nice?"

Sophie shrugged. "You know Mama will never attend. She is too worried about appearances."

"I may go without her. The way he spoke of St. Mary's, it sounds like a simple country parish. I doubt very much that everyone there is conscious of status to the degree they are at Matlock Bath." She smiled hopefully. "I can't go every Sunday, but I would like to go once every few fortnights."

"Very well, if you go I will go with you." Sophie sounded tired, the weight of the world resting on her young shoulders.

Harriet gave her sister's arm an impulsive squeeze. A light breeze tickled her face, sending the ribbons on her dress fluttering.

"I'll come, too, dearie. I've missed Sunday services." Rose looked down at Harriet, her eyes shining with motherly affection.

"Thank you, Rose." Harriet's mood lifted, suffusing her

with a sense of buoyancy. "I cannot wait for the ball to-night."

The ball simply couldn't come quickly enough, though it was just a few hours away. If only this lightness of spirit would last until then. For the first time in ages, she felt like dancing. Not, of course, that the captain would ask her to dance. Heat rose in Harriet's cheeks, scorching her like a flame. He would dance with Sophie, naturally. That was the right and proper thing to do; in fact, the simple act of them dancing together would take Sophie closer to matrimony and the family closer to stability.

So why did she feel a wriggle of discomfort at the pit of her stomach? It wasn't jealousy. Surely that feeling was just…nerves.

# Chapter Eight

The cold, sharp edge of a razor blade scraped across Brookes's chin. He willed himself to stay still and completely in the present, not allowing the feeling of steel on flesh to carry him back to the terrible night at Waterloo. Stoames squinted at him with a critical air, running the blade slightly over to the left. Wiping the blade on a towel, he paused. "You'll have to pull your lips down, Captain, so as I can get the bit under your nose."

Brookes pulled a face, twisting his lips down to lengthen the spot between his nose and mouth. Giving his skin a final swift swipe, Stoames stepped back. "Hot towel, Captain."

Brookes pressed the steaming cloth to his face, inhaling the clean scent of shaving soap and fresh linen. He dabbed at the bits of lather that still clung to his face, and rubbed the linen hard against his skin for good measure. "Shaving is such a nuisance. Perhaps I should be like the men in the field, and grow a beard."

"What's practical in the field isn't fashionable in the ballroom," Stoames replied with mock sincerity. "Are you ready for your evening dress?"

"Yes, and I can put it on myself. I don't need your assistance with tying my cravat, either. I don't want the points so high they choke me or make it impossible to turn my head."

"I'm hardly making you into a dandy. But will you need anything else from me at the moment?"

"Yes. There's a jewel case in my study. Top drawer of my desk. Fetch it for me, there's a good man."

Stoames bowed and left. Brookes strode over to the bed, smoothing out invisible wrinkles in his immaculate suit, which was laid out across the counterpane. From the moment he'd regained strength enough to stand, Brookes had insisted on dressing himself. No one, not even his faithful batman, helped him struggle to ease his trousers over his wooden leg. By the time Stoames returned, bearing a leather case, Brookes stood at the looking glass, tying his cravat.

Stoames handed the blue leather-bound box to Brookes, his lips turned down in disapproval. "What's in there?"

"Mother's jewels. The sapphires and diamonds." Brookes snapped open the case. Candlelight refracted off the precious stones, dazzling his eyes.

"Why are you getting them out now?"

"Don't get yourself in a swither. I'm looking them over, contemplating how they will look on Miss Sophie. Here's what I need." Reaching down inside the case, he dug out a ring—a large, winking sapphire surrounded by glittering small diamonds, a perfect match to the necklace and pair of bracelets the case also contained.

Stoames sniffed loudly. "Sapphires don't suit blondes."

Brookes laughed, regarding the batman with genuine interest. "Oh, no? What does suit blondes?"

"I can't say as I know. Pearls maybe. But I do think that sapphires look particularly striking on brunettes."

"Mother didn't have a pearl ring."

"Maybe you should go to town and buy one. The journey might give you a chance to clear your mind," Stoames retorted with a gleam in his eye.

"I'm not going to propose to her tonight, not that it's any of your business." Brookes slipped the ring into his vest pocket. "But I need to be prepared. I must make my intentions known, and the sooner the better. We'll dance together at the ball. Perhaps it will rekindle old feelings. And by tomorrow, I may be asking for her hand."

Stoames snorted. "Fools rush in, Captain. Fools rush in."

The little lantern bobbed along in the deepening dusk, casting a gentle circle of light ahead of the Handley party as they walked toward the village hall. A gentle breeze ruffled Harriet's silken skirts, and she pulled her shawl closer about her shoulders for warmth. One could hardly tell that her gown of robin's-egg blue enjoyed a previous existence as an elaborate court dress for Mama. Sophie removed the train and stripped off most of the faded trimmings, revealing its simple yet elegant lines. Harriet had teased her sister about the process, which occupied many weeks the past winter. So many practical chores demanded their time, such as new curtains for the parlor, and a new dress was a waste of time. But now, gratitude flowed through Harriet for her sister's handiwork.

"Sophie, you've outdone yourself this evening." Harriet beamed at her sister, resplendent in reembroidered jade velvet, in the dusky twilight.

"Thank you, Hattie," Sophie replied. "Doesn't Mama look lovely?"

"Beautiful." Harriet ran her eyes over her mother's rosy gown, which set off the fading gold of her hair. Reaching out, she squeezed her mother's hand.

Mama squeezed back, but in the fading light, Harriet noticed her face growing pale. "Mama, are you going to be all right?"

"I make no promises. I shall endeavor for us to stay past supper, but if I feel my nerves coming on, I shall need to go home."

"Of course, Mama." Harriet loosened her mother's grip. They had reached the edge of the village. The Village Hall twinkled up ahead, lit with a thousand candles and torches. Harriet's heart beat fast in anticipation.

She had not attended a dance since her London season. And really, those balls were never very much fun. She hated being a wallflower and always disappointed Mama, so pleasure was impossible. Refreshed in spirit after her brief discussion with Reverend Kirk, Harriet cast off the previous year of penury and grief like an ill-fitting cloak. That was the reason, and nothing more.

Carriages, horses and villagers in their country best packed the green in front of the village hall. Harriet clasped her gloved hands together. How delightful to be part of the milling crowd, especially after all those months of being shut up in the cottage. Not that she minded taking care of Mama, of course. Harriet snuck a glance at her mother. Mama's face wore a drawn expression, as though she had tied a ribbon too tightly at the base of her neck. Harriet linked her arm through her mother's. "Come, Mama, we shall find a place for you to sit and watch the dancers."

The ladies handed off their wraps and stood briefly in the vestibule. The bright lights and crush of people dazzled Harriet, and she lost her bearings. She had to find Mama a comfortable place to sit. She peered around the room, her mouth going dry as panic set in. Relief flooded through her when she spied a clutch of dowagers in black, fanning themselves in a corner of the ballroom. She took her mother's elbow, steering her toward the women.

One of the women rose, spying Harriet and her mother. "Lady Handley!" she effused. "Do come and sit with me."

Harriet breathed a sigh of relief. She recognized the

woman as Lady Reese, one of the gentry who had a home in nearby Lumsdale. Harriet blinked. Lady Reese did not seem as concerned about Lady Handley's reduced status as her peers in Matlock Bath had done. Harriet shot her a grateful glance.

Lady Reese beamed in return, and linked her arm through Mama's, guiding her over to a little wooden chair. Straightening her gloves, Harriet looked around for Sophie, whom she had lost in the crush of guests. Two women, one wearing a dancing ostrich feather, parted in front of Harriet. She stopped in her tracks, her mouth dropping open as she stared straight ahead.

Sophie was gazing up in wonder at a tall soldier in uniform, smiling frankly and openly. He smiled down at her carelessly, the smile quirking the corners of his mouth. They stood much too close together. Though they were ringed on all sides by a milling group of guests, they were apart from the crowd, as though covered by a bell of silence. Harriet gave her head an impatient shake. She needed to break through that spell.

"Sophie!" she called, starting forward. "I thought I had lost you."

"Come, Hattie, I want you to meet someone." Sophie smiled up at the young soldier dreamily.

He held out his hand. "Lieutenant James Marable, at your service."

Harriet bobbed a brief curtsy. "How do you do, sir?"

"Very well, thank you." He smiled down at Sophie meaningfully. She blushed and dropped her gaze.

Dangerous territory indeed. What if Captain Brookes walked in at this very moment? She tugged impatiently at her sister's arm.

"If you will excuse us, Lieutenant, my mother wishes to speak to my sister."

"Of course." He bowed low. "Miss Sophie, may I claim you for the next dance?"

"You may." Sophie dropped a little curtsy. "Until then?"

He smiled, flashing brilliant teeth, and moved away.

"Whatever is the matter?" Sophie huffed, her brows drawn together in annoyance.

"You were standing entirely too close to Lieutenant Marable. What if Captain Brookes had seen you?"

Sophie shrugged her shoulders, refusing to reply.

Harriet sighed. "Promise me one thing. Be courteous to the captain tonight. Do not provoke him to anger by flirting with another man."

"I won't provoke anyone. I want to enjoy myself."

"Do not enjoy yourself at Captain Brookes's expense." Exasperation surged through Harriet. How dare Sophie toy with the emotions of a good man?

Sophie flinched. "I will not deliberately hurt him."

The lively little orchestra struck up the next dance, a cotillion, and Harriet watched Sophie glide off toward the dance floor with Lieutenant Marable. Her high spirits evaporated like a puff of smoke. Embarrassment at being left alone rooted her to the spot. Her blue gown was too noticeable. She must look ridiculous. What was the phrase? Mutton dressed as lamb? Harriet's face heated and little drops of perspiration pricked the roots of her hair. Perhaps she should find a comfortable spot to wedge herself, where she could stay unnoticed. After all, she perfected the art of being a wallflower during her London season.

"Miss Harriet?" A pleasant voice rumbled, bringing a smile to Harriet's face.

"Captain Brookes." She sighed with relief, turning to face him. He held two glasses in his hand and extended one to her with a smile.

"Would you care to sit down?" He motioned away from the dance floor with a brief nod of his head.

"Most definitely." She wove her way through the throngs of people, spying two empty chairs along the wall. She sank down in one, patting the seat of the other with her gloved hand.

"Are you enjoying yourself?" He sat beside her, taking a long draft of his drink.

"To be honest, Captain, no, I am not." She took a tiny sip of her punch, allowing it to flow through her body, restoring her spirit.

"Why not?" He turned to face her squarely, cocking one eyebrow.

"Balls are not my favorite pastime, I'm afraid." She took another refreshing taste. "Even during my London season, I never enjoyed attending one." She cast a worried look over the dancers. Would Brookes spy Sophie in the cotillion with his ghost?

"I have not attended a ball since Waterloo," he commiserated. "The Duchess of Richmond hosted one the night before the battle."

"Before the battle!" Harriet echoed, caught off guard. "That seems a rather frivolous occupation before entering the fray."

"It was." He took another drink of his wine. "In the midst of the general merrymaking, we learned Bonaparte had crossed the frontier."

"What did you do?" Harriet leaned toward him.

"Wellington and the Duke of Richmond shut themselves up in a dressing room, strategizing. Then Wellington decided we would attack on the morrow. I left when I got word so I had time to make my men ready."

"Of course," Harriet replied, gently urging him to keep talking.

"But many of the men elected to stay until dawn. They didn't have time to change clothes, and fought in evening dress. The strangest thing of all was that, of all the men who danced that night, I reckon half were dead or wounded by the next evening. I was one of the lucky ones."

His matter-of-fact voice cut her deeply. Her eyes stung with unshed tears. "I'm sorry."

He looked at her, surprise opening his gray-green eyes wide. "Why are you sorry? That is a soldier's lot in life."

Harriet shook her head. "It seems a terrible waste, is all." Her voice sounded so thick she hardly recognized it.

"No tears at a ball." He took the glass from her hands. "I apologize for bringing the matter up at all. It seems strange to me, that this is the first ball I have attended since that fateful night."

She swallowed and nodded her head.

"Would you like more punch? I might take another glass of wine myself." He stood up, looking down at her expectantly.

"Yes, if you please."

In his absence, she struggled to regain her composure. Flicking a glance over the crowded ballroom, she spotted Sophie, still dancing with Lieutenant Marable. A flash of anger suffused her, leaving her breathless. Did her petulant sister, so young and so headstrong, deserve a man like Captain Brookes?

Brookes strode across the ballroom, balancing the two drinks carefully while he navigated the throng. He halted in his tracks, staring at the dance floor. Ah, he had seen Sophie dancing merrily with someone else. Harriet could not turn away.

Brookes stared at the couple a moment longer. His head swiveled toward Harriet, his green eyes locking with her gaze. An inscrutable expression crossed his face. Then he vanished. Harriet peered around sharply. She could no longer pick out his broad shoulders in the crowd. She cast her eyes down, studying her blue kid slippers with intensity.

Where he went was no concern of hers, was it? Perhaps he found a pretty dancing partner to incite Sophie's jealousy.

Two very masculine feet shod in black leather appeared next to hers. She raised her head, heat rising to her cheeks.

"Miss Harriet." Captain Brookes cleared his throat. He started again, speaking in an even tone, "Would you do me the honor of reserving the next dance for me?"

# Chapter Nine

Brookes stood before Harriet, extending his hand. She cast her azure eyes up to him, and he willed his countenance to remain impassive. He refused to allow Harriet to read into his soul and discover his inner turmoil. Seeing Sophie with another man—a man who could have been him a few years ago—fired Brookes with an overwhelming urge to prove himself. His heart thumped painfully in his chest. Could he manage a dance? Riding a horse never troubled him but the hops and skips of a country dance presented a challenge that set his heart racing and his palms sweating. Hedging his bets, he requested a minuet of the orchestra. 'Twas the slowest dance in his recollection.

Time ceased to move. Only Harriet would break the spell. After an eternity, she slipped her hand into his, rising gracefully from the chair. "I would be honored, Captain." Her touch, even through their gloved hands, sent tingles up his arm. He breathed deeply of her violet scent, willing himself to remain steady and composed.

They wound their way through the press of the crowd to the cleared area in the middle of the room. "A minuet, if you please, ladies and gentlemen," cried the village shopkeeper, the impromptu master of ceremonies. Interest surged through the crowd of onlookers, and several of the younger couples began clearing the floor. "A minuet? How very old-fashioned." One young lady laughed, swishing past Brookes on the arm of her partner. Yet Brookes noted with pleasure that some of the older couples, who had not been dancing, stood up. Taking their places on the floor, the faces of the couples reflected surprise and excitement.

The orchestra struck up a few stately opening bars. Brookes stood still, listening for a moment. Like the fifes and drums calling his men to standards, the delicate strains infused Brookes with a sense of purpose.

Brookes steered Harriet beside that mirror image of his youth who had claimed Sophie for the cotillion. Obviously they were proceeding with the old-fashioned minuet. Their second dance together. The young pup had serious intentions, did he? Bowing, Brookes moved to stand next to Sophie.

"Captain Brookes, allow me to present Lieutenant Marable." Harriet indicated the young man with a wave of her gloved arm. He bowed low, and the lieutenant returned the salute.

"Captain Brookes, sir. I've heard tales of your sport at Waterloo." Marable regarded him with something like awe. His openmouthed gaze sent a frisson of discomfort down Brookes's spine.

"Have you, now?" Brookes turned and bowed to Sophie, who returned the honors. Facing Harriet, he made his salute. She curtsied, but kept her eyes trained on his face. She nodded, inclining her head ever so slightly. Her encouragement sent strength surging through his body.

"Oh, yes. The tales of your cavalry charge fill the men of my battalion with admiration." Marable turned and honored Harriet, then Sophie.

Would that young idiot shut his trap? Honestly, 'twas enough to try a man's patience. "Indeed." Brookes took Sophie's hands, leading her around to one side. He bowed to her, and she responded with a deep curtsy. He stepped gingerly at first, unsure if his leg would follow his commands. He shifted his weight slowly to the ball of his foot, then back to his heel, rising and falling in time with the music. He breathed a sigh of relief. Everything seemed to be going well. Time to engage in battle.

He reached out, taking Sophie's hands. They slid a few paces to the left, and he drew her slightly closer. "This reminds me of a ball some three years ago." He squeezed her hands, willing her to understand. He was the same wild lad as before he left for the peninsula, despite the outward changes she saw. Wasn't he?

Sophie rocked forward and then fell back into place. "I don't recall ever dancing the minuet." She dropped her head and peeked at Lieutenant Marable and Harriet, who mirrored their steps.

She only raised her head for the next movement, joining Marable in the middle of the floor, circling him with a coquettish air. She flashed Marable a dazzling smile, which he returned warmly. The couple bowed sideways at Brookes and Harriet. Catching Sophie's eye, he studied her with a curious intensity. He suspected the gulf between them grew wider with each step of the dance. Her eyes reflected glimmers of candlelight from the chandeliers up above, but he could not read her expression. She returned to her place beside him, bobbing down low.

He moved into the middle of the floor, rotating around Harriet. As they joined hands, Harriet hissed, "Do not lose hope, Captain. You are doing most exceedingly well." Then she turned away, giving Marable a brief salute. He had been so engaged in watching Sophie's movements and reactions that he had forgotten to gauge his own. He smiled with relief. Dancing came naturally to him on his wooden leg, just like before the war. His first success. He schooled his features back to an impassive mask, and returned to his place beside Sophie.

The ladies formed a star pattern, holding their hands high. Brookes stared at Harriet and Sophie circling left and then to the right. A fierce need to shelter and protect them both flooded his sensibilities. He blinked in a vain attempt to clear his vision. Harriet's purity reminded Brookes of a courtly maiden of old, granting her favor to a departing knight. He desired her good opinion. He wanted, for her sake, to be a better man. Should he honor his unspoken commitment to her sister only to lose her in the bargain? The problem ensnared Brookes, trapping him like the French regiment ambushed in the valley at Waterloo.

Sophie—well, capriciousness was her stock-in-trade. Yet he recalled the young woman who snipped a lock of her hair for him before he departed for the peninsula. He remembered the years of love letters they exchanged, their affection deepening into adoration with each missive. True, when he returned, she faltered.

So now he faced the most important decision of his life. Which sister desired his affections?

Or, to put it bluntly, which one deserved his love?

The ladies broke apart. He and Sophie spun around each other, their eyes locked. He gazed down at her, trying to read her very soul. Duty and honor won out over his heart. He could not pursue Harriet if an obligation existed with Sophie. His eyes flashed a private message to the slender, lovely creature he held. *Enough caprice.*

Sophie's blue eyes flickered in return. She backed away to the center of the floor again, linking hands with the other women. Had she finally capitulated? The men bowed to the ladies, and Brookes glanced over at Marable. His old competitive urge returned, running high. Brookes did not desire to win so much as he desired to beat Marable at his own game. But his foe smiled happily at the dancers, completely oblivious to all that transpired, in the blink of an eye, between his partner and Brookes. A heaviness settled in Brookes's chest. Marable never saw him as a challenge.

He led Sophie to the center of the floor, bowing low. She swished her skirts and returned the courtesy. Her eyes were cast down, but the color rose in her cheeks, a sure sign that her allegiance to Marable wavered. With an odd twinge of disappointment, Brookes no longer cared if she surrendered or if he won. Bringing the elegant dance to a finale, the ladies drew together, forming a regal line that faced the crowd. Brookes joined Marable and two other men in standing behind them. The twin columns of dancers saluted deeply to the group of onlookers. Polite applause broke out in a wave over the ballroom. He offered his elbow to Harriet, his earlier enthusiasm completely extinguished as he escorted her off the floor.

A hollow ache thudded in the pit of Harriet's stomach, leaving her with no appetite for supper. She toyed with the salad on her plate, stabbing it reluctantly with her fork. Lady Reese leaned over from her place on Harriet's right. "You should eat something more, my dear. Try the chicken, there's a good girl. I know it's the fashion for young ladies to pretend they never hunger. But after dancing, a hearty meal is a pleasant thing."

Harriet responded with a weak smile. She took a bite of the chicken, but it tasted like ashes in her mouth. Why was she so unhappy? After all, she had done everything she could to encourage the captain into reclaiming Sophie. Hadn't she cajoled Sophie into being kind, even throughout the minuet? Hadn't she applauded the captain for his splendid performance? Everything clicked into place just as it should. Her head throbbed, the blood pounding in her ears.

"I wish I had seen the action at Waterloo." Lieutenant

Marable sat across from Harriet, smiling at Sophie. "To be one of that regiment—well, they were the bravest group of soldiers since time immortal. Losing a limb in that battle is as good as a badge of courage, you know. If not for that wooden leg, I reckon Brookes would still be in the thick of army life."

Harriet observed a flicker of interest cross Sophie's face. "Is that so?"

"Oh, yes. Of course, the men of my regiment are green, but we all endeavor to be gallant and as brave as those men. It is our rallying cry." Marable waved a hand in the captain's direction, sitting a few tables over near a window.

Harriet watched her sister cast a glance at the captain. Her blue eyes deepened, a sure sign she was intrigued. So her sister perceived the captain in a new light, as a war hero. She stared at Sophie, trying to discern any spark of special interest.

"Your rallying cry?" Sophie echoed thoughtfully.

Harriet pushed away from the table with a scraping noise that set her teeth on edge. "Excuse me. I must find my mother." Her legs trembled so; she gripped the back of the chair for support.

"Of course, dear." Lady Reese caught her hand and patted it gently. "She is at the end of the table."

When Lady Handley spied her eldest daughter, her eyes widened with relief. Harriet knelt beside her mother's chair. "Mama, I am sure you must be exhausted. Shall we leave now?" Perhaps Mama's nerves could serve as her saving grace.

"Perhaps we should stay until after they serve the final course. Appearances, you know."

Tears filled Harriet's eyes. Another moment at the ball meant another moment of torture. Blinking rapidly, she whispered, "Honestly, Mama, I have such a headache."

Mama searched her face with a curious gaze, and Harriet

schooled her features to hide her roiling emotions, trying to appear headachy and tired—not heartbroken in the least. "I feel ill. Wouldn't you rather leave now, too?"

"Yes. We will leave now. I prefer that, as well."

"Oh, thank you, Mama." Relief flooded through Harriet.

"Go and fetch our cloaks. I shall collect your sister and meet you in the hall."

Harriet rose shakily from her mother's side. Her feet moved as though she swum through molasses, and it took forever to cross the supper room. Entering the hallway, she collided with something heavy. Strong arms seized her shoulders. "Are you all right?" She recognized the voice. She would know it anywhere, at any time.

She rubbed her eyes, clearing the tears away. Then she tilted her head up, looking steadily at Captain Brookes. "Yes," she managed in a shaky voice. "I have such a headache. I must go and rest or I am afraid I might be ill."

He released her shoulders. "I'm sorry to hear that. Give me a few moments, I will get my carriage and escort you home."

"No!" She could not bear the thought of being in an enclosed carriage with him and with Sophie. The mere mention of it churned her stomach. True, she never expected the captain to throw Sophie over for her. She encouraged them both to reunite. But their possible union hurled her heart into her slippers. She must stay far away from the pair of them to protect her emotions, until her heart healed.

His brows drew together in surprise at her tone. She hastened to soften the blow, lest she tip her hand. "I don't wish for you to leave early, simply because I must go."

"I do not like the idea of three women walking home alone this late at night."

"It's not that far," she protested. "There is no need."

He sighed, running his eyes over her face. "We will compromise. I will send you home in the carriage, but I will stay here, enjoying the dubious pleasures of a country dance. Agreed?"

She smiled in spite of herself. "Agreed."

Sophie and Mama emerged from the supper room, just as the carriage rolled to a halt before the village hall. The captain gallantly escorted them outside, and handed each one of them up into his carriage's luxurious interior. Harriet settled on the velvet seat, the touch of his gloved hand still burning into her arm. She shivered involuntarily as he rapped on the door. His hands were large and powerful. Even during their brief contact, his strength overwhelmed her.

"This is most luxurious." Mama sighed, running her hand over the lush velvet. "There was a time when I had a carriage this grand, and others besides. Sophie, if you would but marry the captain, then your family could enjoy this comfort again."

Sophie stared pensively at her mother. "He has not asked me, Mama."

Harriet rested her head on the tufted cushion, closing her eyes. Why couldn't she be a thousand miles away? The carriage was stifling; the walls of it pressed on her nerves. She exhaled slowly, trying to push the walls back into place.

"You have not encouraged him enough. You must show more affection." Mama sounded more like her old self than she had in years. Harriet recalled Mama giving her the same advice, night after night, during her London season.

"Very well. I will show him more affection. I did not know that he could dance on his wooden leg." Sophie paused, and then continued in an awestruck whisper, "Lieutenant Marable says that the captain's regiment's bravery is immortal."

"Ah, well then. Perhaps you should not be so cold to the captain. Restore our wealth to us, my daughter, and you will make your mother very happy. Harriet, how is your head?"

"Achy, Mama, but I will recover." Harriet pressed her skull more deeply into the cushion. Perhaps if she pushed hard enough, she would disappear.

## Chapter Ten

Harriet awoke in the chilly gray dawn with a heavy heart. She lay still in the bed, listening to Sophie's deep, even breathing. A desire for liberation seized her. She slipped out from under the covers noiselessly. Dressing in haste, she cast furtive glances over her shoulder at her sister. If she wakened Sophie, her sister would sail into gossip about the ball—and Harriet did not want to talk about the ball, or anything that happened last night, with anyone.

She stole across the hall and looked in on Mama, whose ever-present bottle of laudanum nestled against an empty glass. A few drops of liquid still clung to the bottom of the goblet. Mama slept soundly—so soundly that Harriet could march around her room banging a drum if she wished. Again, there was that doubt—was Mama taking the medicine too often? Dr. Wallace said a little laudanum would cause no harm, but was Mama only taking a little?

Harriet placed her hand on Mama's forehead, soothing it with a gentle touch. Whatever she might feel about Sophie and Captain Brookes, one thing would come of it all. Mama would become herself again once her former style of living was restored. A tightness seized Harriet's chest. She missed her mother so much it hurt. She missed Papa, too, but his death was a clean break. Mama's suffering was a slow torment.

She glided downstairs, ready to make an excuse for her early rising to Rose, but even Rose still slumbered. For once, no one needed her. Grabbing her cloak, she left the cottage in a swish of skirts, and ran as fast as she could.

She sprinted up the hill in the direction of Brookes Park, but diverted her steps toward the millpond, where she first met the captain on that fateful day of his return. She breathed deeply, gulping great lungfuls of air to clear her clouded mind. Making it to the crest of the hill, she gave out, collapsing on the ground with a thud. Drawing her knees up to her chest, she surveyed the little cottage, which crouched furtively at the bottom of the hill. She had never minded the smallness of the house before, but surveying it from this height, Tansley Cottage stifled her. It was tiny and close and the chimney smoked dreadfully in the rain. Naturally, it had rained all summer. And her mother always wailed about their lost fortunes, and her sister always preened, and though she loved them all with a fierceness that hurt, she simply could not countenance them this morning.

She hugged her knees. Sophie had regained some measure of adoration for the captain last night. And based on the triumphant expression he wore as he led her sister through the last few figures of the minuet, he felt the same. She shrugged her shoulders. What of it? Had they not always planned it so? However his wooden leg might have flummoxed Sophie, her feelings must now have changed.

Dew settled heavily across the grass, seeping through Harriet's cloak. But she didn't care. She struggled with some indefinable foe, and she had to get to the bottom of it all before she saw or spoke to anyone this morning. The captain's feelings should not bother her. Nor should Sophie's change of heart. After all, she had encouraged them both all along.

Did she love him?

Harriet paused. She esteemed him greatly. He was a good man, but she could not allow herself to go that far.

What, then?

Harriet squeezed her eyes shut. Sophie's abrupt change of heart boded ill. She wanted the captain to have someone who loved him with all her heart and soul. Though she loved her sister, Harriet worried about Sophie's flighty nature. Who knew when her feelings would change again?

But the matter was none of her affair. She could watch and guide and try to help, but ultimately her sister held the captain's happiness in her hands.

*Father, help me to understand. Help me.*

"Good morning, Harriet."

Harriet jumped.

Captain Brookes dismounted and strode over to her, settling beside her on the grass. Harriet swallowed. Trying to school her features into a semblance of calm, she waited a beat before speaking. "Good morning, Captain, you surprised me."

"You surprised *me*. Riding over the hills, I didn't even see you. Indeed, if Talos hadn't shied a bit, I might have run you over."

Was he serious? "Are you telling the truth?"

He smiled, his eyes lighting up with mischief. "No, I'm being a bit melodramatic. But it sounded like something in a Romantic poem, don't you agree?"

"It did." She returned the smile, but desperately concocted a plan to get away. 'Twas best to escape now, before he could sense her ruffled emotions.

"What are you doing out here?" His voice betrayed a mixture of confusion and interest.

"I was thinking. Praying a little, as well."

"May I ask why?" He snapped off a blade of grass and began peeling it apart, bit by bit.

She gasped a little. It wasn't exactly a prying question, but a terribly personal one. Her instinct for self-preservation rose to the surface, and she searched for an answer that wouldn't be too revealing. "I prayed for my family's happiness, and for wisdom."

"Why?" He tossed the shredded blade of grass away, picking at another.

"I don't know." His question confused her. "Why wouldn't I pray for my family?"

"Why do you need to pray for wisdom?" He faced her squarely, his green eyes darkening to gray.

She swallowed again. He didn't need to know the answers to these questions—her prayers were none of his affair. Still, she cast about for an answer that wouldn't incriminate her, wouldn't allow him to guess her innermost feelings.

"I prayed for wisdom as I write my book." A small lie, but one designed to protect her. Even so, she cast her eyes Heavenward and made a silent plea for forgiveness.

He nodded, turning his gaze back to the blade of grass in his hands. "Ah, the book. I see."

They sat in silence for a moment. Then he turned toward her again, a purposeful gleam in his eyes. "I cannot pray for wisdom, as you have. I lack your faith. But I would like to ask for *your* wisdom, if I may."

She looked at him warily. "I shall endeavor to help."

His eyes clouded, making it impossible to read his expression. A curious intensity—an aura, almost—belied the set of his shoulders. She found it hard to draw breath.

"About your sister…"

"Yes?" The blood pounded in her ears.

"Is there any reason I shouldn't ask her to be my wife?"

He sat so close that she saw the flecks of gray and brown in his green eyes.

A loud buzzing sounded in Harriet's ears, making it difficult for her to think. She looked away from him, focusing on the view of Tansley Cottage below. He loved Sophie. No use trying to delay or hinder the inevitable. She could not trust her voice, so she merely shook her head.

"I want to make sure there is no reason I shouldn't marry her."

She looked at him in confusion. His eyes were wide, searching. Almost as if they were demanding an answer from her. Whatever he sought, she couldn't fathom. She cleared her throat. "I know of no impediment, sir."

He sat back, as though her answer had knocked him out a little. "Very well."

Harriet stood abruptly, brushing her hands down her cloak. "I should be going, Captain. Everyone will be rising soon, and I wouldn't want them to miss me." She held out her hand in farewell, but he surprised her by grabbing it and using her strength to haul himself up from the ground.

"I shall come calling this afternoon." His voice was quiet and serious. His head was cast down, and she could not seek out his gaze. "Unless perhaps I should wait…"

He might ensure Sophie happiness. And Sophie? Harriet could only hope her sister's capricious nature ebbed away once his ring graced her finger. "No, Captain. I won't say a word. We have no plans today, so you are most welcome." She smiled up at him, her lips trembling a little as she attempted the same encouragement she had given during the minuet. "Most welcome."


Riding back toward Brookes Park, he replayed their conversation over and over in his head. Harriet did not care for him, that much was certain. She needed his help with writing her book, but she did not care for him as a man.

Brookes's gut turned with shame. It was a good thing—a very good thing—that he hadn't admitted any feelings of uncertainty to Harriet. Maybe it was just the minuet talking, but he was thoroughly confused about which Handley sister he should pursue. Along one path lay the call of duty, but his desire ran in quite another direction. Had he said as much to Harriet, he would have looked a proper fool and a blackguard, too. She didn't seem to care a fig about him, except as a good subject for a book.

In fact, Harriet would despise him if he showed his true feelings. She'd regard him as a bounder, a cad, ready to throw Sophie and all their unspoken promises aside after one dance with her. Brookes sighed. Did either of the Handley women want to be Mrs. John Brookes? He had an unspoken obligation to their family, after all. Was his injury so dreadful that neither would desire his suit? Some men probably knew just how to handle this situation—seasoned veterans in the art of love. But confusion and danger seemed to linger on all sides, and he was as green as a lad going into his first battle, knowing he only wanted to come out of it all right.

Why, 'twas exactly akin to charging into battle for the first time three years ago. He literally dodged a bullet—several of them—on that fateful morning. And now, in peacetime? He dodged another. He heard it whistle past.

Transferring the reins to his left hand, he reached into his pocket, feeling for his mother's ring. Yes, it was still there. He must continue helping Harriet with her book. He gave his word. No graceful way to back out now. And if she did not want him, he would simply control his feelings for her. No harm would come of spending many afternoons secretly enjoying her company.

The problem of Sophie remained. Brookes drew Talos to a stop, halting before he reached the gates. Sophie didn't like him anymore, or so it seemed. Even being in her company strained his nerves. But last night, during the minuet, he caught a brief glimpse of the Sophie he remembered. If he couldn't have the richness of a life with Harriet, perhaps he should settle for a life of superficial glamour with Sophie. By marrying her, at least matters resolved themselves. They could all resume their lives again. He would restore her family's fortunes, and Harriet might think kindly on him for that. He could not have the one he loved, so he would settle for the one he should get. He twitched the reins in irritation, spurring Talos to action, speeding past the gates to Brookes Park.

"Oh, Sophie, do be still. Your constant movements are enough to drive me mad." Harriet knelt in their bedroom, pinning a lining into the curtains for the parlor. Sophie blew a puff of air at her sister, drawing her fine brows into a straight line.

"Why do we have to work on this today? It's so dull. Why don't we do something fun?"

"Because we've needed new draperies in the parlor for these six months, at least. It's long past time to put them together. Oh, do compose yourself!" Harriet spat a pin out of her mouth, staring at Sophie in vexation. A prosaic task was just the thing to calm her nerves, and she promised to keep Sophie around the house until Captain Brookes's arrival. In choosing something large and cumbersome requiring Sophie's help, she tied Sophie to the cottage. If not, her sister would be off to gossip with friends all afternoon and miss the captain's visit.

But the dullness of putting together curtains quickly turned into chaos thanks to Sophie's inability to sit still. Harriet smoothed the fabric down with shaking hands. The captain said he would come in the afternoon. But here it was, almost three o'clock, and no captain in sight. A cold hand grasped Harriet's heart—perhaps something had happened to him. He sat a horse fine, but what if he had fallen off or been thrown? He could be lying out on the hill, bloody and broken, and no one would know for hours.

Harriet dropped the fabric on the bed, scurrying over to the window. Scanning the hill with anxious eyes, her heart pounding in her ears, she finally picked out a black horse and a tall rider. No harm befell him. He was fine. And he rode this way to propose to her sister.

"Whatever's the matter? Why are you staring out the window?" Sophie came to stand beside her sister, blocking Harriet's view with her curly head.

"I see the captain, darling. I imagine he's come to pay you a visit." Harriet formed the words with difficulty. Her voice held a breathless quality. "You should go down to the parlor. You don't need my help this time."

"Do you think he's come to propose?" Sophie faced her sister, a look of curiosity sharpening her features. Her sister didn't look at all nervous—indeed, she gave the impression of a spectator at a particularly interesting cricket match. "If so, I would rather have you there. Couldn't you be there, Hattie? To help smooth things along?"

"No." Harriet choked the word out. The walls of the tiny bedchamber closed in on her. "This is between you and the captain. It wouldn't do for me to be there." She turned blindly from the window and plunked down on the bed, heedless of the fabric and pins. "Please hurry, Sophie. It isn't polite to leave the captain waiting."

"Oh, all right." Sophie turned and regarded her sister crossly. "Goodness, you are missish today. Whatever is the matter with you?"

"I am simply tired of playing gooseberry with you and the captain. I want the whole affair to be settled, as soon as possible. And I want you to take charge of it." Harriet ran her tongue nervously over her lips when she finished speaking. Afraid Sophie would pry further beneath her prim facade and discern her roiling emotions; Harriet leaped from the bed and crossed over to the window. Glancing outside, she spied the captain as he dismounted from Talos. "Go at once. He is here."

"Fine, if you insist." Sophie turned and left the room, and the threshold squeaked as she paused in the doorway to fire her parting shot. "But I am not at all sure what I shall say to him."

## Chapter Eleven

Brookes sat in a small, spindly chair across the hearth from Sophie. The fragile thing, it creaked like it might crumple beneath his weight. He ran a finger inside his cravat, trying to loosen it. He tied it perfectly before he left home, but now it choked him. He stood, knocking the chair over in his haste. Sophie gazed up at him, a quizzical look forming between her brows. He bent down and set the flimsy chair upright and then sank down on the settee, which held his weight comfortably.

"I suppose you must know why I have come." His voice sounded strained, even to his own ears. He attempted to loosen the cravat again, but it remained as tight as before.

"Are you going to ask for my hand?" Sophie regarded him with a curious air. "Harriet refuses to come down. She thinks you mean to propose."

His heart pounded at the mere mention of Harriet's name. He took a deep breath to compose himself. "I had thought of it, yes. But I am unsure of your feelings since I returned to Tansley."

Sophie stood up and walked over to the window. Her hands were clasped behind her back. "Your leg bothered

me more than I thought it would. My apologies, Captain. I
had pictured your return very differently from what it was."

Her blunt manner cut through his nervousness and he relaxed a little. He hadn't realized that his shoulders hunched
to his ears. He pressed them down, feeling the tension
across his neck. "I understand." He thought he could understand. But at the same time, he would not have forsaken
Sophie if some accident had mutilated her. This realization
gripped him, and he stared at her back, attempting to see
the real woman beneath her flirtatious facade.

"But dancing with you last night did make me reconsider.
It reminded me somewhat of the past. Before you left for
the peninsula. Do you remember the poem you quoted me
before you departed? When I gave you a lock of my hair?"

How could he forget? He memorized that poem ages ago,
when he was a schoolboy. 'Twas his favorite. He closed his
eyes and began reciting, stumbling a little over the words.

*"True, a new mistress now I chase*
*The first foe in the field;*
*And with a stronger faith embrace*
*A sword, a horse, a shield."*

His throat constricted, and he could not go on. He stared
at Sophie's back, willing her to turn around. She stayed
rooted at the window, but her clear voice took up where he
left off.

*"Yet, this inconstancy is such*
*As you too shall adore;*
*I could not love thee, dear, so much*
*Loved I not honor more."*

Sophie's voice trailed off and silence descended on the
tiny parlor. Brookes watched her, waiting for her to turn and
give him the encouragement he needed to propose. Even the
slightest change of posture would help, but she remained
fixed before the window, unyielding.

Brookes could stand the silence no longer. "Lovelace,"

he noted, looking down at his boots. Why she mentioned the poem remained a mystery. If she no longer loved him, then reciting the verses meant nothing more than a heart-breaking recollection of the past.

Sophie turned and flounced back to the hearth, but remained silent. Brookes resumed command of the situation.

"I kept that lock of hair all those years." Her stiffness made him shrink from telling her he clutched it in his hand that last terrible night at Waterloo.

Sophie sighed, turning back from the hearth with her hands outstretched in supplication. "Captain, you must understand. I was a very young girl before you left. My head was easily turned, and the idea of you leaving for the war was romantic to me. I think I was more in love with the idea of being in love." She crossed her arms over her chest and gazed at the fire. "On the other hand, I feel a need to provide a level of comfort for my mother, who has been ill ever since Papa died."

He furrowed his brows, trying to come to grips with what she implied. Did Sophie mean that she would only marry him for his money? Or perhaps she sought a way out, too. If she wanted to extricate herself from his proposal, then there was hope for both of them yet. He cleared his throat. "We could postpone any formal engagement and allow ourselves the time to get reacquainted. There is no need to rush into matrimony."

Sophie nodded, a relieved smile brightening her features. "I agree, Captain. Perhaps we should give the matter some time. We could delay matters for even a few months."

Sophie had never spoken so practically before. Brookes considered her, tilting his head to one side. Was Harriet's good sense rubbing off on her? Thinking of Harriet, he blurted, "What will your sister think of me, if I don't propose to you?"

Sophie gazed at him, a thunderstruck expression crossing her face. "Whatever are you talking about?"

"I don't want your family to think I have reneged on my commitment." In fact, the idea weighed on his conscience so heavily that Brookes had difficulty forming the words. If he said it aloud, perhaps she would choose engagement rather than face her family's disappointment.

Sophie dismissed his anxiety with a flick of her wrist. "Oh, who cares about that? After all, we were never formally engaged. I'll speak to Harriet and Mama, don't worry. We both need time to know one another. I agree with you wholeheartedly, and at this time, I do not wish to press our relationship further." She folded her arms across her chest, waiting for his response.

Sophie's confession very neatly jerked the rug from under Brookes, and he took a moment to gather his thoughts. On the one hand, not being engaged to Sophie left the door somewhat open for pursuing Harriet. On the other hand, the arrangement was not a clean break. Every possibility remained that he might become engaged to Sophie in the future. He sighed. All right then. Some freedom was preferable to an engagement. 'Twas the best he could hope for at the moment, anyway. "Very well."

"Shall we shake hands?" Sophie extended hers gingerly, as if afraid Brookes would refuse.

He bowed over her hand gallantly. "Good day, Miss Handley."

"Good day, Captain Brookes." She bobbed a slight curtsy.

He shook his head, striding toward the door. The afternoon unfolded very differently than he originally planned. He must go home to Brookes Park and regain his bearings.

Harriet curled herself on the quilt in their little bedroom, waiting for Sophie to come running up the stairs. She steeled herself for the inevitable flash of Sophie's en-

gagement ring, and wondered if she should waken Mama.
Captain Brookes would want to speak to her, to ask for Sophie's hand in marriage. Harriet unfolded herself from the
quilt and rose from the bed, ready to rouse Mama from her
laudanum-induced slumber, when Sophie banged open the
door, striding in matter-of-factly.

"Oof! Now that's done." She sighed and flopped across
the bed, causing the rope mattress to squeak in protest. She
buried her face in her pillow. "What a relief."

"Where's the ring?" Harriet stared at her sister's left
hand, examining it curiously. "Did he not bring one?"

"We decided not to get engaged."

Had she heard correctly? Perhaps the pillow muffled Sophie's voice too much. She poked her sister's side. "Whatever are you saying?"

"Well, I am not sure we suit each other anymore. When
he returned, I knew he wasn't the same man I had known
before the war. And I must confess that I find other young
men—like Lieutenant Marable—charming. So we decided
to become acquainted with each other again. I honestly
don't know if I love him or not." Sophie pulled the pillow
away from her face and rolled onto her side, staring at Harriet.

Harriet's mouth went dry. "So are you engaged, or not?"
She grabbed Sophie's hand with her own, willing an answer
to her prayers.

"No, I am not. And I may not be, ever, to Captain
Brookes. I would like to know him better and then, if we
suit each other, I may encourage him. But Hattie, I honestly
don't know. He's become so serious. And his hair *is* gray, no
matter what you may say about it. He dances well to slow
songs, but could he handle more than a minuet?"

Sophie shook off Harriet's grasp and began picking
feathers out of her pillow, tossing them gently into the air.
"Lieutenant Marable, on the other hand, is very handsome,

and young, and can dance in a much livelier manner. But…
he may not be rich like Brookes. And I do feel the responsibility of having to provide some level of comfort for you
and for Mama. So I don't know what I shall do, but I do not
have any desire for a formal engagement at this time."

Harriet sighed, closing her eyes. Her heart resumed its
normal beat. Sophie was an incorrigible flirt. "In truth,
Sophie, you sound very much like you are encouraging two
good men along."

Sophie laughed merrily. "Not at all. I am merely waiting
to know my own mind before I make a decision that will
change the course of several lives."

Harriet opened her eyes slowly. Was Sophie's answer actually…sensible? Harriet agreed with her sister in theory.
She shouldn't rush into matrimony before knowing her own
mind. On the other hand, her flippancy over the matter
grieved Harriet. She set her heart on stringing two innocent
beaus in her wake until she decided which one she liked
best. But, then, that was Sophie.

"So, is my help no longer needed to keep the captain
entertained while you decide your own mind? After all,
that's why I have been playing gooseberry since his return."
Harriet willed an expression of calm over her face. Sophie
didn't need her, so her book project must end. She could no
longer spend any time in the captain's company. Her life expanded with her friendship with Brookes, and now it must
shrink back to the confines of Tansley Cottage.

"I doubt he will be coming to see us often. If he does
return, you can chaperone if you wish, or Mama can sit
with me. But I no longer fear the silence between us. I
spoke to him frankly—it was my first time to do so, you
know how I dislike confronting anyone—but I daresay it
made things better. I should have done so all along." Sophie
smiled, blowing a feather into the air. She watched as it
floated to the bare wood floor. "I cannot wait for the next

ball, for I can dance with both Marable and Brookes and compare which is the better partner."

"I suppose congratulations are in order?" Stoames came into the study, where Brookes savored an overfull glass of brandy.

"Yes, but not for the reasons you imagine." Brookes poured with a heavy hand, sliding the glass over to Stoames.

Stoames picked it up, regarding Brookes with a wary eye. "What happened?"

Brookes swirled the brandy in his glass, releasing its rich, full bouquet. "Do you recall what it feels like to dodge a bullet?"

"Only too well, Captain."

"Well, my good man, that's what happened to me today. In peacetime, no less." He swallowed a mouthful of brandy, allowing it to burn down into his chest.

Stoames cocked an eyebrow at him and reached out for the brandy bottle. "Unless you're telling me that an irate uncle turned up with a musket and forced you into matrimony, I think you've had a bit too much, Captain."

Brookes pushed his hand away, forcing Stoames to release the bottle. "I'm free, but not as much as I would like."

"Speak sense, man." Stoames sipped his drink slowly, his eyebrows lifted.

"Sophie and I decided to wait and become better acquainted before becoming engaged."

Stoames appraised him carefully. "You're handling it well. I would have expected more fire."

"I'm drinking." Brookes grabbed the bottle, splashing more of the amber liquid into his glass.

"I expect to see you drunker."

Brookes laughed. "I feel relieved. We are very different people now than we were before the war. So the agony of rushing into matrimony is gone."

Stoames whistled long and low. "A mighty close one indeed. And what about Miss Harriet?"

Brookes brought his glass down sharply on the desk. "Miss Harriet doesn't care for me, either. She told me so this morning. I am an unloved fool. None of the Handley women will have me."

"You told me this morning that she only said there was no impediment to your asking Miss Sophie. Have a bit of sense. She could hardly throw herself at you when you were going to propose to her sister." Stoames set his drink down on the desk, crossing his arms over his chest.

Brookes met Stoames's challenging gaze squarely. "I suppose that's true." Perhaps there was reason to be optimistic yet. "What should I do?"

"If you are still tied to Miss Sophie you can't pursue Miss Harriet. On the other hand, you can find ways to make Miss Harriet think kindly of you."

"I could help her with her book still." Brookes sighed. "But I need to find a way to do so without raising eyebrows. An unmarried man and woman alone together—her reputation—"

"I have good news. While you were out, a guest arrived." Stoames turned down one corner of his mouth, grimacing slightly. "She'll be here for some weeks."

"Let me guess. Aunt Katherine?" Father's sister—of course, she would descend on him without warning. And stay for weeks on end. Brookes shook his head, trying to clear his brandy-induced brain fog. "I don't follow. How does this help me with Harriet?"

"Well, she arrived today whilst you were at the cottage. She's having her afternoon nap, but she'll be down for supper. I'm thinking you could use her visit to your advantage. She could chaperone while you and Miss Harriet work on the book. Giving you the means—"

"To help Harriet." Brookes smiled for the first time that day. Hope washed over him, leaving him giddy. "Stoames, a toast, to my Aunt Katherine."

# Chapter Twelve

Harriet shifted the stack of books in her hand, transferring them to the crook of her elbow. She must return everything Brookes loaned her. Make a clean slate of the whole matter. She grasped the heavy brass knocker, allowing it to fall against the strike plate with a small crash. Goodness, everything at Brookes Park was so substantial. Had she knocked on Tansley Cottage's door like that, the flimsy thing would've fallen in.

The door swung open and Bunting smiled at her. "Good day, Miss Handley. Won't you come inside?"

"Oh, no, Bunting. I came to return the books I borrowed." Harriet indicated the pile with a brief nod. "If I gave these to you, would you please return them to Captain Brookes's library?"

Bunting shook his head, pulling his brows together in confusion. "There must be some misunderstanding, Miss. Captain Brookes expected you this morning. Everything is set up in the library for your work."

Harriet tilted her head. Whatever was the butler talking of? "We didn't have any work set up for today, Bunting—none that I can recall."

"Well, perhaps you should wait and speak to the captain

himself. He is at the mill at the moment but should return within the quarter hour. He left very strict instructions for me to show you into the library when you arrived." Bunting stepped back, opening the entrance wider. "This way, if you please."

Harriet stepped inside the vestibule, pushing her bonnet back. Heat prickled along her hairline. She hoped to make a quick trip and an even hastier retreat, but Bunting impeded her plans. She had no desire to face Brookes, not today. If only the butler weren't so...*butler-ly.* She couldn't very well back out without causing some kind of scene, one that might make Bunting's brows fly up in shock. He led the way to the library, which stood open and welcoming. A fire blazed in the grate. Stopping on the threshold, Bunting announced, "Mrs. Crossley, Miss Harriet Handley is here."

"Of course, do show her in." The voice was decidedly elderly, but rich and amused, too. Harriet fell back a step. Mrs. Crossley—who on earth could that be? And why was she here? Bunting crossed the doorsill and waited. Harriet, remembering her manners, stepped into the room, right into the approving gaze of the most astonishing old woman she ever beheld.

Mrs. Crossley perched on a divan near the fire, knitting rapidly. Her face reminded one of an old apple, but a merry twinkle sparked the kind blue eyes that regarded Harriet. A mass of slate-gray corkscrew curls peeked out under a black lace cap, which was tied in a jaunty bow under her chin. She extended a fragile hand, studded with rings of every conceivable color and size. "Come in, my dear. My nephew has told me so much about you."

Harriet took the hand, and with a surprising strength that belied her age, Mrs. Crossley drew her down onto the divan. "Now, let us have a good chin-wag before John returns. Bunting, some tea, if you please."

"Of course, ma'am." Bunting set the pile of books on the desk and bowed out.

She'd lost her manners again. She had been staring at Mrs. Crossley without a word of greeting. She shook her head to snap out of her reverie, and smiled at Mrs. Crossley. "It's a pleasure to meet you. I must confess I am confused. I meant only to return the books I borrowed, but Bunting insisted on showing me in."

Mrs. Crossley took up her knitting again. "John was adamant that Bunting keep you here until he returns. John has told me everything about your book, and I must say I admire your spirit. For a young girl to try and support her own family through her pen—it's fantastic. In my day, all a young woman could do was marry well. My nephew esteems you, too, and he's determined to help with the project."

Harriet blinked. "I don't know how the captain suspected I was on my way. I meant to run over and hurry back home this morning."

Mrs. Crossley smiled, a look of contentment flickering over her wrinkled features. "My John is very good at surmising situations. It's why he became such a brilliant soldier."

Harriet leaned back against the cushions. Mrs. Crossley's matter-of-fact manner loosened her tongue. She shook her head with conviction. "I don't think he wants to continue working on it, since his future with my sister is undecided at present."

Mrs. Crossley clicked her tongue against her false teeth. "Tut tut, my dear. John believes in your project. He told me about your sister, but never mentioned delaying or ceasing your book. It stands on its own merits. If you are worried about appearances, I am only too happy to chaperone. I descended on my nephew as soon as he returned safely home to Tansley, and I can earn my keep by helping you both with the project. No one will think a thing about it while I am here, and I intend to stay for several months. I missed my John while he fought on the peninsula. I have no desire to leave his company so soon."

Harriet glowed. She liked Mrs. Crossley already. She pressed her head against the cushion more deeply and allowed a cautious smile to creep across her face. "Thank you for your help."

"Not at all, not at all, my dear. Now, I will ask you about your family, but before I pry anything out of you, I shall tell you about mine. That way you will be disarmed into telling me everything and I shan't have to go digging."

Harriet smiled. "That seems a very brazen way to go about gathering secrets."

Mrs. Crossley laughed. "You would be surprised at how well it works. Now, let's see. I am John's aunt on his father's side. I married Mr. Crossley, who was a wine merchant, when I was but seventeen years old. In my day, women married very young. How old are you, Miss Handley?"

Harriet smiled at the impertinent question—it was impossible to be cross with Brookes's aunt. "I am two and twenty. My sister is twenty."

"Ah, well, John is all of twenty-eight—mature, you understand, but still young. He will make some lucky young woman a very good husband. And, hark this, that graying hair is from his battles on the peninsula, I am sure. He is not so old in spirit." She paused to draw breath. "What was I talking of? Oh, yes, my husband. We moved away from Tansley, settling in London." She placed her knitting in her lap and sighed. "I've outlived almost everyone, including John's mother and father, and even his brother, Henry. When word came that John survived Waterloo, I made up my mind to see him the moment he returned." She broke off as Bunting entered with the tea. "Ah, I do hope you didn't bring any of that detestable lapsang souchong. I cannot abide the smoky flavor."

"No, ma'am." Bunting set the tray on a small mahogany table, drawing it close to the two women. "Only the oolong, very delicate and flowery, I'm told."

Mrs. Crossley waved him away. "Now, dear, about your family—"

Harriet steeled herself. The wise old woman's scheme worked only too well. A pent-up flood of confidences poised on the tip of her tongue—she longed to confess all to Mrs. Crossley, from the loss of the family fortune to her sister's flippant refusal of Captain Brookes's hand.

"Aunt Katherine, you are a shameless busybody." Brookes strode purposefully into the room, regarding his aunt with a bemused expression.

"Oh, you naughty boy. Just when she was about to tell me everything." She smiled and began pouring the tea. "And now it's only a few moments before you young people get to work and all pleasure will be forgotten." She handed a cup to Harriet, and one to Brookes.

Harriet took a fortifying sip of her tea. "Mrs. Crossley has told me about your plan to continue working on the book. I must confess I am most grateful to you, sir. I thought for sure you would give up the project." She raised her eyes to find him watching her intensely. His gaze brought warmth rushing to her cheeks.

"Not at all." His look softened and he gave her a conspiratorial wink. "I have to keep Aunt Katherine busy, you know." The old lady smiled and sipped her tea, the perfect picture of innocence.

"Come sit at the desk, and we will continue working on your book. You see, I have your paper and pen all ready. When we spoke at the village dance the other night, I told you about the Duchess of Richmond's ball. Would you like to know more about it?"

"Oh, yes, Captain." Harriet rose, and made her way to his desk, clutching her teacup in one hand. "I should like to know everything."

"She is a dear girl," Aunt Katherine said after Harriet had departed for the day. "I like her very much. Too bad I shan't be calling her my niece soon. Tell me, John, what is so wonderful about this Sophie that you are determined to pass Harriet over for her?"

Brookes sighed. Auntie was up to her old tricks, meddling where she didn't belong. It was only a matter of time before she pried the whole story from him. He held up his hand to stem her scolding.

"Auntie, upon my honor, I was a green lad when I left for the peninsula. I saw only Sophie's beauty and charm. I didn't understand the sweetness and generosity of a woman like Harriet. Now I see her worth only too well. But I am bound to honor my promise to Sophie."

"Stupid blunderer," Auntie replied with affection. "You can't let a girl like Harriet slip away from you."

Brookes regarded his aunt with wonderment. She never liked anyone wholeheartedly right away, and she often prided herself on reserving judgment until she had known a person for months, if not years. Harriet was the sole exception to her rule, at least in his recollection. "What makes you like her so much, Aunt?"

She put down her knitting, and stared into the fire. Silence descended on the room, punctuated only by the crackle of the flames in the hearth. Brookes tilted his head. Auntie was never silent—she always had an opinion about everything, from tea to young women, at the ready. How unusual for her to think about anything before pronouncing judgment.

"She is so very still, so deep, John. I know you saw a lot during the war. I can tell from the look in your eyes that you saw things most men dare not contemplate. She is the one who can give you solace. Remember, as the Lord said in the book of Genesis, 'It is not good for the man to be alone.' Harriet is your helpmate. She *is* good."

Brookes's mind shuttered, as it did with any mention of faith. "Aunt, I hope you'll understand when I say I don't like to discuss faith. I lost my belief in God the night I almost died at Waterloo. That kind of talk makes me highly uncomfortable."

She peered at him sharply, giving Brookes the uncomfortable impression that she read into his very soul. "How very modern of you. I am sure your reasons are your own, so I won't try to meddle with your religious beliefs. But honestly, my boy, you did ask my reasons, and there you have them."

He drummed his fingers on the table with impatience. "True, I'll give you that. But promise me one thing, Aunt— don't interfere. I've made a hash of things and I am trying to set everything right. I've already told Stoames to hold his tongue."

"I'll promise no such thing, and hopefully Stoames didn't either. I like Stoames. He's salt of the earth. I expect he and I together will make you see sense." Her voice was as tart and sweet as the lemon curd they had spread on the scones at tea. "On the other hand, I will promise not to meddle within your hearing."

Brookes sighed. It was as good as any promise he could hope for.

The little mantel clock in the parlor chimed one o'clock. Everyone slept in the predawn hush, except Harriet. After the clock ceased its toll, only Harriet's pen scratching across the paper broke the silence. She hunched over the page, her hands frozen in the cold, but there was no time to care about physical discomforts. Harriet poured out her thoughts and ideas about her book onto paper. 'Twas a soldier's memoir, first-person, but she wouldn't pretend to be Brookes. She invented an imaginary soldier, ready to live the war through his eyes: Mr. J. H. Twigg.

An idealistic lad, Twigg fought for the heroic concepts of truth, majesty and heroism. But his first battle awakened Twigg to the reality of war. Harriet paused, rubbing her palms together, trying to ease the stiffness out of her joints. Her hero must suffer the way real men suffered. Men who had fought and died alongside Brookes for king and country. The depths of Brookes's suffering she could not guess, but as a good writer she must at least imagine his torment. Twigg's suffering could not be farcical, only realism would do. If Harriet struck the wrong note, her book might fail to pay tribute to Brookes and his men. Harriet's heart pounded. She could not confess her love for Brookes, but her book could be her declaration of love. He must never know it, of course, but in writing the book, she could speak the words filling her heart. The book had to be her masterpiece. Nothing less would do.

Harriet stilled for a moment, and then allowed the flood of words to wash over her and fill the pages. In time, the little mantel clock chimed four o'clock. Her eyes fluttered closed, and she forced them open for one last moment. She blew a little puff of air on the candle, which burned so low that it was nothing more than a pool of grease and a small, guttering flame. Pillowing her head on her crossed arms, heedless of the drying ink, Harriet fell fast asleep, clinging to the desk as she would a life raft.

# Chapter Thirteen

*He* lay facedown in the mud, scarcely daring to draw breath. The two Prussians looted soldiers less than a yard away, judging by the sound of their voices. Maybe if he played dead, they would pass him over. No, he wore an officer's uniform, which bespoke wealth and privilege, something they would not ignore. He couldn't move, not without attracting attention. He would either die immediately, or simply wait until they reached him. Either way, his life was over. The blood pounded in his ears. His mouth was so dry he couldn't swallow. He dropped Sophie's lock of hair. Groping slowly through the mud, he found the hilt of his sword, buried deep in the muck. If he was going to die, he would die fending them off, as a good soldier should.

He dropped his head back into the mud, but it struck bare wood.

Wood?

Brookes pulled himself up. He shook his head, trying to get his bearings. Slowly, it dawned on him that his head had struck the bare wood floor of his bedroom at Brookes Park. He had been dreaming again, that same nightmare that wakened him in a cold sweat every night since Waterloo. Only this time, he fell off his settee. He groped underneath it and found what he sought—his decanter and glass. With shaking hands, he poured a long draught.

The dressing room door flew open, and Stoames emerged. "Captain, are you all right?"

"Fine, Stoames. I fell off the couch. Here—join me."

Before Stoames could answer, a loud knock shook the bedroom door. A female voice, elderly and imperious, called out, "John? Are you all right? Let me in."

Brookes muttered a curse under his breath while Stoames crossed over and opened the door for Aunt Katherine. Waking her meant answering questions, something he didn't want to do, especially at this hour.

"John? Whatever is the matter with you? It sounded like a pile of bricks hit the floor in here. Woke me up out of a sound sleep."

"My deepest apologies, Auntie. I fell off the settee." He took a long pull of brandy and swallowed. After the dream, he always burned with the same all-consuming thirst that plagued him on the battlefield. Nothing ever quenched that fiery craving, not even the brandy. He smiled, hoping that he appeared nonchalant enough that Auntie would return to bed.

She strode into the room and perched on the sofa, regarding him with eyes that only grew sharper with age. "The settee? Why aren't you in your bed?"

"Auntie, for goodness' sake. I'm still in my dressing gown. Can we have this conversation tomorrow?"

"Tut, tut. I'm not in the least put off by your dishabille, my proud soldier. I used to change your nappies, if you'll but recall. Stoames, clear away this brandy. My nephew doesn't need it. Certainly not at two o' clock in the morning."

Stoames hesitated, his eyes darting between Brookes and Aunt Katherine, assessing who was the better bet.

Brookes sighed. "Take it away, Stoames."

Stoames picked up the tray and quit the room as quickly as his soldierly dignity would allow.

"Now, John. Answer the question. Why are you on the settee instead of your bed?"

Brookes regarded his aunt evenly. When he was a child, he climbed to the top of a tall oak tree at the Park even though his parents had forbidden it. He fell, of course, and sprained his ankle. Though he tried to hide his limp, Auntie discovered the truth. She held no patience for pleasant lies, not then and not now. Honesty proved the best policy. "Auntie, after losing my leg, I find it more comfortable to sleep there than in my bed."

She nodded. "Is there any other reason?"

He swallowed. Only Stoames knew the depths of his suffering during the war, and they never discussed it. No one else knew what happened the night of Waterloo. He tried to form the words, but they choked in his throat. A draught of brandy might have loosened them. But, denied his liquor, he stared into the fire, shaking his head. He finally spat the word out. "Nightmares."

"Ah." Auntie leaned over and patted his shoulder. "My boy, I don't know what to say, because I have a feeling that anything I would say would be inadequate to the situation. But know that you are home now, and loved."

He would never cry in front of a woman, least of all his aunt. He stared straight ahead at the fire, allowing the heat and light from the flames to dry up any suspicious moisture. He swallowed again, and reached up, patting her hand. "Thank you."

"I don't know much about war, John, but I have a feeling that, if you were to find a confidant, you could pour out the horror of all you experienced. Perhaps, by talking about it with someone, you could begin to recover."

Brookes looked up at his aunt, his brows drawing together in confusion. "Only Stoames knows what happened,

Aunt. We've both lived through it. Why would we wish to talk about it?"

"Oh, I didn't mean Stoames. I meant Harriet."

He turned and faced his aunt, opening his eyes wider, focusing on her wrinkled face. "Harriet? Why would I tell these things to Harriet?"

"Well, you did promise to help her with the book. And that girl is a good listener. Like I said, very quiet and still. I imagine it would do you good."

He shook his head, quirking the corner of his mouth into a half smile. "I could never tell Harriet the truth of what happened."

"Why not?" Aunt Katherine drew her legs up under the settee and wrapped her shawl more tightly around her shoulders.

"She's led a very sheltered life, Auntie. Hearing the truth about war would horrify her."

"Balderdash." Auntie pronounced the word with a flourish that would make Stoames proud. Brookes regarded his aunt with a frank stare.

"Something in that girl's eyes tells me she's suffered, too. Didn't you say her father was Sir Hugh Handley? Handley Hall was a famous manor house in its day. A library that rivaled Alexandria, my dear. And now the mother and sisters reside in a poky cottage on the outskirts of Tansley Village? What caused their downfall? That girl has seen some truth in life, depend upon it, my boy."

He pondered his aunt's words. "But she still has so much faith…" He was unsure of what he was trying to say, except he didn't understand why she had faith and he had none. Did her surfeit of faith hide her personal troubles?

"To me, that sounds like the mark of a strong character. You don't have to take an old woman's advice, but I do feel most strongly that talking to Harriet could only help." She drew herself up from the couch with a yawn. "Upon my word, these ancient bones creak more than they used to. This old woman needs her sleep. Will you be all right?"

"Yes, Aunt." He smiled at her, but remained sitting on the floor. His wooden leg was beside the couch, and he didn't relish the trouble or embarrassment of putting it on in front of her simply to show her to the door.

She smiled, as if reading his mind. "After I leave, why don't you try sleeping in your bed? Only for tonight. You might find it more comfortable."

He couldn't smother the grin that crossed his face. Auntie was bound to meddle, in every aspect of his life. His heart surged with love.

"I'll try, Aunt. Good night."

Harriet had one duty: committing the soldier's life and thoughts to paper in a manner that was believable, but never exploitative. Brookes gave her access to the outer aspects of his existence as an officer, but a wall he built prevented her from understanding his innermost feelings. If only she could break down that wall. Once she knew what he felt the day he almost died at Waterloo, she would get to the very soul of the man she admired.

She had chastised herself at first for riding roughshod over Brookes's soul, but now she needed to know the truth or she would never pay honest tribute to his suffering without his trust. Staring off into space, Harriet nibbled on the end of her pen. She shrank from prying too deeply into Brookes's experience, but her character was a mere puppet on a stage without his help. If she could only break through the captain's reserve, Twigg might become fully human. And since Twigg was her homage to Brookes, he must be as brave, heroic, and vital as the real man.

Harriet tapped her pen on the desk. How could she loosen his tongue without prying? Mrs. Crossley certainly had no trouble loosening Harriet's during her visit. How was the old woman able to inspire such confidence from others? She had been a complete stranger to Harriet, and yet, within moments Harriet was prepared to pour out her life's story. Harriet blinked. Ah, yes. Mrs. Crossley had shared her confidences first.

Of course, that made perfect sense. How could Brookes trust her with his most private and painful memories if she never shared hers? Shame flooded Harriet's senses, leaving her cheeks hot. All she had done was fire questions at him, neglecting to develop a bond with him. They must share mutual concord and faith for their partnership to be a success. Today, she wouldn't be so inquisitive. She would share instead.

Sophie opened the door to the parlor, breaking Harriet's privacy. "Are you going to Brookes Park today?"

"Of course, after Mama starts her afternoon nap. Why do you ask?" A prickle of unease worked its way up Harriet's spine.

Sophie sidled in, closing the door behind her. "I feel I should come along. Since the captain and I are trying to get to know one another, I should make an effort to see him more."

A bubble of frustration welled in Harriet's chest. If Sophie called on the captain, too, then the day would be lost. No, not only the day, but perhaps Harriet's chance at forging any kind of bond with Brookes. For Harriet never knew, one day to the next, if he would finally tell her he was done with her prying questions. And if Sophie came, she would remind him of his obligation to establish bonds of love and trust with her. But Harriet needed to forge a bond of her own with Brookes. She cast down her pen and faced Sophie squarely.

"I won't be able to do much work with you there. You'll distract him."

"Oh, la, that's what I should be doing." Sophie smiled and patted her golden ringlets. "Don't you agree?"

Harriet could think of no sensible reason to deny Sophie's request—not without exposing her own true feelings of regard for Brookes, or telling Sophie of her plan to connect deeply with him. She sighed; she would have to take her chances. "Very well. But mind, if he decides that we should work, you must allow us to talk without interruption."

Sophie shrugged her shoulders in irritation. "Oh, fine. But I doubt very much that the captain will care a fig about work, when he sees how well my new bonnet suits me."

The two sisters walked up the courtyard and Sophie tilted her head back, regarding the massive stone facade. "Oh, just think. I might be mistress of this someday. If I choose the captain," she breathed, and squeezed Harriet's arm. Harriet resisted the urge to shake her off. After all, Sophie was only stating the truth. Within a year, Harriet might well be coming to visit her sister here. Or—Harriet shuddered, shrinking a little inside—might be living under this same roof with Brookes and Sophie and her mother. Surely they could have their own cottage. Harriet would gladly keep Tansley Cottage, smoky chimney and all, if it meant she wouldn't be living in close proximity to Sophie and Brookes's domestic bliss.

Bunting showed them into the library, where everything was set up as usual, awaiting Harriet's arrival. Mrs. Crossley and Brookes sat before the fire. Brookes read a book, and Mrs. Crossley knitted her same interminable shawl.

Brookes thumped the book on a table, starting out of his chair. Peering closely at it, Harriet recognized the volume of Donne she borrowed weeks before. She turned her eyes back to his face. Judging by the quick lift of his brows, Sophie's arrival surprised him. She dove into the social graces without delay, hoping to smooth over his shock. "Captain, my sister wanted to come along today. She hasn't made your aunt's acquaintance, and I speak of Mrs. Crossley so often and so highly, that she simply had to meet her. Mrs. Crossley, may I present my sister, Miss Sophie Handley?"

Mrs. Crossley rose, inclining her head toward Sophie. "A pleasure to meet you, my dear."

Sophie bobbed a curtsy. "I am most grateful to meet you, ma'am."

For a brief second, Harriet didn't know what to do. She knew she needed to broach the subject of work with the captain, but it seemed rude to begin talking about the war with Sophie there. Her mere presence made it a social call rather than an opportunity to learn.

Mrs. Crossley entered the fray, motioning for Sophie to join her on the settee. "Now, my dear, you and I shall sit here and discuss lovely frivolous things, while those two labor away on Harriet's book. I am sure our chatter will interrupt the muse, though. Perhaps, Brookes, you should take Harriet for a walk around the estate, and you two can discuss the war. That way, you won't be disturbed by my chat with pretty Miss Sophie."

Harriet peered at Mrs. Crossley, who had taken up the social reins smoothly and gracefully, manipulating everything to suit her needs. Even Sophie was disarmed by the flattery, and appeared to think nothing of Harriet leaving with Brookes—though her entire purpose in coming was to spend time with him. Harriet smiled in gratitude. She might have a chance to start bridging the gap today after all.

Brookes nodded, and offered Harriet his elbow. Mrs. Crossley called after them, "Brookes, take Miss Harriet to the hot spring—it's an ideal setting for working on the book. You will find the peace and quiet there you need."

## Chapter Fourteen

A steady cool breeze blew across the hills, ruffling the long grass. Brookes paused for a moment, drinking in the sweet smell of drying hay. The scent of summer reminded him of the long months he spent swimming in the spring, climbing trees in the park, or riding horses with Henry. He snapped off a piece of moor grass and twisted it in his fingers, releasing its musty scent. He stole a sidelong glance at Harriet, who delicately picked her way through the field, skirts slightly raised. "It's up ahead, not much farther," he said, waving the grass at a squat, gray stone building that gave the appearance of springing up from the meadow.

Harriet uttered a surprised cry. "I knew you had a spring, but I never expected to see a proper bathhouse."

"My grandfather built it many years ago. The waters are nice and warm, not burning hot like you find in Matlock Bath. My brother and I often swam here, not only in the summer, but the whole year 'round."

"Have you taken the waters since your return?"

An innocent question, but it put his hackles up immediately. How well might his leg fare with swimming? But then, he hated the sight of the ravaged stump by daylight.

"No." He winced at the curt reply. More gently, he added, "I haven't had time, you see."

"Oh." She fell silent.

He tossed the grass away with an irritated flick of the wrist, and motioned for her to follow. The bathhouse had a single oaken door that the family never bothered to lock, but it often swelled and stuck with the humidity. Grasping the latch, he leveraged the door open with his shoulder. It creaked in protest as he swung it open. Turning back to Harriet, he offered his hand. "Come inside, it's quite nice."

She grasped his hand. A tingle shot through his being, elicited by her mere touch. He glanced around briefly to make sure no animals had made the bathhouse their permanent habitat during his few years away. Fortunately, it seemed deserted. A fine layer of dust covered the gray stone floor, and a layer of grime muted the daylight streaming in through the windows. Brookes made a mental note to send the servants out to give it a good scrubbing. But the dirt wouldn't prevent their work, and the spring water gave the air a pleasantly sour odor. Other than the layer of grime, the bathhouse remained as pleasurable as he remembered. Harriet's mouth had dropped open in amazement and he smiled.

"It's wonderful. If I had a bathhouse like this, I would swim every day." She brushed past him, striding into the main room that housed the spring.

"Careful, the stones become slick with the damp," he cautioned.

She nodded, slowing her steps. "May I sit here on this bench?"

"Sit with care, Harriet. Sometimes the benches are wet, too." He opened a chest that stood inside the vestibule, and drew out a few rough hemp towels. "Here, allow me." He joined her in the main room and draped them over the stone bench. "This will keep out some of the damp."

"Thank you." She sank down on the bench and peered around. The unnatural echo of their voices accompanied the hissing of the spring in the bathhouse. Warmth cocooned them, sheltering them both from the outside world. Brookes sat beside Harriet, scuffing his boots along the gritty stone floor to make some kind of sound, anything to break the spell.

Harriet sighed. "I wonder if something like this would do my mother good."

Brookes tilted his head at her. "What do you mean?"

"Mama is suffering from what Dr. Wallace calls nervous hysteria. He has her on laudanum." She paused. "I am not sure if it's helping… She sleeps all the time." The words rushed out of her in a torrent, as though she were finally allowing a dam to break. "I wonder if something else could be more help. Taking the waters somewhere—anything to strengthen her constitution."

Brookes's eyebrows lifted slightly in surprise. Harriet never mentioned her troubles before. From outward appearances, he surmised that her family lost their fortune but pulled through the ordeal with no great trouble. But her voice held a slight tremor, and the way she allowed the words to pour out caught his attention. Life at Tansley Cottage was not at all rosy.

He cleared his throat. "I'm very sorry to hear it, Harriet. You could bring your mother here to take the waters. It's not as far a journey as Matlock Bath, and no one would even know you were here."

She whipped her head around, smiling as if he had offered the moon. "Oh, thank you, Captain. I would try that, if I may."

A burning desire to hear her speak his given name seized Brookes. "It seems unfair that I can call you Harriet, but you always refer to me as Captain or Sir. Please, do call me John."

"Thank you, John." Her voice hushed, and her head bowed.

He had never thought much of his given name, but from her lips it sounded honeyed, sweet, almost cherished. He shook his head. It was a name. No call to get all starry-eyed about it.

"The collapse of my father's affairs has proven too much for my mother," Harriet continued in an even tone. "You see, we had no idea how far his debts reached until after he died. And then, when we discovered how badly things were, there was nothing more that could be done. We had to retrench to Tansley Cottage."

"Why didn't any of your father's family come to your assistance?"

Harriet's eyes clouded over and she swallowed. Brookes sensed that she measured how much to tell him. "Perhaps you don't know this, but my parents' marriage is considered something of a misalliance. Papa was a knight, you know, and my mother was a commoner."

"But that sort of thing happens all the time." Brookes quirked an eyebrow at her. Dislike of his future extended family left a bitter taste in his mouth. The Handleys sounded like a prejudiced and priggish lot. "It seems most ungenerous of them."

"Well, if you must know the truth, Mama was an actress before she married Papa." Harriet turned and faced him as though she faced down a lion in his den. "Below a commoner, you might say."

He ran his eyes over her face, trying to understand why she told him all this. After all, he could have been the sort of man to cut ties and run after hearing such a tale. An actress in the family—many men would shy away from the possibility of such relations. Her honesty and trust humbled him.

Harriet sat ramrod-straight save her bowed head. He

knew the defensive position well. "It's a relief to tell someone," she whispered, keeping her eyes fixed on the floor.

"Thank you for telling me." He stared into the pool, watching the bubbles rise to the surface. "I appreciate your trust in me."

"Thank you for allowing me to confess. I feel better talking about it with someone." She rose from her seat and circled the pool, gazing into it. "May I ask you something?"

His defenses rose, unsure of what she wanted to know. He watched her cagily, trying to guess what she would say. "Yes."

From the opposite end of the pool, she turned to face him. "Does your leg hurt?"

He exhaled slowly through his nostrils. "No. It's strange because sometimes I get a pain in my foot or feel an itch on my calf, but my leg is no longer there. But it doesn't hurt. I think—" he surprised himself, not knowing if he should continue or not "—I think the nightmares are infinitely more disturbing."

"You have nightmares?" She turned and wandered back to the bench, stepping carefully over the slick stones.

"Every night since Waterloo. I hate the thought of sleeping, because I know it's only a matter of time until I begin reliving that night on the battlefield."

He hesitated, waiting for her to press him for further details. But instead, she joined him back on the bench, admitting, "I had nightmares for a long time, too."

"About what?" He turned to face her, studying her expression.

"The day the duns took our home away. They went through everything. It was like a plague of locusts." A shudder ran through her body. "It was the most savage invasion of privacy I ever experienced. They even took the quilt from my bed. A part of me died that day. I know it sounds dramatic to say it, but it's true. While the duns went through Handley Hall with a fine-tooth comb, I burned every manuscript I had ever written."

His mouth dropped open. She may well have told him she cut herself with a knife, her revelation was so shocking. "Why would you do such a thing?"

"Because writing about people who never existed seemed like a frivolous thing to do when my world was collapsing around me." A single tear ran down her cheeks.

The urge to embrace her overcame him and he stood up to fight it. He wanted to protect her from any more of life's fierce storms, giving her the security and love she so desperately wanted and deserved. Stepping away from the bench, he paced halfway around the pool and back, handing her his handkerchief. "I am so sorry. I know that's not much to say, but I am."

"No, I have to apologize. I don't know what came over me. I've never cried about it before." She blew her nose and clutched the handkerchief in both hands, twisting it into a little rope.

They sat in silence for a moment. Brookes crossed his arms over his chest, attempting to overpower his desire to reach out to Harriet. Why had Harriet's father allowed his situation to deteriorate so badly, without retrenching sooner? It seemed a wretched folly on his part. More than ever, he admired Harriet for all she was attempting to do to save her little family. Neither her mother, drowsy with laudanum, nor her sister, preening about the village, were making the same decisive strides to improve the family's fortunes.

Harriet sniffed a few times. "I feel better now. Thank you."

"Not at all."

"I wish there were something I could do to help you." She

looked up at him, her eyes and the tip of her nose slightly—and adorably—reddened.

He quirked one corner of his mouth into a little smile. "No need. Talking with you about the book is most helpful."

She looked at him with a purposeful expression, her introspective gaze sizing up his deepest needs and wants. "I think you should go for a swim."

Harriet could have bitten her tongue out the moment those words escaped her lips. Why did she blurt it out, without even thinking? The blood pounded in her ears when he swiveled around to face her squarely.

"Swim in the spring? Why?"

She clutched her hands together, willing them to stop shaking. "I don't know. I don't see how it could do any harm. A bath might help the restlessness and the strange feelings in your leg." She raised her eyebrows in an attempt to sound nonchalant. "You have this bathhouse here at your disposal. Why not use it?"

An awful silence descended over the bathhouse, broken only by the hissing of the hot spring. Harriet's heart plummeted to her half boots, and she turned her gaze to the floor. She could not see his face, but his silence told her she overstepped a boundary.

"Perhaps I will," he replied slowly. "I shall take the waters this evening, after my work is done."

"I think you should." Harriet paused, seeking a way to remedy the situation, lighten the mood—anything to break the tension her words had caused. "May I try it? Just dip my toes in?"

His eyebrows shot up in surprise, but a smile broke across his face. "Of course, if you wish."

She turned briskly on the bench, efficiently removing her boots and stockings while keeping her legs covered.

Picking her way over the damp stones, she bunched her skirts in her fists. Then she found a reasonably dry patch near the edge of the pool, sat on the edge and dipped her legs in.

The water was warm and caressing. She smiled. It *was* wonderful. She relaxed for a moment, and then half turned to look at Brookes. "I am sure a bath will do you good, sir. The water feels lovely."

He smiled in return. "Is it invigorating? Are you glad you gave it a try?"

"Yes." She kept her skirt tucked around her knees and her legs modestly submerged, so no part of her bare flesh peeked above the foaming water. "But I shouldn't stay long. We should be going back to the house."

Brookes nodded and took one of the scratchy hemp towels from the bench. Harriet scooted back from the edge of the pool, making sure that her skirts still covered her legs. She reached out a hand for the towel, but Brookes sank down beside her instead.

"Allow me." He reached for her foot, rubbing first one foot, then the other briskly with the rough fabric.

Harriet's heart pounded in her chest, but she kept her countenance impassive. He was just being a gentleman. If she started acting missish now, she would seem ridiculous. On the other hand, both feet were now thoroughly dry. She reached behind her for her stockings, but Brookes grabbed her right foot, tracing the arch with his forefinger. Harriet's breath caught in her throat and she jerked, attempting to draw it away.

He ignored the small struggle. "Your foot is so little," he said with a wondrous air, as though he had never beheld something as perfect as Harriet's foot. He ran his finger over her arch once more.

Alarm coursed through Harriet, and this time she jerked

free. "We should be going," she gasped, her throat tightening in shock.

He looked up at her, his eyes reflecting the dark gray of the stone walls. With the kind of precision that he might have used to issue orders, he snapped, "Yes. Yes, we should."

## Chapter Fifteen

Brookes rolled over, yawning, and then bolted upright with a start. What happened? He stared around his bedroom, noting the sunlight streaming in through the windows. Judging by the pale sunlight slanting through the curtains, it was midmorning. Brookes rubbed his eyes with the heel of one hand. His back pressed not against the hard arm of his settee, but against the soft pillows that stacked in fluffy piles against the headboard of his bed. He fell asleep last night in his bed. Not only that, but he slept through the night without nightmares, for the first time since Waterloo. The shock of these twin revelations washed over him, leaving him giddy. With a knock, Stoames entered, bearing a heavy breakfast tray.

"Sleep well, Captain?" He placed the tray on the corner of the bed, and reached behind Brookes to push the pillows into a more comfortable fit for sitting up.

Brookes waved him away and regarded the tray with a wary eye. "What is that?"

"It's a bit past ten. Cook sent up some rashers of bacon and eggs." Stoames removed the cover of the dish with a flourish.

"I can't believe I slept this late. I haven't slept in past

five o'clock in years." Brookes sat up, the wonder of it still clouding his reason.

"Well, I think it's a good thing, Captain. You've needed it." Stoames carefully balanced the tray over Brookes lap.

"I didn't have any nightmares, either, Stoames." Brookes reached gratefully for his coffee.

"Another good thing, Captain." Stoames gave him a measured look. From their many years' acquaintance, Brookes recognized that expression. Stoames was trying to think of what to say. "Enjoy your breakfast. I'll be back in a bit."

Brookes took a hearty swig of his coffee, allowing it to burn down the back of his throat. The whole morning was vaguely disorienting and slightly off-kilter. He needed the strength of the black brew to bring him back to reality. He breathed in deeply, allowing the bitter steam to permeate his senses.

But even while he struggled to waken more thoroughly, a dawning sense of wonder flooded his being. He triumphed over the night. The pale light of morning woke him, not the shock and sudden fear of death. The fuzz of a two o'clock nightcap didn't cling to his tongue; instead he only tasted clean, harsh black coffee. After Waterloo, he'd surrendered the hope of sleeping through the night, or the possibility of a night free of horrific nightmares. But tucked up in his bed, warmth suffused him, leaving him refreshed and…happy. For the first time in ages, he was happy.

This transformation he laid at her door. Gratitude surged through him. Eagerness to see her again made his heart beat faster. He wasn't a man who believed in messages of faith of any kind. And yet, recalling the fit of her tiny foot in the palm of his hand, he decided she was made only for him.

But did Harriet share his feelings? He recalled her brisk movements as she drew on her stockings and boots, shielding herself from his eyes. She had been silent when they ambled over the hills, returning to the Park. He couldn't imagine himself with any other woman, but did Harriet regard him with the same intense devotion? Brookes set his coffee cup down carefully on the tray, and rolled his head back on the pillows.

He must improve himself. Only by bettering himself would he be worthy of Harriet, but what improvements could he make? He should take the waters at the bathhouse every day. He would work like a dog to make the mill profitable. He would continue to keep his tenants well-housed and fed. He would see to it that Lady Handley received the best of care. He would arrange matters so that Harriet and all of her family were safe and secure for the rest of their lives. And then, when he had finally proven himself worthy, he would beg for Harriet's hand. He had a sudden vision of pouring his mother's sapphires and diamonds out at her tiny feet. He smiled. Harriet deserved all of that, and more.

Brookes looked up from his breakfast tray, focusing on a spot on the wallpaper across the room. Only one problem remained.

Sophie Handley.

That knocked the wind out of him. It was akin to the sickening feeling he had experienced during his boyhood fall from the tree. He still remained under some obligation to Sophie. And Harriet, fine and good, would never betray her sister, even if she felt the same sense of destiny he did. Trapped by his own sense of duty, his soldierly instinct failed him. He tried to remember the way he and Sophie had left things. Weren't they only going to try to become better acquainted? No obligation existed beyond that. Except, of course, that polite society might frown upon a man leaving one sister for another. Or that Harriet might feel she was betraying Sophie by marrying him.

Obligation, however vague, trapped Brookes. He needed an exit strategy. His sense of wonder and optimism refused to be deterred. He would find a way.

* * *

Harriet's eyes burned as though tiny grains of sand abraded them, and her stomach churned so violently that she had turned away her luncheon. She sat, balancing her elbows carefully on the table, and peered over the rim of her tea cup at Sophie, who chattered away at Rose.

"Rose, I think old Mrs. Crossley liked me very much. She said I was so pretty and kept complimenting me on my hair and dress. I am sure she is going to speak well of me to the captain, don't you?"

"Oh, I am sure she will, dearie. It's a good thing that you're already getting the approval of the captain's family." Rose leaned over and patted Sophie's arm.

A bitter taste flooded Harriet's mouth, and she swallowed convulsively. Sophie might not be so merry if she had known what happened in the bathhouse between Harriet and Brookes, while she worked her charms on Mrs. Crossley. Harriet's cheeks burned with embarrassment at the memory of the hurried moments of pulling on her stockings and boots. She'd dared not meet John's gaze. And the awkward walk back to the Park, knowing that guilt and shame must be burned on her face for all to see. But Sophie hadn't noticed anything unusual. She spent the entire rest of the day—and a good portion of the next—discussing her good fortune with Rose. If Mrs. Crossley noticed anything, she kept her surprise well-concealed.

But a devastating remorse overwhelmed Harriet. Perhaps she should cancel her visit to the Park that afternoon. Yes. She would send a quick note around after they had finished their meal.

"Hattie," Sophie snapped, breaking through Harriet's trance. "Don't you think Mrs. Crossley liked me?"

"Oh, yes. She found you quite charming, I'm sure." Harriet managed a weak smile for her sister.

Sophie sat back in her chair with a satisfied puff, allowing Harriet to return to her problem. No, she couldn't cancel her trip. Canceling might send the wrong message. If she refused to come, John might realize how deeply their conversation in the bathhouse had affected her. He might surmise that she was developing a *tendre* for him. Mrs. Crossley had said he was a master tactician. If she reacted wrongly, then he would guess the truth, and all would be lost...

"I'm sorry, Sophie, what did you say?" Harriet set her teacup down with a little crash.

"I was asking how many rooms Brookes Park has." An irritated pout pursed Sophie's rosy lips. "Goodness, you're vague today."

"I have such a headache." Harriet rubbed her brow with shaky hands.

"You poor dear, I noticed you didn't seem to feel quite yourself. Why don't you run along for a nice rest?" Rose bustled around the table and pressed her hand to Harriet's forehead. "Ah, you feel clammy. Off to bed now. You've been working too hard on that book of yours."

"I'll go to the Park later, after I've had a nap." Harriet stood up, hoping her knees would support her unsteady legs. "Sophie, you'll come with me, of course." She couldn't run the risk of being alone with Brookes again. She would only make a fool of herself, and compromise her sister's chance at happiness.

"No, I don't think I will. I promised Mary I would visit this afternoon." Sophie smeared a ridge of butter across her bread, daintily biting a crescent out of the middle.

"Off you go, then." Rose turned Harriet by the shoulder and sent her on her way with a tender shove. "I'll check on her ladyship and make sure she's partaken of her lunch tray. Don't worry about a thing."

Harriet trudged up the stairs. Closing the door to the little room she shared with Sophie, she pressed her back against the doorjamb. Tears pricked at her eyelids. She lay down across the quilt, fully clothed, and let the tears wash over her the way the water at the bathhouse had caressed her feet. She was the worst, most deceitful sister in the world. She loved Sophie's beau. She coaxed the most private, innermost thoughts from Brookes and then tempted him by challenging him to bathe in the hot spring. Disgust at herself and her behavior made the bile rise in her throat.

None of these things were done willfully, but the end result was the same. She was in love with John Brookes, but for all intents and purposes, he belonged to Sophie. What he may or may not have felt was irrelevant. Honor bound him to Sophie, at least until she finally made up her mind, and any part Harriet might play in trying to break that bond was reprehensible.

Her sobs finally eased, and Harriet turned her pillow over to find a dry spot. She thought that a bath would help with the torments he felt. She hadn't meant to become any kind of siren. In fact, she was surprised to find that she could wield that kind of power over a man, because she was not attractive. Not compared to Sophie. But she had, and now she had to face up to the consequences.

Squeezing her eyes shut, she sought comfort in prayer. Harriet prayed for strength, wisdom and guidance. She lay still on the little bed until the familiar feelings of comfort and peace filled her soul. Her work at Brookes Park must proceed, no matter what happened. She must continue writing her book, and ask John for his help. This was the only way she could write the book that might reverse her family's fortunes. But she would do all this without letting John know that she loved him. There was no need, for he was not a free man.

Harriet sat across the desk from Brookes, pen poised in hand. She scrubbed her face with soap and water before leaving the cottage, hoping that she erased every trace of her tears. The urge to close her lids over her burning eyes was almost unbearable, but she could not drop the mask of her customary efficiency and good cheer. In keeping with her scheme, she kept silent, never mentioning the bathhouse, or her family's troubles. She made excuses for Sophie and peppered John with mundane questions about the war. Dates, facts, figures. No need to ask any more questions about his feelings or the suffering he had endured. Those queries might lead to dangerous territory.

Aunt Katherine snored gently in the corner, punctuating the scratching sound of Harriet's pen as she hastily scribbled her last few notes. Coming to the end of her sentence, it was time to end her day and go home. Setting the pen into its holder, she offered him a bland smile. "I think that's all the questions I have today, Captain."

"Are we back to 'Captain' again? I thought you were going to call me John."

"Of course, John. Old habits, you know." Harriet sanded the pages, waiting for the ink to dry.

"Before you go, I would like to talk to you about something more, if I may." Brookes put out his hand, lightly clasping her wrist to hold her still. "Can you stay for a bit longer?"

Thunder rolled outside, followed by a brief flash of lightning that made Harriet jump.

"See?" Brookes indicated the window with a nod. "The weather's turning nasty again. Better to wait it out for a bit."

Harriet peered out of the window, watching the rain slant against the pane. "It does look rather bad." The weather had been fine when she left the cottage. The sudden change in the weather impeded her escape, and her brows drew together with irritation. She looked over at Mrs. Crossley, who still snored contentedly, undisturbed by the downpour. Nothing too intimate could happen with his elderly aunt nearby. If she refused, he might suspect that something was amiss.

She sat back down, pulling her pen back out of its holder. "Very well, John, what did you wish to tell me?"

"Come and sit by the fire. Sometimes, having you sit across the desk from me—it makes me feel as though there are obstacles in our way." He stood up, beckoning her to follow.

Harriet's eyes widened at his words. Perhaps he had guessed her innermost thoughts, even though she had tried so desperately to conceal them. "I beg your pardon?"

He turned and smiled at her. "I don't know. Some things are easier told when we sit side by side near the fire."

If he hoped to disarm her, it worked. "Very well." Harriet rose from the desk and strode purposefully over to the hearth, choosing a slipper chair. She sank into its depths, noticing that she sat within Mrs. Crossley's line of vision should the old woman awaken. Brookes settled in a leather armchair across from her. "What is it?" Her heart pounded heavily, like a cannonball in her chest. Surely, he guessed her thoughts and decided to let her down easy. Or perhaps even upbraid her for betraying her sister in the first place.

He stared into the fire, his jaw hardening. Then he slowly turned to face Harriet.

"I want to tell you the truth. Everything that happened at Waterloo. What happened to me the day I lost my leg."

# Chapter Sixteen

Harriet folded her hands in her lap. Without a graceful way to bow out, she waited. The firm set of John's jaw and the deep gray color of his eyes indicated his all-too-familiar determination. But aside from his usual resolve, she sensed his vulnerability. This confession drove him. Refusing him this chance would be cruel. She pressed her back against the chair, softening her glance to encourage him to continue.

"Waterloo was a mess, make no mistake. Most people don't understand how confusing a battle can be. Throughout my career, I had seen it all before many times, and I could usually impose my own corner of order upon the chaos I witnessed. And I did, the moment we were given the order to charge. I honed in on my duty, and I performed my tasks precisely." He paused, and ran his tongue over his lips.

"You must know that as a soldier, it was my job to kill with a mechanical efficiency. And I did… I shouldn't tell a woman about this. It may upset you." He ran his eyes over her face, as though assessing how candid he could afford to be.

Harriet shook her head. She must allow him to keep on, no matter how nightmarish his experiences might sound to her ears.

"Waterloo was different from other battles. I am a career soldier, and still, the horror of it stays with me to this day." He swallowed, and locked Harriet's eyes in his own gaze, compelling her to understand. "It was slaughter. We outnumbered the French and outflanked them. One of the Scots Greys captured the French standard, and when he carried it off the field in triumph, the will of our enemies went with it."

Harriet nodded her head, keeping her eyes soft and her voice low. "I understand, John."

His shoulders unclenched a bit at the sound of her voice. "There was no one left to kill, Harriet. We had completely obliterated the French. Our orders were to cover the other regiments while they withdrew from the field. It was supposed to be over. But that's not what happened." He broke off, and cleared his throat.

Harriet said nothing, but kept her expression neutral. A sudden movement or change might cause him to shy away, like a wounded animal.

"My men began charging the French artillery. They were maddened by victory and bloodlust. My own horse gave out under me, so I found another mount and rode after them. But Harriet, I couldn't stop them. God help me, I tried. Stupid fools. I shouted at them until my voice went hoarse, and rode like mad, trying to make them hear sense. But they were cut down before my very eyes." His voice grew hushed, awed. "The precision of the gunfire was quite astonishing to behold."

Nausea broke over Harriet like a wave but she kept her shoulders relaxed and her countenance still.

"I was keeping abreast of Major Ponsonby, whose mount—not one of his usual ones, but a lesser one he must have found on the field—got mired in the mud. Harriet, the mud at Waterloo was more debilitating, in some ways, than the gunfire. The horse got stuck knee-deep in the muck and

Ponsonby could go no farther. He surrendered to the French, but he was killed by one of the lancers anyway."

Harriet swallowed, but held still. The devastation he felt that day was palpable, but John pressed forward, not ceasing his confession.

"About that same moment I was hit with grapeshot. The force of it was so strong it knocked me off my mount. I fell, and rolled over into a wagon rut to escape notice. I must have blacked out, because when I woke up, night had fallen."

He fell silent. Goose bumps broke out over her arms, causing an involuntary shiver to run down her spine. She tried to suppress the quiver through her body, but her shoulders made a sharp, jerky movement despite her best effort. If John noticed, it didn't break his concentration. He stared into the fire, as though what had occurred on the battlefield of Waterloo could be answered within the flames.

"Are you tired of listening?" His voice sounded as though it came from a million miles away.

"No." She kept her tone soft and neutral. "Tell me more."

Brookes held on to Harriet's voice as he would a life raft. She would help him through this. "When I awoke, I had no idea where I was or what was happening at first. But then I heard looters going over the field. Did you know that soldiers often loot the dead or dying?" He leveled a glance at her face.

Harriet shook her head, but her eyebrows were raised in shock and disbelief.

"I never did it, and I wouldn't allow my men to. To me it's a disgusting and disrespectful practice, but I suppose to some men, it was a way to earn a living. These looters were Prussian, I could tell by their uniforms. They were picking through the dead, taking anything of value. I'd never suffered through the aftermath of battle before. Always, I had ridden off the field in triumph. But not the night that followed Waterloo." He noted the dawning horror in Harriet's eyes. He paused for a moment, unsure if he should go on, but then the words poured out of him in a rush. "The looters weren't just pillaging among the dead, they were murdering the living. If you had been lucky enough to make it through the battle, they would kill you for whatever possessions of value you might have."

He faced Harriet squarely. "I was next. I could tell they were only about a yard away. I knew they would go over me with a fine-tooth comb, for I was in my officer's uniform, which denoted some wealth. I had no idea what I would do, except I wanted to die honorably, like a good soldier. So I grabbed my sword and waited."

His breath came faster now, while he relived the moments in which his life hung in the balance. "Stoames found me. He had been looking for me all day and most of the night. The Prussians saw his lantern beaming and dropped down amongst the corpses, playing dead." His mind flashed back to that night…Stoames sank down beside him, trying to find a way to move him out of the rut without making his injuries worse. "I whispered to him what they were doing, and where he could find them. Stoames located the looters and took care of them in the same way they had taken care of the injured in their path. And then it was over. The nightmare of the field was done. We had only to wait through the night for help."

Harriet's soothing voice broke through the clouds of his memory. "Why weren't the wounded escorted from the field at once?"

Brookes shook his head. "We had orders from Wellington himself. No man was to be moved until the battle was over. Otherwise, you ran the risk of too many deserters. Stoames told me the battle ended at dusk, so there was no way to collect the wounded until the next day."

He turned away from Harriet, focusing on the fire again. "Sometimes I cannot stop the terrible, burning thirst I felt that day. It's why I drink to excess sometimes. There was no water. The farmhouse well at La Sainte Haye had been polluted by mud and blood. Stoames gave me the last few drops of his gin ration, and that was all the drink there was for the next day or so, until we reached Brussels."

Something gentle pushed against his arm. He looked down in wonder at the top of Harriet's glossy dark head. She was now sitting beside him on the settee. The warmth of her body flowed through him, easing the anguish he still felt from that terrible night at Waterloo. Her presence was natural and right, like the warm water from the hot spring that had caressed his wounded leg the day before. Still lost in thought, he leaned into her warmth and stroked her hair. The shiny strands slipped through his fingers like ribbons.

"Do you understand why I lost faith?" He muttered the words, unsure if she could even hear him. "After seeing the worst of mankind, I cannot believe there is a God. If so, why would He let innocent men, dying men, suffer so?"

Harriet turned her face up to his, unshed tears sparkling in her eyes. "I don't pretend to know everything there is to know about faith. And I would never insult you by assuming I understood the depths of how you and your men suffered that day." She paused, her lips trembling. "I—I feel that God won't stop the terrible things that people do to cause each other pain. Unfortunately, that's what makes us human. But I do feel most fervently, John, that God was with every man who died that day. He was beside you when you fell, and He was with Stoames, who risked his own life to rescue yours."

Brookes ceased stroking Harriet's hair, allowing her words to wash over his soul. His heart expanded with love and peace. During his boyhood summers, he would lay in the field, staring up at the stars. The constellations he had observed then held infinite mystery and promise. He gazed deeply into Harriet's ink-blue eyes, fathomless and deep as that summer night's sky.

He loved Harriet Handley.

He would spend the rest of his life learning from her, helping her, endeavoring to be worthy of her.

He wasn't sure how. But it had to be so.

Harriet drifted back from where John's words had taken her, over the battlefield at Waterloo. Slowly, she became aware that she was sitting beside him, closer than propriety allowed, and he was stroking her hair. Despite all her best efforts, here she was in yet another intimate position with John. She didn't remember moving near him. Holding still, she allowed her body to rest against him. She couldn't break the spell yet. Not just yet. In a few moments, she would release him to Sophie with a full heart. Until then, she would savor this kinship whilst she could spin it out. She shifted her gaze to Mrs. Crossley, still snoring on the settee. At least his aunt was unaware of everything that transpired.

They sat together in silence. His hand rested in her hair, and his touch filled her with longing. His story had shaken her to her core, and she wanted to care for him, easing his burden of suffering for the rest of their lives. Harriet gathered her wits, and it dawned on her that she could no longer bear to write the reality of what he had suffered. "I don't want to write the book anymore." She whispered the words, not wishing to change the mood, but needing to tell him just the same.

"Why? Because of what I said?" He looked down at her, his eyes hooded and inscrutable.

"No. Because I am unequal to the task. If I didn't write it well enough, I would feel like I had failed you and everyone who died on that field." The shame of it scalded her skin, but she spoke the truth, and the sooner he knew it, the better.

"Write the book. I believe in you. I wouldn't have told you everything that happened if I didn't trust you."

Their gazes met and locked. His words had been a challenge and a confession. "I will depend upon you even more—" Harriet waited, half expecting to hear him turn her away.

A gentle smile illuminated his features. "You have only to ask."

She realized she had been at the Park for hours, now it was long past time to be home. Harriet pulled away from him reluctantly, breaking the spell. "I should go."

John looked out of the window. "The rain has eased, but not much. I'll ring for my carriage." He rose and extended his hand, drawing her up from the settee. The brief touch sent a jolt of awareness through Harriet, but she carefully schooled her features so it wouldn't show. He gave the bell-pull a tug, while Harriet smoothed her hair and her dress.

"Bunting, the carriage for Miss Handley." John barked the order the moment the door to the library opened, without even turning around.

"Right away, Captain." Bunting bowed out.

John offered her the crook of his arm. "I'll escort you to the door."

They stood together in the entry hall, waiting for the carriage to pull up to the front door. Harriet could think of nothing sensible to say, so she remained quiet. She looked up at the ceiling, where candlelight flickered in a simple brass chandelier, and down at the floor, which was rubbed to a highly polished gleam. Brookes Park was very much like its owner—masculine, unadorned and yet very handsome. Sophie expressed such intense pleasure at seeing the Park, and gushed about how she longed to be mistress over everything. How would her sister's lovely but slightly florid style transform this house?

Harriet breathed a sigh of relief when the carriage rounded the courtyard and neared the door. She took a step forward, but John drew her back. Sliding his hand down her arm, he clasped her hand and brought it quickly to his lips. The kiss burned through Harriet's glove, leaving her light-headed and breathless.

"Thank you." It said everything, yet it said nothing. Then he handed her up into the carriage. The coachman flicked the reins, and they were off. Harriet peered at John through the curtains lining the carriage window. Before they rounded the curve of the courtyard, John disappeared into the house. Settling back against the cushions, Harriet fought a rising fear that he would likewise disappear from her own life.

# Chapter Seventeen

Auntie's silence was an accusation. She sat across the supper table from Brookes, toying with her dish of beef-steak and shallots, not saying a word. Her lack of conversation disconcerted him more than anything. Usually Auntie held a ready opinion on every subject, so when she kept her counsel it was an almost incriminating act. Had she heard what transpired in the library this afternoon?

Brookes regarded his aunt with a watchful eye. Then he turned his gaze down to the steak on his plate as fatigue rolled over him like a wave. How nice his warm bed would feel at the end of this evening. His confession to Harriet tired him, but beneath the exhaustion an inexpressible feeling of lightness lingered.

"Nephew, I have a wish to go to Bath." Ah, there it was. Auntie's imperious voice broke through his weary fog.

"Matlock Bath? Of course. I'll make sure the carriage can take you tomorrow."

"No, my beloved idiot. I meant Bath proper. I'm feeling achy in my joints and bored to tears and I think Bath would be the best cure for it all." Aunt Katherine bestowed a warm and loving smile on him.

"Very well." He looked up at her, lifting his brows. "How long will you be gone?"

"You must come with me. I couldn't possibly travel alone." She rested her fork beside her plate, folding her hands in her lap.

"I would love to, but it would be impossible, Aunt. There's too much for me to do around the Park and the mill."

Aunt Katherine smiled, glossing over his work at the mill and on the farm as though they simply didn't exist. "I'll bring Harriet Handley along as a travel companion, and the pair of you can work on her book."

He blinked. His aunt, with her acute powers of sensibility, read his mind. If Auntie brought Harriet along, he could find a way to win her hand during their excursion. But it wouldn't do to be too obvious about it. He racked his brain, trying to find the right answer. Harriet's book. Of course. "There's an old army chum of mine, living in Bath. Charles Cantrill. I will see if I might visit him, and bring Harriet along. It might help her book if she talks to another soldier who was there. Cantrill lost his left arm, Aunt, so he's taking the waters until his health improves."

His aunt regarded him, eyes sharp and bright. "Perhaps taking the waters would do you good, too, my boy."

Brookes couldn't recall the last time he blushed, but it had been many years. He hoped his aunt couldn't see the flush creeping up his cheeks now. He felt like a lad caught stealing gingerbread from the larder. Attempting to put her off the scent, he smiled. "True, though the bathhouse here might be effective."

"The Park is lovely, but the waters of Bath are incomparable. And you'll have the chance to visit your friend. I shall write to Harriet's mother after dinner and beg her to release Harriet for a few weeks. How long will it take you to ready yourself for the journey?"

He made a rough mental calculation of the state of affairs at both the mill and the farm. "I could be ready within three days."

"Excellent. We will travel in easy stages, my boy, none of your breakneck speeds for me. We could be down there within a week and a half, and then spend a month or so there. It would amuse me and I am sure the waters will improve my health. And you will be able to work with Harriet whenever you wish. It's the best solution." She picked up her fork again, biting into her steak with relish.

Perhaps she slept through his interview with Harriet this afternoon. But Brookes rather doubted it. She was up to her old tricks, meddling and manipulating to help others find happiness. A sudden grin broke out over his face. Only this time, he would allow himself to be manipulated. It suited his needs perfectly.

"Harriet! Come here at once." Mama's voice rang down the stairs, startling Harriet so that she dropped her pen. Precious ink splattered across the page, and Harriet blotted it in haste. She capped the inkwell. Why did Mama sound so angry?

Dashing up the stairs, Harriet tried to think what she could have done wrong. By the sound of her voice, Mama was upset. Perhaps she found out that Harriet had all but embraced the captain yesterday. Or perhaps she knew that Harriet went to the bathhouse with him. That last thought slowed her steps. None of her actions had been consciously calculated to harm Sophie's chances or show her true feelings to the captain. But Mama wouldn't care about Harriet's reasons. Elevated to polite society through marriage, Mama cared only for decorum and appearances—she did not care a fig for intentions.

Entering the room, Harriet steeled herself to make a full confession. She sank onto the foot of the bed. "Mama, I—"

"Harriet, I must know why Mrs. Crossley wrote, asking me if you would be a companion to her on her journey to Bath." She regarded Harriet gravely, peering at her over the sheet of foolscap she was clutching. "Have you been pushing yourself at her too much? We are too poor to mingle with people like Mrs. Crossley, at least until Sophie marries the captain."

Harriet snatched up the letter, scanning through its contents. Yes, there it was. Mrs. Crossley had written to ask her mother to spare her for a few weeks. Harriet raised her eyes to her mother's face, hoping her confusion registered with the dawning hope in her expression. "Mama, I had no idea. I've spoken to Mrs. Crossley quite often, and the subject of Bath has never come up. Honestly. This is the first I've heard about it. All I have been doing is working on the book with Captain Brookes."

"Oh, your book." Mama waved her hand and sighed. "If anyone should be going to Bath, it should be me. I am the one who is ill. There was a time when I went to Bath once a year to take the waters, see the plays, hear the concerts. Now it's all gone."

Harriet nodded, hoping her mother would cease her reminiscences there, instead of working herself into a hysterical fit. Mama snatched the letter back.

"Well, I will simply write her back and tell her no. I couldn't possibly spare you for all those weeks. What if something should happen to me?" She sank back onto her pillows.

Disappointment surged through Harriet, and tears blurred her vision. She never thought of going to Bath, but Mrs. Crossley's invitation stirred the excitement in her blood. A change of scene—what a lovely thought. Determined not to let the tears show, she blinked and nodded slowly.

"Besides, we are too poor. You haven't any clothes fit to

wear in Bath, and I wouldn't have you looking like a poor relation. You are Sir Hugh Handley's daughter, though some might want to forget it." Mama cast the letter aside and faced Harriet squarely.

Harriet sighed, hoping to stem the litany that was sure to follow. Her mother would start listing all of her grievances against the Handleys, and grow so upset that she would have to take a dose of laudanum. Harriet hated when Mama took the laudanum. Her now-constant reliance on the medicine sent a prickle of unease through Harriet, and the marathon naps she took after a single dose was troubling. If only they could find a different, or at least less worrisome solution for Mama's illness.

Mama sharpened her gaze, regarding Harriet with the air of one trying to read her soul. "And besides, shouldn't Sophie be the one getting to know the family better? Book or no book, you spend entirely too much time at the Park."

A need to justify her visits compelled Harriet to speak quickly. "But I am writing the book to benefit our family, Mama. If I sell it, we might have some money, and I could take care of the whole family."

"The book is a nice gesture, Harriet, but there is no guarantee you can write it well enough that it will sell. I have indulged your dream of your book, but in truth I do not approve of young girls working for money. It's simply not done. The only real chance we have is Sophie's marriage to the captain, and I won't have you ruining that by keeping them apart for any reason." Mama dismissed Harriet's novel with a shrug of her shoulders.

"Harriet, be a good girl, go and fetch me some fresh water. Mix a little tincture for me, won't you?" Mama gave her a rare, cajoling smile, and patted her hand. "I will write to Mrs. Crossley while you prepare everything, and send my response straight away. No use allowing the question

to linger. Become a companion for her? What nonsense.
You're already my companion, aren't you?"

The next morning, Harriet had no idea what the future
of her book might be. The chances of finishing grew slim-
mer by the moment. If Mrs. Crossley left for Bath, her daily
trips to Brookes Park to work on the book must cease, as she
would have no chaperone. And Mama did not want her to
continue anyway. So Harriet sought comfort in the garden.
Putting her pen aside was like an act of treason, but she did
so anyway. Her manuscript hindered her sister's courtship,
and nothing more could come of it.

The sound of carriage wheels ground to a halt in front
of the cottage. Harriet stood up, shielding the sun from her
eyes with one dirty, gloved hand. That was Brookes's vehi-
cle. While Harriet gazed in wonderment, a tiny old woman
alit gracefully, stopping in front of the house. Mrs. Crossley. What on earth? Stripping off her gloves, Harriet stepped
across the path, picking her way through the muddy garden.

She doused her face and hands with chilly water at the
pump, wiping the droplets off with a corner of her apron.
She must look a mess, but nothing could be done about it
now. She entered the cottage through the back door, tiptoeing though the kitchen. The sound of voices carried in
from the parlor, where Sophie and Rose had congregated
with Mrs. Crossley. The old woman's imperious tone rose
above the rest. "No, thank you, no tea. I am here to speak
with Harriet and Lady Handley."

Harriet strode into the room, extending her hand. "Mrs.
Crossley—what a nice surprise. I am so happy you came
by for a little visit. Are you leaving for Bath soon?"

"Yes, it so happens that I am leaving in two days' time.
And that's why I am here." Mrs. Crossley rose from her
chair by the fire. "I received a most upsetting letter this
morning, from her ladyship. She says she cannot spare you

to be my companion for my journey. I should like to speak to her, if I may."

"Her ladyship is very ill, Mrs. Crossley. She's taken a little tincture of opium this morning to ease her nervous exhaustion." Rose's eyes darted from Mrs. Crossley to Harriet, silently pleading for assistance. "I don't think she's well enough to receive anyone."

"Oh, tosh. I shall only need a few moments of her time." Mrs. Crossley rapped her knuckles on the back of the chair. "Her ladyship needn't come down. Show me the way to her room, and I will visit with her there."

Harriet glanced at Sophie, who hadn't uttered a word. Her sister's eyes grew wider, but if Sophie was shocked, she tried to carry the moment with appropriate social grace. "Oh, Rose, do take her up to see Mama. I'm sure she would hate to miss speaking with Mrs. Crossley. We receive so few visitors."

Harriet's heart surged with gratitude. Her little sister had handled the situation with style. Sophie would make John a fine wife, one who would run Brookes Park with elegance, if she continued to grow in refinement and poise.

"Very well, dearie. Follow me, if you please, Mrs. Crossley." Rose ushered her out of the room and up the stairs.

Sophie turned to Harriet, her eyes sparkling. "What is this about Bath? Will you travel with Mrs. Crossley?"

Harriet shook her head. "I am needed here—I cannot be spared. I only learned about the journey yesterday, and Mama told me I could not go."

Sophie jumped up from her chair, pacing the room. "Oh, but you must! It would be a wonderful experience for you, Harriet. Such a nice change of scene. And you might be able to finish your book, if you were away from home and all of your usual responsibilities."

Harriet regarded her sister closely. "You aren't jealous?

You should be the one going, not me. And I do have so much to do here—"

"I'm not jealous." Sophie smiled at Harriet. "I shall get to see Bath often, if I choose to marry the captain. And I couldn't go along now, before we are engaged. It might cause talk. But if you were to go, it would be quite proper. Captain Brookes isn't your intended, after all. And you could finally finish your book, without the task of caring for Mama at the same time."

Harriet sank down into a chair. She held no envy for Sophie's supposed future—or at least she told herself she was not jealous. Sophie's words made sense. She could finish the book if she could leave home duties aside for a few weeks. Still, she resisted. "I haven't a proper wardrobe."

Sophie grasped Harriet's shoulders, smiling and giving her a little shake. "For goodness' sake, you can borrow some of my made-over dresses. Who cares about your appearance? You'll be scribbling away on your book, or helping Mrs. Crossley as her companion. It's not as though you are making your debut."

"True." Harriet sighed. Of course no one would care what she looked like. "Even so, I doubt very much Mama will change her mind, no matter what Mrs. Crossley says."

A footstep sounded in the doorway. "Depend upon it, my dear, I can be most persuasive." Mrs. Crossley beamed as she stepped into the room. "Begin packing your trunk, Harriet. We will leave in two days' time."

## Chapter Eighteen

Harriet turned away from the carriage window and faced Mrs. Crossley, who had snoozed for the better part of an hour. During this restful part of the journey, Harriet pondered over how she was able to make the journey. She shook her head in disbelief. The mystery of how Mrs. Crossley convinced Mama to let her come on this trip still remained. After a terse command to Harriet to begin packing her trunk, Mama remained silent on the subject. When Harriet left, her mother simply presented her left cheek for a kiss, with no words of farewell. The coldness of the gesture stung, but Harriet learned to take her mother's temper with a grain of salt. She could ask Mrs. Crossley about the discussion, but shied from the prospect. It did not matter what caused this to happen, anyway. It was enough that she was here.

She glanced back out of the window. Brookes rode alongside the carriage, Stoames trailing a few paces behind. Both usually did so, unless the weather turned nasty or Brookes's leg troubled him. The arrangement caused Harriet mixed feelings of relief and disappointment. She missed his company but things were better this way. Every moment spent with him meant another moment in which she fell deeper in love. Since his engagement to Sophie loomed in the near future, it would be foolish indeed to build up her regard only to break her own heart in a matter of weeks.

Mrs. Crossley awoke with a little snort. "So sorry, my dear." She yawned, stretching her thin arms into the air. "The swaying of the carriage always lulls me to sleep."

"It's all right. I was mulling things over in my mind." Harriet yawned in response and smiled. "Though I feel a bit tired as well."

"I'm so glad you got to make this journey with me. How bored I would be without you here. Although I imagine I am boring you with my endless naps. Never mind. Now that I am awake, we can have a nice chat." Mrs. Crossley opened her reticule and pulled out a tiny round tin. "Have a sweet."

Harriet selected a sweetmeat, savoring the raspberry flavor that melted on her tongue. "Thank you, Mrs. Crossley."

"Oh, my dear, call me Aunt Katherine. Everyone does. I'm liable to forget whom you're addressing, if you call me Mrs. So and So." She popped a sweetmeat in her mouth and settled back against the cushions with a purposeful air. "Now, then, let's gabble. I want to talk about John."

Harriet's heart leaped into her throat. The deception was over. Aunt Katherine guessed her true feelings, and was preparing to put Harriet on her guard. She knew it. Her love for John Brookes was apparent to everyone who saw her. "Yes?" She must remain alert and wary.

"I think what you are doing with John is marvelous, and I wanted to tell you so. Keep up the good work, my girl."

"Good work? Do you mean the book?" Harriet tilted her head and regarded the old woman, keeping her own features bland. Perhaps her secret was safe for the time being.

"Well, I think the book was an excellent start to get Brookes going in the right direction. But I was talking more specifically about his faith. I overheard a little of what you told Brookes the other day, when he told you about Waterloo." Despite her best effort, Harriet's eyebrows shot up, causing Aunt Katherine to giggle. "Don't worry, my dear. I wasn't trying to eavesdrop, but I awoke in time to hear you discussing your faith, and I didn't want to intrude on a private moment. So I kept still until you left."

Harriet closed her eyes, willing the blush creeping over her face to vanish. Surely Aunt Katherine saw her leaning against John. Her actions were most improper, and Auntie probably meant to take her to task—most kindly, of course.

"My dear, I understand why John lost faith. And I know that you have suffered, too. Not that anyone has told me anything—John isn't the type to gossip. But it seems that suffering can make us grow, or imprison us in perpetual bitterness. It seems to me that your devotion has deepened in adversity. I am sure you are opening John's heart by sharing your beliefs." Aunt Katherine leaned forward and pressed her hand over Harriet's, giving her a warm smile.

Harriet took a deep breath to steady her racing pulse. "I have experienced some unpleasant things in my life, Aunt Katherine. But enduring the loss of Handley Hall and the death of my father seems very slight indeed compared to what John has borne. I was not trying to pander to him, but rather, offer some small comfort."

"I understand, my dear. And I think that we can't compare our troubles to someone else's lot in life. What seems an insurmountable obstacle to you might seem nothing at all to me. If we keep our faith, it will carry us through." Mrs. Crossley drew her hand back and sank farther into the cushions. "When I was a young girl, newly married to Mr. Crossley, I lost my baby. You know, my dear, it isn't proper to talk of these things with a young girl, but I feel you are an old soul. I became violently ill after the loss of my child. Truly, I would have died without Mr. Crossley's love, and without His grace."

"Oh, Aunt Katherine, that is terrible. I am so sorry." Harriet crossed the carriage floor to bridge the gap between them. She settled down beside the old woman and turned to face her, clasping her wrinkled old hand in her own.

"Do you know, I am in my seventy-second year, and not a day goes by but that I don't think of my child." Tears welled in her dark eyes, dimming their usual spark. She squeezed Harriet's hand. "Mr. Crossley and I were never able to have another baby. That is why I became so close to John and Henry. They were like my own sons. And I hold John's happiness most dear. It pains me to see him floundering around, talking like a skeptic."

Harriet returned the pressure on her hand. "You must have been devastated, Aunt Katherine. I am so sorry. I can only say I am glad your love and faith carried you through."

The older woman leaned forward, peering into Harriet's face. "My dear, I make a habit of meddling in John's affairs. Ask him, and he will be only too happy to agree. But I do feel that this time, I have a special license, so to speak. I want John to be happy. He's suffered so much. And I think your influence can only bring about the best results. So I urge you, please continue to speak to John about your beliefs. I have a feeling that you can open his heart, where others might not be able."

Harriet warmed under Aunt Katherine's praise and trust, but the enormity of everything the older woman said overwhelmed her. Harriet rested her head against the carriage cushions. "I don't know what more to do, other than to talk to him, and listen, and finish the book."

Aunt Katherine released her hand. "Don't worry, my dear Harriet. I've a feeling that's all John needs."

Brookes strode down the musty corridor of the inn, thanking his lucky stars that this was the final night they would be staying on the road. The prospect of a luxurious apartment and good food was most appealing. He hated to admit any weakness, but his leg ached from the wearying daily rides. Stoames rode beside him all the way, and for his companionship, Brookes was grateful. He could have chosen to ride in the coach, and sometimes did, but Auntie's relentless prying got on his nerves. More importantly, every moment he spent with Harriet left him reeling with frustration. He wanted to marry her right away, but he still hadn't ascertained Harriet's feelings on the matter. He would not relish the prospect of sitting across from Harriet in a game of whist. She could be holding all the right cards or nothing, and a man could never read her expression.

He entered the supper room, only to find it empty. Harriet and Auntie were still refreshing themselves from the long ride. He spotted a decanter and goblets that appeared clean enough, arranged carelessly on the table. He poured out a glass of watered-down claret. Disgusting, really, the quality of it, but 'twas the best he could hope for until tomorrow. On cue, the innkeeper bustled in, rubbing his hands. If only all these chaps didn't look the same.

"Well, sir? And what can we bring for you?"

"A light supper, I think, for myself and the two ladies."

"Very good, sir. We could bring pigeons in a hole."

Brookes's stomach churned. Exactly what they had eaten last night. He sighed. "That'll do."

"Well, Nephew, what have you bespoken for us to eat? I am famished." Auntie sailed into the room, holding her hands out to Brookes.

"Same as last night, Auntie. I shall be happy to get to Bath and eat properly again."

"What? No spirit of adventure? Surely a soldier dines on far worse every night." Aunt Katherine reached up and tapped his cheek with her forefinger.

"Yes, but I didn't pay for the privilege. Where's Harriet?"

He poured a glass of water for his aunt, and handed it to her with an overly chivalrous air.

"Here I am." She stepped into the room, smiling. "Don't tell me, we're having pigeons again."

"Indeed." He poured another glass of water for Harriet. She was looking particularly lovely, even after the long and dusty journey, in a simple blue dress. Blue suited her best, though he never saw her in a color he didn't like. "Has the food on this journey lessened your taste for travel?"

"Oh, no. I enjoy traveling very much. If I were home, I would be having potatoes again with the same two people I always dine with. There's so much more fun in eating pigeons for dinner in inns that look remarkably the same, but are countless miles apart."

"And the company?" Aunt Katherine demanded, raising her empty goblet for more.

"Most enjoyable, I assure you." When Harriet made her declaration, a becoming flush stole over her cheeks. Brookes searched her face, trying to read the answer to his question in her eyes. But she kept her glance cast down at the floor. Yes—she would be a formidable card player indeed.

Aunt Katherine set down her fork and leaned back in her chair, yawning openly. "Well, wonderful though that tough pigeon was, I don't think I will stay for fruit and cheese."

Harriet looked over the rim of her glass. "Should we retire?" Aunt Katherine *did* look pale and weary. Perhaps she should help her into bed early.

"No, no, my dear. You stay and enjoy the rest of this rather dubious supper. I am going to read for a while and then have a nice early bedtime. Good night, children." Aunt Katherine rose from her chair and patted Harriet's shoulder. Then she crossed over to Brookes and kissed his cheek.

"'Night, Auntie." He returned the gesture briefly.

When Aunt Katherine quit the room, the air grew still. Harriet had trouble catching her breath. Perhaps if she spoke about the subject weighing heaviest on her mind, it would ease some of her anxiety. "John, I would like to ask a question, if I may."

He lifted his brows. "Of course." He poured another glass of wine, downing it in a single swallow.

"Mama believes that the book is a waste of my time and yours. She doesn't feel that I can write well enough to have the book published. She doesn't like for me to work. And she feels that my sister's marriage to you is—" Harriet floundered, trying to think of a delicate way to introduce the subject of money. "—more important." Well, that sounded weak, but polite.

"Your sister and I are not engaged, Harriet." The intensity of his gaze seared her. Surely he peered into her very soul. She rose to break the spell—and to protect her privacy.

"Well…I understand that, and I know that you and Sophie are trying to become better acquainted, but Mama has very high hopes that an engagement would be imminent."

He shrugged his shoulders and sat back in his chair. "What are you trying to say?"

"Would you read my manuscript?" The question ended with a squeak. She cleared her throat awkwardly and grasped the back of her chair for support. "I want your opinion on the matter. If you think it has promise but needs work, I will keep going. But if it doesn't have a hope, then I would rather hear it from you first. Your opinion means more than anyone else's." The words poured out in a torrent of anxiety.

"Why does my opinion mean more?" He lifted one eyebrow.

"Because—you lived it."

Was that a flinch? Harriet couldn't tell. Somehow her answer had displeased him.

"Yes." His voice was quiet and neutral. He toyed with the stem of his empty wineglass.

"You'll give me your honest opinion? I would rather you be absolutely truthful with me."

"Would you?" His fingers clasped the wineglass with a sudden tightness, and a little snap sounded through the room. He dusted the shards of glass from his hands with his handkerchief.

Harriet rushed over to his side. "Did you cut yourself?"

"No. Who knew that clunky thing could be so delicate?" He extended his hand to her.

Harriet grasped his rough fingers, a shiver coursing through her at his calloused touch. "Are you all right?" She turned his hand over. No, he hadn't cut himself. She dropped his hand as though it were on fire, and bit her lip. She must refrain from any physical contact with John. A mere touch was simply…too dangerous. And she couldn't show her attraction or her confusion.

He nodded, turning one corner of his mouth down with a rueful expression. "Yes. Nothing but wounded pride."

She nodded and backed away a few steps. "The manuscript's in my trunk. I'll go up to bed now, but I'll leave it outside your room. I would like your honest opinion…"

He gazed at her speculatively. Then he grinned, a devastating smile that sent her heart aflutter. "Harriet, I promise to be completely honest with you in everything from now on."

## Chapter Nineteen

Brookes strolled down the streets of Bath, balancing his umbrella in one hand as he negotiated the crowds of tourists. The foul weather failed to deter the hordes of fashionable people who came to Bath to see and be seen. The rain hadn't eased for the three days they'd been here. He hated to admit it, even to himself, but the dampness of the summer made his bones ache. Not that he was all that old, of course, but still—it slowed a man down. He would venture to the Pump Room this afternoon and try some of the curative waters. It wouldn't do to get old and decrepit before his time. After all, he wasn't even thirty. He must still appear spry to Harriet. Not that he could court her just yet—but still, he desired to appear only virile and strong.

Cantrill had rooms in Westgate Buildings, just around the corner from Aunt Katherine's flat on Bilbury Lane. 'Twas a mere stroll, even on a wooden leg. Yet Brookes hungered for a rest and a bracing cup of tea—if not something stronger—by the time he knocked on Cantrill's door.

The door swung open, revealing a thinner and more serious Charlie Cantrill than Brookes remembered. "Greetings, man, it's good to see you." Charlie grinned broadly, the somber expression fading as he swung the door open fully to allow Brookes inside. "Come in out of this miserable weather." His sleeve covered most of his mutilated left arm. How surprising—he was not wearing his artificial limb. Why not?

"Cantrill, good to see you. Sorry to see old Boney couldn't finish you off." Brookes left his umbrella in the vestibule and stepped inside, removing his greatcoat.

"Toss your coat over that chair, there, and come in. No, old Boney could only take my arm, and of course he made off with your leg, my good fellow. Let's have a drink and toast Wellington, our fearless leader." Cantrill led the way into a small sitting room, where a fire burned cheerily in the grate. "Cognac or scotch?"

"Thank you, Cantrill. I feared you might offer me tea."

"Well, I myself will have tea. I gave up spirits a long time ago, but keep it around for sinners like yourself," Charlie rejoined with a wink.

"Really, old man? A teetotaler, are you? Well, this old sinner will have a scotch, if you please, and keep it neat." He chose a chair near the hearth, and regarded the ease with which his comrade could pour and mix drinks, even with one hand.

"So, what brings you to Bath? The waters or the beautiful weather?" Cantrill questioned with a wry grin.

Brookes took a fortifying sip of scotch. Pleasantries first, then business.

"Where's your wooden arm, Cantrill? Are you too proficient without it?"

"Ah, I usually don't need the ridiculous thing unless I am out in society. Around my home, I don't even bother. Taking the waters has vastly improved my strength. Now, why the visit? Here to improve your health, too?"

"I'm here with my Aunt Katherine, who descended upon me not long after I arrived home in Tansley, but immediately got bored and wanted more amusement. So I am here acting the part of the chaperone." He grimaced and Cantrill chuckled. "I've been taking the waters at our hot spring back home, but who knows. Maybe the waters of Bath will make me feel like a new man."

Cantrill swirled the tea around his cup with a contemplative air. "How's the leg?"

Brookes smiled. "I hardly notice it. Even danced a minuet some weeks ago."

Cantrill raised his brows. "Did you perform on a bet?"

"Not at all, my good man. It was part of an overall plot to win a lady's favor."

A grin broke out over Cantrill's thin face. "And did you?"

Brookes sighed. "It's hard to say. I may have won her favor, but now I am not sure I want it. In truth, Cantrill, I find I am no longer interested in the young lady. But now I have a great attraction to her older sister. I am trying to extricate myself, so to speak, with honor before I can pursue the one I love."

"What makes the elder sister so extraordinary?" Cantrill peered closely at Brookes over the rim of his teacup.

"She is an original, I suppose. I fell madly in love with her younger sister before leaving for the war. But when I returned, the changes Sophie perceived in me weren't at all agreeable to her."

Cantrill nodded sagely. "Had an experience with that, myself."

"Have you?" Brookes snapped his head up, studying Cantrill closely. "It's an awful mess, isn't it?"

"It is. Yet, I feel somewhat relieved. Now I know her true character. Had I spent my life shackled to such a vapid creature, I might feel ready to end it all." Though Cantrill laughed, a trace of bitterness threaded through the sound.

"Well, Harriet isn't vapid. She is an extraordinary woman. She's the other reason I am here." He set his glass down and faced Cantrill squarely. "Harriet is writing a book about a soldier who lives through Waterloo, and has been talking to me to get an accurate picture of what the war was like. I have shared some of my deepest memories with her, and I find her to be a trustworthy and honest person. I would be honored if you would consider speaking with her, too."

"Of course I will." Cantrill gazed thoughtfully into the fire. "I may not share all of my confidences with her because I am not yet acquainted with her, but if you say she is reliable—"

"I would trust her with my life. Upon my honor." Brookes locked gazes with Cantrill. His use of the military oath caused Cantrill to stare at him from under hooded lids.

"I'll talk to her. Indeed, I look forward to meeting the woman worthy of that boast," Cantrill responded. "You can bring her round tomorrow afternoon, if you like. Have you read her work? Is it any good?"

Brookes recalled the sleepless night he spent reading her manuscript from beginning to end. Was it good? No. He remembered flipping through the pages, his heart racing while his own life was outlined in graceful yet precise prose. No, good was definitely not the word for it. "The book is astonishing," he replied, shaking his head in wonderment. "I cannot believe a sheltered young woman could vividly capture life in the field, but she has managed that feat. If she finds a publisher worth his salt, it should be an immediate success."

Harriet yawned, shifting around in her little gilded chair, hoping to find a more comfortable position. She hadn't visited a modiste in years, not since her London season, and she had forgotten how tiresome the clothing selection process could be. Sophie would be in her element, fingering fabric swatches with glee, but Harriet could only try to conceal her boredom out of politeness. She wished she were back at Aunt Katherine's home, reading some of the books Brookes brought along from the Park, or writing her own. Brookes returned the manuscript with a terse "Keep at it," and she worked feverishly on it ever since gaining his approval. This morning, for example, she could have finished the chapter where Twigg faced the aftermath of the battlefield. But she agreed to tag along with Aunt Katherine. The old woman proved such a gracious hostess, Harriet was obligated to feign interest.

"Oh, look, Harriet. Isn't that charming?" Auntie passed a fashion plate over to Harriet. "Look how elegantly the fabric is draped. It would look stunning on you, my dear."

"Do you think so?" Harriet ran a glance over the dress. In contrast to many of the other fashion plates, a modest and simple cut distinguished this gown, leaving one's charms to the imagination. Harriet smiled. It was the prettiest one she had yet seen. "Oh, I think you should order it for yourself, Aunt Katherine. I think a deep purple would be most becoming on you."

"Stuff and nonsense! Fashion is wasted on an old woman like me. Marie-Elise, do you have something similar to this already made up? Something that could be adjusted to fit my friend here?"

The modiste scurried forward, scooping up the picture. "*Mais oui,* I had one almost the same made for another young lady, but she refused to take it. She said it was cut too high across the bosom. *Un moment,* I will fetch it for you." She disappeared behind a velvet curtain to the rear of the shop.

"Oh, Aunt Katherine, I couldn't possibly—" Harriet waved her hand, trying to interrupt the older woman's command of the situation.

"Tut! Let's see how it even fits before we make any rash decisions." Auntie pulled Harriet to her feet and claimed the little gilt chair for her own.

Marie-Elise returned, carrying a mass of ink-blue bombazine proudly before her. She shook out the folds of the gown, pressing it to Harriet's shoulders. "Ah, yes. Very nice. What do you think, Madame?"

Aunt Katherine gave her gray corkscrew curls a decisive shake. "I cannot tell. Harriet, put it on. We'll see how it looks."

With a little shove, Marie-Elise hustled Harriet in and out of the dressing room. Heat washed over Harriet—what to do now? She could not take advantage of the elderly woman's astonishing generosity, and yet she could not very well pay for the dress herself. Catching a glance in one of the mirrors, Harriet paused. She did not recognize her reflection. The girl in the mirror looked graceful and well-borne, not pretty like Sophie but attractive nonetheless. Inadvertently, she put her hand up to touch her hair, making sure it was indeed her own reflection she saw.

"Ah, my dear! Now that dress suits you beautifully. That color brings out the blue of your eyes." Aunt Katherine clapped her hands, her rings sparkling in the afternoon light that streamed through the windows.

"It needs some adjustment through the shoulders. Mademoiselle is much thinner than my previous client. But that can be done very quickly, and I can send it around this evening."

"Oh, no, thank you," Harriet interjected. The heat flamed her face again, stifling her. "It's a lovely dress, but I am afraid I cannot afford it—"

"Let it be my gift to you," Auntie interrupted. "You have been an excellent companion to me on this trip, and I would like to express my thanks."

"No, I should be thanking you, Aunt Katherine. Besides, Mama would never allow me to accept such an extravagant gift." Harriet turned around, preparing to undo the tapes at the top of the gown.

Marie-Elise clicked her tongue with a frustrated sound and took Harriet by the shoulder, leading her into the dressing room.

"No, wait. I have a better idea." At Aunt Katherine's command, Harriet spun around.

"What if you paid me back for the dress out of the proceeds of your book? Once you become an overnight success and earn your daily bread working as an authoress, you can pay me then if you wish. Or it shall be my gift to you, for all you have done for John." Aunt Katherine favored Harriet with a wheedling look, opening her eyes wide and smiling broadly. "Marie-Elise, take the measurements for the alterations you need to make in the shoulders. Have it sent around this evening, if you please."

Harriet's heart surged with love and gratitude. "Aunt Katherine, you are too generous and good to me."

"Not at all, my dear, not at all. Besides, how could we let a beautiful gown like that waste away in a storeroom? That would be a tragedy."

A letter waited for Harriet when they returned to the flat for the older woman's afternoon rest. Recognizing Sophie's handwriting, Harriet tore it open at once. How she missed her sister and Rose, and even her mother. What had happened in Tansley since she was gone? She wanted to know every detail—if Mama's nervous condition had improved, and what the weather was like, and if the garden was flourishing in her absence.

Unfortunately, Sophie was never much of a correspondent, as evidenced by the very brief missive.

*My dear Sister,*

*I hope you are doing well in Bath. Rose and Mama send their love. I send mine, as well. Tansley is very much the same as when you left it. Mama's nervous fits come and go and seem to get worse if she is very tired. But we have not had to call Dr. Wallace in many days so I believe that is an improvement. Rose says to tell you that the potatoes and onions are storing nicely in the root cellar. I haven't had much time to garden because I have been making over a new gown. Mary and I are tearing apart one of Mama's old court dresses. Just wait until you see it, it will be the first glass of fashion.*

*Dearest Hattie, since you have been gone I have done much thinking about my future with Captain Brookes. I have reached the conclusion that I cannot love him. I will marry him only if you insist I should. I know Mama needs me to marry very well in order to improve her condition. But I cannot love Captain Brookes. I have known that only too well since he returned. I have tried to convince myself otherwise but it is no use. He is far too serious and I do not find him at all attractive. I know you must think it's because of his wooden leg but I am not so shallow. He is a different person now than when he left. I must wait until I find the man of my dreams.*

*Please write and tell me what I should do. Again, I say I will marry John Brookes if you say I must. I am torn, for while I want Mama to be well, I also want my own happiness. I am, as always—*

*Your loving sister, Sophie.*

Harriet dropped the single sheet of foolscap. The farce had ended. Sophie no longer wanted the captain.

# Chapter Twenty

Sophie's letter contained the key that unlocked Harriet's fetters. How often had she wondered what she would do if she were free to love John Brookes? And here was that freedom, wrapped in foolscap, delivered from home. Sophie no longer cared a fig for him. But Harriet cared—oh, yes, she cared with all her might. She loved the way Brookes's eyes changed color from green to gray depending on his mood. She loved his mischievous streak and the way he teased his Aunt Katherine. But most importantly, she loved the man who had lain in the muddy field at Waterloo, preparing to die like a soldier. His loss of faith on that night revealed a vulnerability that Harriet found more alluring than any manly bluster. She wanted to spend the rest of her life making John Brookes whole again. And now, she could.

She glanced at her reflection in the looking glass. Her face drained of all color, but her eyes burned like sapphires in the dim afternoon light. She must conceal her shock and surprise until John understood that his obligation to Sophie was no longer justified. She must restrain herself from running headlong down the stairs, hurling herself headlong into his arms when he returned home this afternoon. Harriet bit her nail absently, a habit she conquered during her girlhood, but which returned in moments of great emotional upheaval. Realizing her actions, she clasped her hands in her lap. 'Twas time to think clearly. All right, if Sophie no longer wanted Captain Brookes, he must know the truth. But who would tell him? And when?

She closed her eyes. Sophie must tell him. It was, in fact, the right thing to do. Once Sophie released him, then perhaps Harriet could begin to show her affection. But not before—no, John would think she was being disloyal to Sophie. She sprang up from the bed, dashing over to the little desk by the window. Time to remind Sophie of her responsibilities. She pulled a sheet of foolscap out of the drawer and uncapped the inkwell with a flourish. Her handwriting, usually so neat and precise, quivered all over the page. She tossed the ruined sheet of paper away and took a deep breath to steady her hands. She began again, concentrating on the banal until she steadied her nerves. She spoke of her trip to the modiste, and the constant rain in Bath, and finally—

*But Sophie, enough polite chatter for now. Let me get to the heart of your letter. Of course I would never force you to marry where you don't love. Marrying any man you don't love simply to secure your own comfort is indecent. But you must write to Captain Brookes yourself and tell him so. He is a good man and it would be dreadful of you not to make a clean break. If you release him, he is free to love whomever he chooses, and you are, too. You should write to him at once, whilst we are still in Bath. That way the entire matter is cleared up before we return home.*

*If you change your mind, please let me know at once. I do not know how to behave around the captain unless I know whether he is my future brother-in-law or not.*

*Give my love to Mama and Rose, and keep a bit for yourself.*

*Your loving sister—*

There. Harriet reread the letter with a scrupulous eye. Yes, she concealed her desires neatly within the framework of spinsterly concern for the proprieties. Sophie, not much given to reading between the lines anyway, would never suspect her sister was in love with the captain. She signed the letter with a grand gesture. The letter would arrive at Tansley Cottage within a few days. If Sophie answered at once, then Captain Brookes would be a free man by the beginning of next week. And she would still have a week with him in Bath—seven glorious days in which she could begin demonstrating her affection—before they returned to Tansley.

She sanded the pages, making sure the ink wasn't the least bit smudged before folding and addressing the envelope. She wrote the address with great precision and care. There must be no chance that it might be misdirected. Then, rather than leave the letter on the table in the hall, she rang the bell for Ada, the maid that had been assigned to her when she arrived in Bath.

"Yes, Miss?" Ada popped her head around the doorjamb almost the second after Harriet pulled the bell.

"Ada, I need this letter posted at once. Can you do it for me?" Harriet nibbled on her thumbnail, and stretched the letter out in her other hand.

"Of course." Ada grabbed the letter. "I will do it right away, before Madame wakes up from her rest."

After the maid quit the room, Harriet plunked down on the bed. She handled the situation as best as she could, and she could only wait patiently. The next few days promised to be agonizing, but there was nothing she could do but endure them. She bowed her head briefly in a prayer of thanks. In a matter of weeks—or even days, if one was feeling optimistic—her own happiness might be assured.

A knock sounded on Harriet's door, some hours later when she retired to dress for the evening. Aunt Katherine decided to take Harriet and John to a recital featuring a famous French soprano, and afterward they planned to dine *en famille* in the flat. Harriet gazed dismally in the looking glass, trying to coax her hair into a more becoming style. A desire to look lovely seized her, but there was no hope for it with her dowdy gown and flat locks. She cast her hairbrush away.

"Come in?" Harriet turned halfway round from her dressing table.

Ada entered the room, bearing a large pasteboard box. "Your gown from the modiste, Miss."

Harriet stood up, smiling with pleasure. "She did promise to deliver it this evening. How lovely! Ada, would you help me with it?" She undid the tapes of her old afternoon dress, letting it slide to the floor in a careless heap.

"Of course. Oh, how pretty it is!" Ada lifted the dress out of the box, giving its folds a brisk shake. Then she draped it over Harriet's head, allowing the fabric to whisper over Harriet's arms and shoulders before tying the tapes in place. The bombazine caressed Harriet's skin richly. The heavy, luxurious fabric rustled when she moved, unlike her cotton gowns, which hung limply from her shoulders. Once she had owned dresses this fine, but never appreciated them. With a pang of regret, the image of the boxes arriving from the modiste at her father's London home flashed across her mind. They contained fine lawn chemises, silk afternoon dresses, cotton morning gowns and even tailored wool riding habits. And the matching kid slippers, so thin she could feel the pebbles of the driveway at Handley Hall crunching underfoot. But those material pleasures vanished long ago. Any of the dresses that still had worth were snatched up by the duns who invaded Handley Hall for sale on the secondhand market. Only the simplest cotton dresses remained. Mama hid most of her gowns under a loose floorboard in her bedroom, and that was why Sophie had a wealth of dresses to make over.

She examined her reflection in the looking glass. The adjustments Marie-Elise made to the shoulders allowed the bodice to fit smoothly against her bosom, highlighting her collarbone. She could never call herself pretty, but this gown improved matters a great deal. She smoothed her hands over her waist. She must become a successful authoress now, if only to repay Aunt Katherine for this exquisite pleasure.

She glanced away from the mirror and saw Ada regarding her with a thoughtful air. "What is it, Ada?"

"I was thinking that we might arrange your hair in a new fashion, Miss. To complete the picture, so to speak."

Harriet laughed, a wry grin passing over her face. "Ada, my hair is stick-straight. There's very little I can do to make it look pretty. It won't hold a curl for more than a few minutes."

Ada shook her head decisively. "Curls wouldn't suit you. But your hair is shiny and thick. We might try a new low chignon, weaving some braids in and out of the back. Something soft and relaxed, not as severe as your usual style."

"I'm entirely in your hands, Ada. Work your magic at will."

Brookes raised his head, heart pounding in his chest, when Harriet walked gracefully into the vestibule. Her appearance was markedly different. His eyes narrowed as he studied her. Had she changed her hair? It looked different—still dark and glossy, but more attractive than usual. The gown she wore was looked richer and more elegant than her customary style of dress. He flicked a glance over Harriet again, allowing his eyes to briefly caress her figure. This was no mere cosmetic change. No, indeed. A glow emanated from her, illuminating her features. What made her so happy? A wayward thought grabbed him. Was she in love? The question made his mouth go dry.

"My dear, you look divine." Aunt Katherine crossed over to her and took her hands. "That gown is the perfect shade for your complexion. Look, John, how it brings out the sapphire of her eyes. She is stunning."

Brookes struggled in vain to keep the heat from rising to his face. Trust Aunt Katherine to point out the obvious. To cover his blush, he made a low bow in her direction. "Harriet, you look lovely."

"Thank you." She smiled, dazzling him with the warmth of her gaze. It was on the tip of his tongue to ask why she looked so blissful. But he bit the question back. Perhaps she met someone in Bath. It wasn't any of his business, was it? They had only shared one dance together. Indeed, Harriet must regard him more as a business partner than a suitor. So it was far too personal to ask her any intimate questions until he was a completely free man. He ran his eyes over her graceful collarbone. Stoames was right. His mother's sapphires would suit her beautifully.

"Shall we go?" Aunt Katherine tucked her arm around Harriet and led her through the door to the waiting carriage. Brookes handed both women up with courtly grace, allowing himself the momentary indulgence of holding Harriet's hand a bit longer than was absolutely necessary. Settling beside Aunt Katherine, he rapped the window of the carriage and they were off.

"Well, my dear, I shall have to chaperone you closely this evening. There's no telling how many eligible young men will crowd around you once we arrive." Aunt Katherine patted Harriet's shoulder, but smiled meaningfully at Brookes.

Jealousy chewed at his gut like a ravenous wolf. He glowered at his aunt, willing her to be quiet.

"Oh, no, Aunt Katherine," Harriet demurred with a pretty

wave of her hand. "I am on the shelf, you know that. I am going simply for the pleasure of hearing such glorious music."

"Tut, tut." Aunt Katherine reached over and patted her shoulder. "Hardly on the shelf, wouldn't you agree, John?"

Was choking a meddling aunt a punishable offense? He shot her a warning look from under his brows and turned pointedly to Harriet. "You look very well tonight, Harriet, and most of all, you look happy." He sat back, hoping he had made his point to Aunt Katherine. She didn't need to coax flowery compliments from him. And feeding the fire of his jealousy would not help matters either.

"I had a letter from home that made me overjoyed, but I cannot discuss it until later." Harriet smiled, turning her head so she could peer out the window. He could not see her eyes, but watched in fascination while a blush crept up her smooth neck and over her right cheek.

"Ooh, a secret. I do love a mystery. But I shall try to pry the answer out of you soon, my dear." Aunt Katherine rubbed her hands together with glee.

Brookes's head ached. Why would Harriet be so happy about news from home? He closed his eyes, trying to drown the drumbeat throbbing against his temples. Perhaps her mother was improving. But if so, why keep the news a secret? He sighed. He might never understand women.

Aunt Katherine patted his shoulder. "Are you all right, John?"

He opened his eyes, turning toward his aunt a bit to put her mind at ease. "Yes, of course. Bit of a headache is all."

"Ah, well, this fine company will soon put you in the right spirit." Aunt Katherine smiled.

"Some people have a most lifting effect on my spirit," Brookes replied in a low tone, meant for Harriet's ears only. He noted, with pleasure, the deepening of her blush and the way she cast her gaze to the floor of the carriage.

Tomorrow he would take Harriet around to meet Cantrill. Perhaps when they were alone, without Aunt Katherine meddling and scheming, he could find out what was behind that special glow of hers. The path still had to be clear for him to pursue her. If she was happy about her mother or some benign news from home, all would be well. But if she had another admirer—Aunt Katherine seemed so sure—his heart flipped in his chest with jealousy. He gripped the carriage seat and willed the organ to return to its normal beat. Harriet might love another, younger man. A man who was whole—not bitter or broken and lame and sometimes a drunkard. If she loved such an Adonis, well, it was up to John to prove himself worthy of her. 'Twas his duty to make Harriet see she was meant to be Mrs. John Brookes.

# Chapter Twenty-One

Harriet's stomach lurched as she followed John to Captain Cantrill's door in Westgate Buildings. Ada, acting as Harriet's chaperone, trailed a few paces behind. Twice on the brief walk from Mrs. Crossley's flat, she decided to turn back, grasp Ada's arm and ask John to make her excuses. But the prospect of admitting her nervousness kept her from following through. If he faced French artillery fire, she could complete a simple interview.

Brookes rapped on the door with one gloved hand, and looked down at her. "Cantrill's a good fellow. I wouldn't bring you by if I didn't like him so much."

Harriet nodded. His solicitude calmed her nerves a bit. "Thank you."

The door swung open, and a masculine voice—a little more tenor than Brookes's bass tones—called, "Brookes, come in. Do you have your colleague with you?"

"Of course, man, she's here."

Cantrill stepped into the doorframe. He was about an inch or so shorter than the captain, and thinner, too. Brown hair curled back from his forehead in a wave, and his brown eyes held warmth. Harriet liked him on sight. He was not dangerously attractive, like Brookes, but his open and friendly countenance gave him a brotherly air. She had no reason to fear him. Harriet extended her hand. "Lieutenant Cantrill, thank you so much for agreeing to speak to me. It will be very helpful to my book."

He grasped her hand and pulled her inside. "Not at all. If Brookes says you are trustworthy, then I have no reason to doubt it. In fact, I have been looking forward to meeting you. Let's sit in the parlor. It's the only room I've got besides the kitchen for entertaining, and the kitchen gets dreadfully hot. Mind you, it's nice during the winter." Cantrill led the way into a tiny parlor, almost the same size as the one at Tansley Cottage. Harriet looked around, trying not to let her surprise register on her face. Cantrill was the second son of one of the wealthiest merchants in England. Aunt Katherine told her so. But these were decidedly reduced circumstances, even for a second son. Did his treatment regimen cost too much? Perhaps he couldn't earn a living while missing one arm.

Cantrill pulled a few chairs over next to the two already by the hearth with ease and assurance. He gestured to Harriet and then to Ada to sit, but Ada bobbed a curtsy and retreated to another corner of the room. She silently pulled out her knitting, leaving Harriet free to pursue her interview without interruption or censure.

Harriet glanced over at Cantrill. No artificial limb protruded from the sleeve of his jacket. Again—why? Cantrill was definitely an enigma. Her curiosity piqued, questions filled Harriet. She sank down into one of the chairs, preparing to start her interview. Cantrill sat before her, and John chose the chair slightly to her left. Cantrill bent down and poured three cups of tea from a pot resting on the table between them.

"First, a toast. To Wellington." He raised his cup high.

"To Wellington," Harriet and Brookes echoed.

"Now, Brookes says you want to know more about the

war." Cantrill set his steaming cup on the table and sat back, as though ready for her to proceed.

Harriet set her cup on the table, too, prompted to begin her tasks. "Yes. You see, I understand a bit about the cavalry charge, but I would like to know more about your regiment. Captain Brookes told me that you were at Hougoumont?"

"Yes. I'm a Coldstreamer. My men and I engaged in conflict with the French at the front gate of the farmhouse."

Harriet nodded. "Lieutenant, you can tell me whatever you think is important for me to know. I shrink from asking questions that might seem too intimate, since we've only met. But I would love to hear anything you wish to share."

"I won't tell you any of the facts and figures surrounding the war, Miss Handley, because I am sure Brookes has already told you everything you need to know. And of course, Stoames can fill you in on any details you may need. The man's a walking military encyclopedia." He paused, and sighed. "The thing that I remember most is the confusion. You know, I am a career military man. I was well used to battle. There was no precision to the mess. Waterloo was a mass of misunderstandings. No one knew when the battle began, or what our orders were, and the orders changed by the minute. Most puzzling battle, eh, Brookes?"

Harriet glimpsed Brookes's nod out of the corner of her eye. "Stoames said no one knew what to do when it ended. Even Wellington has said that after Waterloo, he has no desire to fight again. Everything was a muddle."

"Everything was mud, too." Cantrill shrugged. "The stickiest muck you could imagine, Miss Handley. Hard to march through, I can tell you that."

Harriet curved her lips to acknowledge the little joke, but stayed quiet. Interruptions and unnecessary chatter could sidetrack their memories.

"I lost my arm when one of Soye's brigade cut me through. Two of my men carried me into the farmhouse, against orders. They wrapped what was left of my arm in bandages and went out to rejoin the fighting. Their actions, I am sure, saved my life. I blacked out for most of the battle. When I awoke, Hougoumont was secure, and two other men of my regiment were carrying me to the field doctor. The courage and selflessness they showed that day are the reasons why I am here, and able to talk to you about my experience."

Harriet beamed. Thank God his soldiers looked after him properly.

"I was very fortunate to have such stalwart men under my command. But Miss Handley, I must say that I feel more compelled to talk about my recovery than my experience during the battle. Is that all right?"

"Of course. Tell me whatever you wish." Harriet sat back in her chair, seeking a more comfortable position.

Cantrill sighed. "War is about death. That much is certain. But for me, war was also a chance for rebirth. My journey, learning to live without my left arm, has been a most rewarding one. I would not trade it for anything."

"Indeed?" John interrupted in a surprised rumble.

"Yes. I can't say I am glad I lost my arm, but I am blessed by the journey I have taken. Before the war I was an empty-headed fool. But losing my arm made me realize how very fleeting physical beauty and strength can be. I began to delve deeper, to find a truer meaning to life than playing cards and flirting with pretty girls." His brown eyes twinkled merrily at Harriet. "Not that I mind those things now. The difference is they are no longer my *raison d'être,* as the Frenchies say. I began to regain the faith I had put aside from childhood. And now, I find that my belief in God—my true faith—is more rewarding than any material possession I cherished before the war."

Harriet's heart expanded as she listened. "That is beautiful. I have found my own faith carrying me through some very difficult times. Nothing compared to what you and Captain Brookes suffered, of course." She nodded in Brookes's direction. "But I, too, lost a good deal of material things, and I find myself stronger for the loss thanks to my faith in Him."

He nodded and quirked his mouth in a half grin. "I take the waters to speed my physical healing, but it's my own spiritual well-being that is paramount in my life. I live simply, you see. I've made sure that all the families of the men of my regiment who perished received some sort of financial reparation."

"Out of your own pocket?" Harriet raised her eyebrows in surprise.

"I didn't say it was much." He chuckled ruefully. "Besides, mere coin could never replace the husbands and brothers and sons who died. But sometimes, it eases the burden they left behind. Those of us who survived meet every few fortnights to talk and laugh about old times. It eases the strain of getting used to civilian life again."

Harriet shook her head in wonderment. Cantrill's tale of recovery and rebirth opened endless possibilities for J. H. Twigg. No longer would his wound be a millstone, hampering his life. It could instead be a reason for a new start. Seized with a sudden need to write, she sprang from her chair. "Goodness, I almost forgot. I promised Auntie I would accompany her to the shops this afternoon."

Brookes and Cantrill looked up at her in confusion. Brookes began to rise from his chair. "Aunt never mentioned it. But I would be happy to walk you back."

"No. Her home is around the corner, and I would hate to break off your visit simply because I was silly and forgot an appointment. Ada will go with me." Ada glanced up sharply from her knitting and rose. To put everyone off the scent, Harriet waved her hands with a flighty air, hoping the gesture would cover her urgency and still allow her to leave and get to work. "Lieutenant Cantrill, it was a pleasure. I hope I will see you again before I leave Bath."

He rose. "Please do. I'm usually at the Pump Room in the late afternoon. Drop by, and I will be happy to talk with you more."

Harriet curtsied, nearly knocking the little table over with her knee. "Goodbye, gentlemen. I'll see myself out." She fairly flew to the door and out into the street, hearing the hurried patter of Ada's footsteps behind her.

Brookes shifted over into Harriet's vacated chair, staring at his comrade. He never knew that Cantrill personally provided for the families of his fallen men. Hearing him speak of faith at all was baffling. He showed precious little of it before the war.

Cantrill stared out the doorway, as though Harriet's retreating figure could still be seen. "What a lady."

Brookes looked at him, quirking one eyebrow. "What's that supposed to mean?"

Cantrill looked at him squarely, tapping the arm of his chair with his forefinger. "If you won't marry her, I will. She's one in a million."

The same savage jealousy that tore at Brookes the night before returned with a vengeance. "I'll marry her."

"Is that so?" Cantrill smiled, with the hint of a challenge in his eyes.

Brookes's fingers curled around his cup. "Yes, to be sure. But first I must extricate myself from Sophie."

"Well, if you can't, then I will be most happy to court Harriet. You said she was an original, but she's actually an incomparable. Pretty, intelligent and deeply spiritual. I doubt very much that any young woman in Bath can hold a candle to her."

Brookes's jealousy flared. Cantrill needled him often in this same manner during the war. But when he teased

Brookes about Harriet, it didn't seem the least bit funny. Brookes cleared his throat and shifted in his seat. "Let's cease praising Harriet for the time being. I'll still plant you a facer even if you're a good friend. I've said I'll marry the lady, and I will."

"Plant me a facer? With my bum arm and your bum leg, we'd be an equal match." Cantrill laughed. Brookes couldn't resist the urge to laugh, too, and the tension was broken.

Brookes drained the dregs of his tea. "I never knew about your work after the war. Helping the soldiers' families and all that."

"Well, I never told anyone before. I was hoping to impress Miss Harriet." He ducked as Brookes pretended to throw a punch. Their sparring was familiar—comfortable, even.

"Enough balderdash, man." He cleared his throat. The words were forming in his mind with the greatest difficulty. Why was his own spiritual growth harder to discuss than his physical health? He sighed. "Harriet spoke with me a while ago. She believes that God—" He broke off and tried again. "She believes God was with every man who died that day. Do you believe that is true?"

"I do." Cantrill gazed at Brookes with a contemplative air. "He was with us all that day. I survived, others didn't. I don't know why I stayed alive while others perished, but I feel that God had a purpose for me in life that I could not accomplish in death. So I have spent my time since Hougoumont trying to live in a manner that celebrates Him."

"But what of 'Man's inhumanity to man'?" Brookes leaned forward, as if he could will the answer he sought from Cantrill's thin form.

"'Makes countless thousands mourn,'" Cantrill finished. "God cannot stop the things we do to each other. He can only be there to help us all pick up the pieces. That is what I am trying to do with my men and their families. Pick up the pieces. Move on. Live more deeply and fully. It's what I wish for you, my friend."

Brookes sat back in his chair and closed his eyes. "I've never really given much thought to my spirituality, you know. I always lived for the moment. Cards, women, drink. Later, soldierly dignity, worth, honor. But never with a deeper meaning. Never with a higher purpose. What you and Harriet have told me—I am afraid of it, a little."

Cantrill pressed his lips together in a thin line. "Of course. It's terrifying to turn yourself over to the unknown. But trust in Him, Brookes. He will grant you peace. Of that, I am certain."

Brookes shook his head. It was so difficult to wrap his brain around the concept. He wanted to believe. He wanted to begin. "How do I start?"

Cantrill shrugged. "I can't really tell you, Brookes. You'll have to find your own way. But I'll tell you one thing. Harriet can help you on your journey. That's why I say, marry her. And if you don't, I will." He held up his hand as Brookes's mouth dropped open to protest. "I know what you've said, and I won't dally where you've marked your territory, my good fellow. But I feel that she can set you on the right path, and be a loving and caring helpmate for you. A lot of women aren't. Beth Gaskell wasn't."

"Your betrothed?"

"Betrothed no more. And yes, she couldn't adjust to an idea of living simply and giving to others. She wasn't prepared to be my wife. I harbor no ill will toward Beth. But I also recognize a good thing when I see it now. And I would hate to see you squander it on any supposed connection to Sophie Handley."

Brookes sighed. "I am trying to find a way out."

Cantrill stood, taking the teapot back to the kitchen. "Find it, then," he barked. Brookes recognized his attitude.

Lieutenant Cantrill issued commands to his men in the same tone of voice. The desire for battle burned through Brookes. Thanks to Charlie, he had his marching orders.

## Chapter Twenty-Two

Harriet paused before the bookshop, swallowing nervously. Her heart pounded like a big bass drum as she clutched the parcel more tightly to her chest. She couldn't believe what she was about to do. But there was no other choice. Papa told her the truth long ago. Most publishers would never assume the grave financial risk of publishing an untried author's work. In all likelihood, Harriet would have to bear the cost of publishing the book herself. She bowed her head. The Handley family coffers could not afford a gamble on Harriet's publication. She prayed on it and this was her only hope. She must earn the money on her own.

She opened the door, and the tinkle of the bell announced her entry to a bespectacled man hunched over a desk. His eyes widened in surprise. "Yes, Miss?"

"I have some books I would like to sell." She placed the package carefully on his desk. "They were part of my father's library."

The bookseller gave a deep sigh and rolled his eyes. "Miss, with all due respect, I don't see a lot of valuable books come in here. The pricey ones never make it to Bath, but go straight to London. I can take a look, but I doubt they would fetch more than a few pounds at most."

"My father was Sir Hugh Handley." Harriet pushed the books closer to the old man, noting the sudden gleam of interest in his eyes.

"Sir Hugh Handley's library? Well, then, let me take a look." He grabbed at the parcel and ripped it open. "Such a pitiful few left. I've heard his library contained thousands of volumes. Of course, they all went to the London booksellers and a few made it as far as France."

Harriet nodded, tears stinging her eyes. "Yes. There were thousands. This is all that's left."

He pawed over the pages with delight. "Ah, I see you kept the Homer. A rare edition, fine engravings. Lovely, isn't it?" He looked up at Harriet and blinked. "What else have you here? Aristotle? A Bible? Edmund Spenser? Ah—the Aeneid, very lovely, the Dryden translation. And a book of verse. A rather ragtag lot. No real common theme uniting them."

Harriet cleared her throat, not trusting her voice. It might have a telltale quaver, and she couldn't cry in front of this stranger. "No, and they weren't the most valuable in my father's collection, sir. Only the ones I loved best."

He rubbed his hands together briskly. "Well, Miss Handley, these books aren't worth very much on their own. But, since they are remnants of the fabled Handley library, and because the Homer is rarer than the others, I can offer you twenty-five pounds for the lot."

Harriet sighed, relief flowing through her being. "Twenty-five pounds? That sounds fine."

He stacked the books neatly and smiled. "In truth they are probably only worth twenty, but I will add in the extra fiver for a tribute to the great Sir Hugh. What a collector. Last of a breed, you know. One of the few who understood the art of amassing a fine library. Now, I will need to go to the back room to retrieve the money. Wait here, if you please."

Harriet stared down at the books, bidding each one a silent goodbye. Selling them was like selling off members of her dear family, but she must let them go. Seeing them desecrated by the duns was insupportable. By saving them, and then selling them to finance her own career, she gave herself the security she lost when Papa died. Harriet sniffed. No matter how practical she tried to make it sound, it still left a bitter taste in her mouth. The sooner the transaction was done, the better.

The bookseller scurried back, and counted out the money with a flourish. "There you go, Miss Handley. Good luck to you."

Harriet tucked the coins and bills into her reticule, and nodded. "Thank you, sir. Have a pleasant afternoon."

Back out on the street, Harriet paused to rub her temples. The preceding two weeks had whizzed by in a flurry of activity and anxiety. After her conversation with Cantrill, she submitted to the throes of finishing her novel. Recalling her ability to write at home was so proscribed by family concerns and social engagements, Harriet wrung every moment of writing time from her remaining visit to Bath.

She begged Aunt Katherine's permission to submit to her muse, and the old woman acquiesced with touching alacrity. Scarcely an afternoon passed without a servant bringing Harriet fresh ink, new sheets of foolscap, or tempting refreshments. Auntie admonished all the servants to remain quiet about their daily tasks, and shooed Brookes off to the Pump Room and card parties in the company of Stoames and Cantrill. Thanks to the old woman's generosity, Harriet finished the book as her journey to Bath was drawing to a close. And now, it only remained for Harriet to find a publisher.

She directed her steps toward Aunt Katherine's flat. Now she secured the funds to pay for the printing of her book, if only she could find a publisher willing to take it. Of course, most publishers wouldn't do business with a woman. Her steps slowed. Perhaps she could prevail upon John to negotiate on her behalf. No one else could help her, since Papa's death.

Her days were spent in such a flurry of writing activity that she almost had no time to speak to John, a good thing indeed. Until Sophie wrote to him and severed all ties, Harriet could not trust herself in his company for long. And of course, Sophie had chosen this moment to become the slowest of correspondents, delaying her letter to the captain these two weeks at least. Harriet frowned. Had Sophie changed her mind yet again? Sophie deserved a good shake sometimes.

She climbed up the steps to the front door and crossed the threshold, taking off her bonnet. Stoames crossed the vestibule, smiling at her.

"Good day, Miss Handley. How are you?" He paused, nodding at Harriet.

"Very well, Stoames," Harriet replied distantly, still trying to puzzle out the whole question of obtaining a publisher. "Is the captain at home?"

"I think he's in the library, Miss. Working on a few business matters. His mill manager wrote today."

"Good." If he was already in a businesslike frame of mind, perhaps she could approach him without too much awkwardness. She smiled. "Thank you, Stoames."

Harriet stepped over to the library, the elaborate Persian rug in the hall muffling her footsteps. She rapped twice on the partially closed door.

"Come in." John's voice sounded curt and distracted. Harriet paused. Perhaps now was a bad time. On the other hand…she touched her reticule, heavy with her bitter fortune. There was no time like the present.

"Good day, John." She crossed into the room and smiled at him.

He glanced up from a ledger book and pile of papers with a brief smile. Closing the ledger, he leaned back in his chair. "Harriet, come in. I haven't seen you much during the past few weeks. How goes the manuscript?"

She stood in front of the desk, her legs trembling. What if he said no? What would she do then? She was likely to fall over if she wasn't careful. Abruptly, she sank into one of the leather chairs beside John. "That's what I am here to tell you about. If you aren't too busy." She waved a hand at the paperwork stacked in front of him.

"No, in truth, a pause might do me good. So, how close are you to finishing?"

"I'm finished now." His eyebrows lifted in surprise and she smiled tightly. "Finished earlier this week. Thanks to your help, and your aunt's, of course. And now I am in the position of finding a publisher. I was wondering if I could obtain your assistance yet again."

"Of course." He regarded her with a quizzical air. "What do you need me to do?"

She cleared her throat, hoping her voice would not betray her nervousness. "Most publishers won't deal with a woman. I was wondering if you could make inquiries on my behalf. There's a publisher in Town, Samuel Eagleton & Co., that might be willing to take it. They've published military memoirs and histories before. A novel might interest them, too."

He nodded and pulled out a sheet of foolscap. "Samuel Eagleton, London," he echoed in a low tone. "Anything else?" He looked at her from under lowered brows, pen poised in midair.

"Any publisher, including Eagleton, will want me to cover the cost of printing the books." He set the pen down, his eyes boring into her. "With untried authors, that is the accepted practice," she hastened to assure him. "I've managed to put together a small sum, enough to cover the first printing, if Eagleton accepts."

"How much money?"

"Twenty-five pounds." She patted her reticule for emphasis.

His gaze narrowed speculatively. "Harriet, what did you do to gather together that much pin money?"

Harriet looked down at her lap. She could not meet his gaze. "I sold Papa's books."

"You *sold* them? To whom?" His voice lowered, betraying his disapproval.

"Whitstones Ltd. In the High Street."

"Why would you do a thing like that, Harriet? I know how much those books meant to you."

His words grated harshly on her nerves, causing tears to prick at her eyelids. After all, the books were hers to sell, weren't they? Who was he to judge her? "They were all I had, John. If I am going to publish the books, then I need money for the printing process. I have nothing else of value, and my family can't afford to gamble on my success."

He sighed. "Well, Harriet, that was a great sacrifice you made. I can't say I am happy you did it, but I understand why. I would have happily loaned the money to you. Aunt Katherine would have, too, you know."

"Oh, I couldn't possibly." Of course, John didn't know she was already in debt to Aunt Katherine for the new gown. Publishing the book was the only way Harriet could repay her, as well.

"Why not? We're going to be family soon."

She shook her head. "I am indebted to both of you already, more than you even know." The heat crept over her face, drying the tears in her eyes. Of course, Sophie's letter hadn't arrived yet. He still thought he would become Sophie's husband. Would he accept the elder sister in her place? Doubt flooded Harriet's soul.

A tense silence filled the room. Harriet finally dared to look up, only to find Brookes staring at her with a curious intensity. He nodded briskly, signaling his decision.

"I'll write to the publisher right away." His voice softened. "Thank you for trusting me with this task, Harriet. I know how much this means to you and your family. I'll do what I can to help."

Relief and gratitude coursed through Harriet. She was glad she was sitting down. Had she been standing, her legs would have given out. "Thank you, John." She opened her reticule. "Do you want the money now?"

"Let's wait to see what the publisher says." He smiled. "I know you are good for it."

Brookes alit from the phaeton, glancing up at the address. Whitstone's Booksellers. Yes, this was the place. The shop was smaller than he imagined. In fact, he had driven past it many times without sparing it a second glance.

"Back in a moment." He nodded to Stoames, who slid over and took the reins.

"Take your time, Captain." Stoames saluted and leaned back against the seat.

The door stuck as he opened it, so he pushed it with his shoulder. His effort caused the bell to swing violently, giving an alarming jangle. A little old man, bending over a stack of books on a scarred mahogany desk, jumped at the sound. Brookes strode in, his boots echoing on the bare floor.

"Can I help you, sir?" The old man regarded him closely. "Is there a particular book you want?"

"Yes." Brookes removed his hat and stared at the bookseller, sizing him up. "I believe a young lady came in today and sold a few books to you. I'd like to buy them back."

"Of course." The bookseller rubbed his palms together.

"Now, let me see. There were five books altogether, at a cost of ten pounds each. That will be fifty pounds, sir."

Brookes nodded, tossing his hat onto the desk. "Allow me to be frank, my good man."

"Yes?" The bookseller smiled, like a dog baring his teeth.

"The lady sold you an edition of Homer. As a collector, I know that book alone is worth about three times the sum you quoted me for the lot."

"Indeed, sir. I am passing the bargain on to you. Being friendlylike to a fellow collector."

Brookes shook his head in astonishment. This old black-guard's cheek knew no bounds.

"I'll take the lot for the price you paid for them. Twenty-five pounds." Brookes held his gaze, waiting out the old man's bluff.

His adversary flushed deeply, but kept his countenance. "Honestly—I should make something off the deal."

"You'll sell them to me for the price I named, and count yourself lucky. Otherwise, I'll have to make it known that you like to fleece unsuspecting and trusting young women. You won't be able to sell a drink of water in the desert when I finish with you."

The old man swallowed and his flush deepened. "Twenty-five pounds. I'll wrap them up."

"No need." Brookes smiled, counting out the money. "I'll take them as they are. I'd like to make sure I have the right titles before I leave. It would be dreadful indeed to return home with the wrong books."

The bookseller nodded, accepting the money with trembling fingers. "Just as you say, sir."

## Chapter Twenty-Three

Brookes stared at the page in front of him, and then sealed the envelope with a sigh. After a few discreet inquiries among his acquaintances, he learned that Samuel Eagleton was a legitimate publisher, not a scoundrel like that bookseller. He never wanted Harriet to be cheated again. He yanked the bell-pull and gazed down at the stack of books on his desk. He hid them in his desk drawer since his visit to Whitstone's two days earlier. How to return them to Harriet, he hadn't a clue. He wanted it to be a welcome surprise, but Harriet was such a proud young lady. If she knew she had been swindled and Brookes saved the day, her mortification might consume her. Brookes didn't want to add to her distress. He ran one hand over the worn leather cover of the volume of Homer. Then he scooped the books up and locked them back in the lower left-hand drawer of his desk. Until he could solve the larger problem of telling Harriet his true feelings, the books were the least of his troubles.

Brookes had not said a prayer in years. Only once did he attempt to plead with the Lord for help and comfort, on the night he had lost his leg. Throughout that endless and terrible night, he could not even form the words in his mind.

But now, overwhelmed by frustration and longing, he bowed his head and prayed.

As soon as he was done, a tremendous burden lifted from his chest. He had always been the one others leaned on for support. His men trusted them with their lives. Relinquishing some control to a higher power was a welcome relief. Invincibility exhausted him. He found an unexpected comfort in prayer.

Knowles, Aunt Katherine's butler, knocked discreetly on the door and paused on the threshold. Brookes waved him in. "Knowles, I have a letter for the post. See to it at once, if you please."

"Of course, Captain. A letter arrived for you this morning." Knowles handed him an envelope.

Brookes looked at it, bewildered. The handwriting, all loops and curves, was familiar. Sophie Handley's writing. He furrowed his brow. Why would Sophie be writing to him? He handed the Eagleton letter over to Knowles. "Make certain that letter leaves in today's post," Brookes admonished him.

"Very good, Captain." He bowed and left the room, as silently as a cat.

Brookes sank back down into his chair, ripping open Sophie's letter so quickly that he almost tore it in half.

*Dear Captain Brookes,*

*I am writing to release you from any further obligation for an engagement between the two of us. In the days since your return I have pondered our affection in my heart and have come to the conclusion that I cannot love you, and any fondness I might have felt was heightened by the distance between us during the war. I am not insensible of the fact that, in ending our understanding, I am severing the possibility of increasing my family's fortunes. I have consulted with my sister, Harriet, on the matter and have told her that*

*I would marry you if she wished. Harriet feels that my marriage to you would be indecent.*

The words blurred into a single black line. Brookes dropped the letter. Confusion gripped him. Did Harriet mean that marriage to him was indecent? If that were so... The pain was overwhelming, more unbearable than anything he had experienced. Sophie was repulsed by his injury. But did Harriet, despite his best efforts, see him in the same light as her sister? He tried to read the words again, but her handwriting remained grotesquely distorted.

His jaw tightened as he tried to think. As mortifying as Sophie's letter was, his concern focused on Harriet. Had he tipped his hand? Did she guess his true feelings and pity him? Harriet was the type of woman to marry a man out of mercy. And her campaign to reform him, to bring him to God was another part of this sympathy she must feel. He loved her. She pitied him. Nausea threatened to overwhelm his senses. He needed a drink.

Yes. A nice tall scotch would settle his stomach and calm his nerves. He heaved away from the desk toward the silver tray glistening on a nearby cherrywood table. Auntie always kept fine scotch around the house. With shaking hands, he poured a tall one and knocked it back. He swallowed so fast he didn't even taste the liquor. He downed another, but neglected to savor that one, too. Then he splashed an extra draught into the glass and staggered back to his seat. Snatching up Sophie's letter, he sat on the corner of the desk and continued reading.

*I hope that this letter finds you well and you aren't too angry at me or my family. I do believe I loved you at one time, John, but I cannot love you any longer. The changes the war wrought are too difficult and final for me to overcome. Please do not think too harshly of me, and accept my best wishes for your future health and happiness.*

Brookes's head spun. To clear his mind, he finished off

the scotch and tossed the glass across the room, aiming for the hearth. It splintered into a million pieces with a satisfying smash. That was better. Much better.

Stoames flung open the door. "What the...?"

"Join me, Stoames. Another drinking bout caused by the Handley women." He grinned at Stoames's alarmed expression. "No, seriously, my good man. Pour another round. I am free, entirely free, of those two chits. Time to get on with my life." He did not intend to say those words aloud, but they poured out of him like scotch from a flask.

Stoames quirked an eyebrow, but strode over to the decanter anyway. "You sound like you've had enough."

"No, only three large ones. I'll need about two more before I begin feeling it."

Stoames measured out two more glasses, handing one to Brookes. "So, what happened to bring about this dubious celebration?"

"I received a letter from Sophie Handley, releasing me from any understanding."

Stoames raised his brows. "That's good news, that is."

"It is, and it gets better. Why is the lovely Sophie releasing me? Because Harriet says that marriage to me would be indecent." He spat the last word out and drank deeply.

Stoames sighed. "Are you certain?"

Brookes waved his hand at the letter. "Read it yourself, my good man."

Stoames picked up the letter and read through it carefully. He took so long about the business that Brookes's temper began to rise. "Well?"

"I don't think Miss Sophie means it the way you are taking it." Stoames looked the letter over closely again. "Or at least I am certain that's not the way Miss Harriet meant it, if she said it at all. You know Miss Sophie. She's a flighty lass. I am sure Miss Harriet said one thing, and Miss Sophie took it another way..."

"Enough. As I said, this is good news. I am now free from all obligations. I am liberated. No longer must I strive to be a better man. I am going to forget I ever heard of these two wenches."

Stoames set his glass down. "You are drunk, and you don't know what you are saying. Do whatever you want to with your life. But I won't allow you to call Miss Harriet a wench."

Dizziness overwhelmed Brookes and he lurched forward off the desk.

Stoames rolled his eyes and extended one hand. "Get up, man. I am going to make some coffee and pour it down your throat until you are sober."

"No." Brookes shook his head, which was heavy as lead. It rolled around unsteadily on his shoulders. "I don't want to sober up. To think, Stoames, I believed in Harriet. To think I began *praying* again because of her." He shook his head. "I'm drunk, Stoames, haven't been this drunk in ages."

Stoames pulled him up from the floor and grabbed him by the shoulders. "I don't care what the letter said. I am certain Miss Harriet would never say such a thing. And she would never intentionally hurt anyone. Her motives are sincere. I've been around enough women to know. Now, I am going to force you into a cold bath and make you drink enough coffee to float a boat. You are going to be sober, presentable and polite for the rest of Miss Harriet's stay here."

Brookes held his head. The library was spinning around. "I love her, Stoames. I want her to love me back."

Freed of her writing duties, Harriet plundered Aunt Katherine's library on a regular basis. She was deep into a new book when a knock sounded on her door. Harriet cast the novel aside and sat up.

Ada popped her head around the door. "A letter came for you today. From Tansley. I thought you'd like to see it."

At last. Sophie had finally written. Harriet breathed a sigh of relief as she grasped the letter. "Thank you, Ada."

"You are most welcome, Miss." She closed the door with a gentle click.

Harriet sank down onto the bed and ripped the letter open. Yes, Sophie was as brief a correspondent as ever. After two weeks of waiting, Harriet had hoped for a longer missive.

*Well, it's over—I wrote to Captain Brookes and will send my letter to him in the post with this letter to you. I simply told him what you told me. It's all over and you can regard him as a friend as you wish, but there is no longer any connection between us.*

*Hattie, I informed Mama of my decision not to marry Brookes and she has been most distressed. She takes the laudanum too often for my peace of mind. Hattie, I beg of you, please come home. I am worried about Mama and have no idea how to help her, as I am the cause of her distress.*

Harriet cast the letter aside and rubbed her temples. Mama's condition was worse. She must go home. Aunt Katherine was going to return to Tansley in another week or so, but Harriet could not force Sophie to wait that long. She must return faster than that—at once, if possible. She had to find Aunt Katherine and get her help securing the use of a post chaise.

She quit her room in search of Aunt Katherine. It was late afternoon, so perhaps she would still be in her boudoir, dressing after her afternoon nap. Harriet, heedless of servants and decorum, ran to the old woman's bedroom and rapped on her door.

"Come in," an elderly voice commanded.

Harriet felt better just hearing her. Auntie brooked no hesitation. She would assume control of the situation and everything would be fine.

Harriet shut the door behind her. "Aunt Katherine?"

"Harriet, my dear. Come in. I am giving my hair a good brushing before I tuck it up again. It becomes so disheveled when I rest."

Harriet cleared her throat. "Aunt Katherine, I received a most distressing letter from home today. I am afraid I must beg your help, though you've been so generous already."

"Of course, my dear, anything you need. Whatever is the matter?"

Harriet paused a moment. She didn't want to reveal the whole truth to the kindly old woman. Deal with the emergency first and then wait a little longer to inform Aunt Katherine of Sophie's rejection. "Mama suffers from nervous exhaustion, you know. She is getting worse, and my sister cannot handle Mama's tantrums alone. She wrote to beg my early return."

Aunt Katherine's brows drew together in concern. "Is your mother under the care of a doctor?"

"Yes. Dr. Wallace in the village. I know I promised to stay in Bath another week at least, but I must go home and attend to my mother. Would you help me find a post chaise? I've a little money, and I can pay the fare."

"A public post chaise? Nothing of the sort. That is highly improper, especially on such a long journey. I will return with you. In fact, we should all depart early. John has business waiting for him at home, and I begin to find Bath tiresome."

"No, I couldn't possibly ask you to cut your trip to Bath short. I need your help in securing passage on a post chaise. I would even be happy for a seat on a mail coach. No one would think anything of it, and I could be home in a matter of days."

Aunt Katherine set her hairbrush down with a decisive clink. "Indeed, you will not travel by mail coach." She gave a snort of laughter. "I will have the berlin made ready for you, and if you insist on traveling alone I will send one of the servants to go with you. I will secure your lodging every night under my name at the inns. That is the best I can do for you, although I do wish you would reconsider and allow us to escort you home."

Harriet sat on a nearby settee with a sigh. "No indeed, but thank you, Aunt Katherine. I want to travel as fast as I can, and I would worry about your comfort."

"I can see you are determined, so I will let you go. Though the very idea that you could tax my nerves by traveling too fast is so much nonsense. When you get home, you must write to me at once and tell me how your mother fares. When I return to Tansley in a few weeks, I will come to call."

Harriet smiled, her lips trembling with relief. "Of course. How quickly can I depart? Can I leave tonight?"

"It's a bit late for travel, my dear. It will be dark soon and you would only be a few miles outside of Bath. Take my word for it, start fresh in the morning. Have a good dinner and a good rest. All will be well, you'll see." Aunt Katherine stabbed the final pin in place and turned to face Harriet. "I know you are concerned, Harriet, so put your faith in the Lord. I will say a special prayer for your mother's recovery tonight."

Harriet bustled over to Aunt Katherine and embraced her impulsively. "You are so good to me. I can never repay you enough."

Auntie pulled back, regarding Harriet at arm's length. "Tut, tut. I rather think you shall. Someday."

# Chapter Twenty-Four

"Well, John, you can come out from hiding. She's gone." Aunt Katherine bustled into the private den adjoining Brookes's bedroom, where he had taken refuge behind a stack of ledgers. She pulled a chair directly across from his desk and sat down, looking at him with the glint of battle in her eyes.

Brookes sighed. "Aunt, I haven't the slightest idea what you mean. Where has who gone?" He barely gave Aunt Katherine a glance as he concentrated on the balance sheets before him. Perhaps she would get the message and leave him in peace.

"Listen, dear idiot. Harriet has returned to Tansley." She nodded as he raised his startled glance at her. "Yes, you see? By getting so far into your cups that you couldn't come to dinner last night, and then sequestering yourself in your private study all morning, you missed out on a great deal."

"Why has she gone back to Tansley so early?" He floundered under the intensity of Aunt Katherine's gaze.

"Her sister wrote and begged her to return. Their mother has taken a turn for the worse." The old woman shifted in her chair and rapped her knuckles on his desk. "Although I think all of those Handley women, saving my dear Harriet, need nothing more than a good kick in the bum."

"Aunt Katherine, really!" He would never get used to hearing her use coarse language. His surprise did not surpass his shock over Harriet's departure, but he shrugged his shoulders with a nonchalant air. "Her mother is truly ill, I suppose."

"Oh, tut. Those women expect someone else to swoop in and rectify their situation. Meanwhile Harriet has been writing her fingers to the bone trying to save their worthless hides. I had a private conversation with Lady Handley, before we left for Bath. Honestly, I am sure that woman has delusions of ruined grandeur. Face the facts and move on, that's what I always say. The Lord will provide."

"Not everyone has your strength of character, Aunt." He winced at her mention of faith. The effects of last night's drinking bout lingered in both mind and body. He had no desire for a theological debate today.

She waved her hand carelessly, as if shooing away his words. "Now, did Harriet ask you to negotiate on her behalf for a publisher?"

"She did." He leaned back in his chair, folding his arms over his chest.

"And did you write to the publisher?"

"I did." He laced the two words with a polite tone of warning.

"Excellent. Now, where does that leave you, my dear nephew?"

"I don't know what you mean. None of this is my affair, though I am sorry to hear of it." The words were frosty and precise. Surely Aunt would get the message.

"Hush, Nephew." She held up a warning hand to stem his words. "It has been under my notice for some time you are quite besotted with Harriet."

Brookes opened his mouth to protest, and then shut it

with a snap. There was no use pretending with Auntie. She saw through every subterfuge, just as she had when he was a boy and fell out of that tree. So he merely shrugged his shoulders.

"In truth, I want you to marry the girl. Not to bring her family any material comforts, though that would follow. No, mine is a purely selfish reason. I like to see you happy. And Harriet brings you joy. She would be an excellent wife for you. And I think she opened your heart to faith, which makes me most exceedingly pleased."

He cleared his throat. "Auntie—"

"If you are worried about Sophie still, I think you could call off any supposed connection. It's been long enough, and she's shown little interest."

"Enough." He pushed away from the desk and leveled a gaze at his aunt. He allowed the intense pain he felt to shine through his eyes. His expression was so stormy even she, as talkative as she always was, fell silent.

"There is no need to fear any connection with Sophie. She wrote yesterday, informing me our understanding is off."

Aunt Katherine clapped her hands. "Oh, famous! Perfect. Now the way is clear for you to wed Harriet."

"It isn't." He paused, measuring his words carefully. "Sophie said Harriet told her a marriage to me would be indecent."

She raised her head, searching his face for answers. "Whatever does that mean?"

"Is it not plain? Harriet finds me so appalling that she would call marriage to me an indecent thing." The raw pain of it sounded in his ragged voice. A drink would taste so good right now. But there was no decanter in the den, and he knew Aunt Katherine would not let him quit the room until she had all the answers she wanted.

"I'm sure Harriet never meant such a thing." She lowered

her voice, speaking softly as she used to when he was a boy, and had injured himself in some escapade. "John, upon my word, I feel most certain that Harriet is in love with you. I have seen her look at you with such esteem and affection. I know she must care."

He shook his head. "Aunt, I know you think you are right in everything. And usually I indulge you in that conceit. But you are wrong in this case." He pulled the letter from his desk drawer and tossed it into her lap. "Here, read it yourself."

She lifted her quizzing-glass and read through the letter, a frown of distaste creasing her brow. "Goodness, what a vulgar letter. Whatever did you see in this girl, besides her beauty? Consider yourself lucky, John, that you didn't marry her before the war. To be saddled with a piece of baggage like that the rest of your life…"

He looked down at his desk. Was Sophie really a common woman? He remembered her the way he knew her, before the war, when they were both young and lively. A vulgar chit? No, not really. "She's not so bad, Aunt. She has been indulged throughout her life. Her beauty commands things from other people—extra sweets before dinner, a pretty dress from town. From birth, I am certain her mother groomed her for a great marriage. And once their fortunes reversed, I was their backup plan. Although I must say it shows some strength of character that she refuses to marry me because she doesn't love me." He purposely avoided his aunt's eyes and directed his gaze out of the window, his voice distant even to his own ears.

"I don't harbor any ill will toward Sophie. But I am—" A telltale tremor sounded in his voice and he cleared his throat again in an attempt to steady it. "I am most hurt by what Harriet said."

Aunt Katherine placed the letter on the desk and regarded him with a grave air. "It's not like you to give up so easily,

John. I would rather you confront Harriet, even in anger, and demand an explanation than to simply fold like this." Her tone changed, reverting to its usual bossiness. "Here's what you do, my boy. Write her a letter, demanding an audience when we return home to Tansley. When she arrives, show her Sophie's missive. Then tell her to clarify exactly what she meant—"

"No." He clenched his jaw and watched his aunt through narrowed eyes. "No confrontations. I don't want anything, except to be left in peace."

"Then I will ask Harriet myself. After all, she is a friend of mine, too, and you are my nephew. If she says disparaging remarks about you to others then I want to know why."

He sighed, rolling his eyes. "No, Aunt. Give me some time. I must navigate this on my own. I must find the right way to confront Harriet, and I cannot allow you to fight my battles for me. I am a seasoned soldier, after all." His mouth quirked with a rueful grin, but there was no joy in his heart.

She sat back in her chair and folded her hands. "Very well. I shall give you more time. But I won't allow you to lose Harriet simply because of one thing her silly chit of a sister wrote. Depend upon it, Nephew—we will revisit this subject again."

He shrugged his shoulders in exasperation. "I've no doubt of that, Aunt Katherine."

Harriet leaned her head against the cushions of the Crossley berlin. Travel was incredibly fatiguing when one didn't have someone to talk to or even a decent book to read. She looked across the carriage at her traveling companion, an elderly maid named Hannah. She had slept most of the trip and when she wasn't asleep, her conversation was brief and boring. And of course, she had no books. Aunt Katherine offered her the run of their library before she departed, but Harriet refused. Her debts ran so deep already that even borrowing a single novel was an imposition. With no conversation and nothing to read, she could only turn inward, mulling over the same worries and troubles which plagued her during her long journey.

The thought of Brookes Park turned Harriet's attention to another well-traveled road: her departure from Bath. Everything had been accomplished in a blur. The moment she left Aunt Katherine's room, she packed her trunk. A light supper, and the next morning, she departed before dawn. The luxurious post chaise was ready and waiting for her. When Harriet climbed inside, Hannah was already tucked in a corner. They stopped at two of the same inns she remembered from the journey to Bath, so her excursion was comfortable and familiar as could be. There was no reason to regret her trip—except she hadn't said farewell to John.

Stoames had come down to the supper room, announcing that the captain was unwell and would have to stay abed. A brief word exchanged between the batman and Aunt Katherine floated to Harriet's consciousness. "Drunk." John was too intoxicated to come downstairs.

Sophie's letter affected him profoundly. That was the only explanation which made sense. That's the reason he drank too much and couldn't dine with the family. If he took Sophie's rejection that hard, then it meant he really cared for her. Tears crowded Harriet's eyes, and she flicked a nervous glance at Hannah, snoring blissfully against the cushions.

She wept because John was hurt. She loved him and never wanted him to feel pain. His life had already been marked by so much loss that Harriet wanted to protect him from ever experiencing unhappiness again. And, if she were going to be honest, she shed tears for herself. It was all right to let go in the relative privacy of this carriage. Hannah slept, and no one else could witness her selfishness.

Though she hated to admit it, she wept, too, because her little sister meant so much to Brookes, and she did not.

There it was. She said it to herself here and now, but she must never think of it again. Allowing herself to give in to maudlin despair over John's lack of affection would bring nothing but unhappiness. She could only thank God she had the friendship and support of such a remarkable man, and leave it at that.

Hannah snorted and shifted in her sleep. Harriet furtively wiped the tears away with her gloved hands, hoping her eyes hadn't turned a telltale shade of red. She would be home soon and would have to assume the reins of leadership when she alit from the carriage. Striding into the little cottage with bloodshot eyes and a tear-streaked face when she was supposed to be the voice of calm authority would never do.

She folded her hands in her lap. Closing her eyes, she prayed to God for strength and wisdom in the coming weeks. She prayed for what she knew He would provide. One couldn't pray to God for material possessions. Rose taught her long ago to do so was folly.

She remembered, as a child, when Rose listened to her evening prayers. Once she had asked God to give her an extra piece of cake for tea the next day. Rose laughed and held her close. "The Lord isn't a kind of celestial good fairy, bringing us treats, dearie," she had admonished in her kindly way. "He can only give us the strength and support we need to cope with life—you had better pray for the strength to do without that extra cake." She grew up with this knowledge deep in her soul, and it comforted Harriet to know He was not responsible for granting material goods in this world.

In all the tales of Greek gods and goddesses Harriet devoured in Papa's library, she grew frustrated at how little mortals had control of their own destinies. They were mere pawns in the hands of the gods. How comforting to know she was no pawn and she could only pray for the intangibles—peace, love, strength, wisdom, serenity—the values which would help guide and shape her, no matter what life threw her way.

And yet, there were times when one wished for a cosmic fairy godmother, someone who could wave a magic wand and set everything back to rights.

The carriage jolted and swayed on the road. Harriet caught herself. These rocky roads meant home—they were drawing closer to Tansley. There was no sense in praying for material goods, and yet Harriet held on to a thread of hope. Even if Captain Brookes never loved her, she could still adore him from afar, caring for him secretly for the rest of her days. Her tenderness was in every page of the book she had written, in J. H. Twigg's story as he negotiated life's path from downfall to triumph. *Call to Arms: A Soldier's Memoir of Waterloo* was Harriet's declaration of love for Captain John Brookes.

*Oh, please God,* she breathed. *Give me the grace to accept what comes.*

## Chapter Twenty-Five

The berlin pulled to a jerky stop before the mounting block at Tansley Cottage. How very small her home looked after weeks of viewing the classical facades of all the grand buildings in Bath. The little house impressed her more than ever with its sense of secrecy—it had much to hide.

Hannah awoke with a startled jump as the rolling motion of the carriage wheels stopped. She peered out the window. "Is this your home, Miss?"

"It is." Harriet gathered her reticule and pulled her shawl more closely about her shoulders. "Would you like to come in for tea, Hannah?"

"Thank you, but no. We are expected at Brookes Hall. The other servants will probably be holding dinner for us."

Harriet nodded. "Thank you for being my companion on this trip. I appreciate your help." The door to the cottage opened, and lamplight spilled out into the front garden, forming a perfect rectangle on the grass in the deepening dusk.

"No trouble, Miss." Hannah smiled for the first time during the trip, revealing a row of gapped teeth. "I hope your mother fares better."

The carriage door opened and the footman extended his

hand. Harriet alit only to be smothered by Sophie's embrace, the force of which almost knocked her over.

"Hattie! You are home," she wailed, burying her face in Harriet's shoulder. "Oh, I am so glad. Please, come in. We have missed you so much."

Harriet patted Sophie's shoulder and glanced up at the footman, who was regarding Sophie with a bemused gaze. "Thank you, sir. I appreciate your kindness on this journey."

"Of course, Miss." He gave a brief salute and stepped back into place. With a jolt, the carriage took off, tracing a C in the mud as it moved on.

Harriet and Sophie walked into the cottage together, leaning on each other for support. When they crossed the threshold, Rose ran into the entry hall, her arms extended. She squeezed Harriet warmly and Harriet breathed deeply, inhaling Rose's familiar scent of fresh bread. How she missed them both.

"Bless you, dearie. We have missed you so. Come into the kitchen and have a nice cup of tea."

They gathered in the coziness of the kitchen. Rose put the kettle on and sliced a loaf of bread into squares. Sophie bustled about, obtaining the sugar and butter from the larder, impressing Harriet with her initiative. So often in the past, Sophie would simply wait, expecting others—namely Harriet—to serve her. Perhaps her trip to Bath had forced Sophie to grow up a bit.

The kettle's whistle rent the air with a piercing scream. Rose poured the scalding water into the teapot, carefully ducking her head to avoid the steam as it rose. She and Sophie set the small repast down on the smooth wooden surface of the table.

"Before we tuck in, a little prayer," Rose reminded the girls gently. As they had since childhood, they bowed their heads with obedience.

Sophie poured the tea. She certainly was taking the initiative this evening. Harriet peered at her sister closely. Noticing Harriet's puzzlement, Rose smiled.

"Sophie has been most helpful to me while you were gone, Harriet." She nodded in Sophie's direction. "Such a fine help in the kitchen and good with your mother, too."

"Rose taught me how to make scones." Sophie offered Harriet the little ceramic pot which held the sugar. "Mine aren't as light as hers, but it was great fun to learn."

Harriet spooned the sugar into her cup and stirred it. "You've always had a hand for needlework. Now you've mastered the kitchen arts, so you shall make some lucky man an excellent wife."

Sophie blushed under the gentle ribbing, but smiled. "I enjoyed learning something new. Rose is going to teach me how to bake bread next. Perhaps Mama would like some fresh bread with supper tomorrow night."

"Tell me about Mama." Harriet set her cup down in its saucer and steeled herself for the news. She could delay the inevitable no longer. Better to know now than continue in dreadful worry.

Sophie's eyes filled with tears, and Rose patted her hand. "It's my fault," she whispered. "When I said I would not marry Captain Brookes, Mama was most distressed. She said I was throwing away our one chance at money and comfort. That I was denying her the life she deserved for some silly notion, like love."

"But surely there was never a greater love match than between our parents," Harriet interjected. "After all, actresses don't marry nobility every day. In fact, they hardly ever wed at all. So if Mama enjoyed a love match, why can't you?" As soon as she said it, Harriet regretted the words. Her voice held a harsh and unforgiving tone. She tried to soften the blow. "I know Mama's health would improve with a return to our previous style of living, but don't despair. Captain Brookes is negotiating with a publisher on my behalf. If my book is published, we will have enough money to live modestly and comfortably."

"That's a fine idea, dearie." Love lit Rose's kind brown eyes. "I always knew you would become an authoress. Ever since you were a little girl, scribbling notes on the back of my housekeeping lists. I am proud of both of my girls. You are both growing and maturing into fine young women." She beamed at Harriet and Sophie in turn, but the proud expression faded when she spoke again. "Dr. Wallace has put your mother on a diet of milk and honey, Harriet. This change, as well as the laudanum, is supposed to help. I fear that neither treatment is very helpful."

Harriet's stomach dropped like a stone. "Tell me what the doctor says."

Rose sighed. "Well, he says her ladyship's condition has worsened, and now she is suffering from melancholia in addition to the nervous hysteria. She refuses to leave her room. She won't speak to us very much anymore. All she does is lay abed and sleep, or stare at the walls. Dr. Wallace thinks the milk and honey will strengthen her and that plenty of rest is good for her nerves. He left a new bottle of laudanum yesterday and will return late tomorrow evening."

Harriet stood up, shaking the dust from her skirts. "I would like to see Mama. I need to judge her condition for myself."

"Please don't be angry with me when you see Mama," Sophie cried, and grabbed Harriet's arm. "Truly, Hattie, I will marry Brookes if I must."

Harriet placed her hand on Sophie's, giving her sibling her best "elder sister in charge" expression to calm Sophie's outburst. "None of this is your fault. And marrying the captain should not be a requirement if you don't love him." She quit the kitchen and walked up the stairs, her feet heavy as lead.

* * *

Mama's breathing was labored and rough, but her eyes were open and staring at the ceiling. A raw, primitive grief engulfed Harriet when she regarded her mother's emaciated and sallow body. She was so small, so powerless. As aggravating as Mama could be at times, Harriet still loved her mother with all her heart. Harriet grasped one of Mama's hands and kissed it, trying to will life and hope back into her mother's form.

Mama tilted her head toward Harriet. Her eyes reflected no spark of recognition, and her gaze remained glassy and flat.

"Mama, I have returned from Bath. I came quickly as I heard you were worse." Harriet could not tell if Mama could understand her, so she kept talking. "I made the journey in four days' time, a record I am sure."

Mama blinked. Another deliberate movement—a good sign. Harriet smiled to encourage her mother.

"Mama, I have good news. I finished my book while I was in Bath. Captain Brookes is negotiating with a publisher on my behalf. If my book sells, I can provide a comfortable living for us all. Isn't that nice?" She adopted a bright and cheery voice, entirely unlike her own. Her tone leant an air of forced gaiety to the somber little bedchamber.

Mama ran her tongue over her dried lips. She mumbled something, but Harriet couldn't understand her words.

"Say it again, Mama, I couldn't hear you." Harriet leaned closer.

"Book won't sell." The words were repeated with tremendous effort.

Tears sprang to Harriet's eyes. "It will be all right, Mama, truly it will. Captain Brookes said the book was good enough to sell. He doesn't lavish praise on everyone, so I believe it to be true."

Mama simply closed her eyes in response.

"Mama, where there is life, there is hope. We have a roof over our head and clothes on our backs. Many people cannot boast even that much."

Harriet rose from her mother's bedside and grasped the Handley family Bible, which rested on her dressing table since they moved to the cottage. The book never seemed more than a mere decorative piece of art, but Harriet seized it. That book held all the answers she could not put into her own imperfect words. She turned to the book of Matthew and began reading aloud, finding comfort and peace in the words.

She looked up from the worn leather Bible and regarded her mother's countenance. Was she even listening? Harriet could not tell. Her eyes were closed and her facial muscles were relaxed, so Harriet began reading the passage where she left off.

After a few verses, she paused again. Mama's eyes opened and she looked straight at her eldest daughter. "Water."

Harriet poured a glass of water from the pitcher next to her bed. Mama sipped it, the movement sapping most of her energy.

"I am a frivolous woman." Her words were heavy and slow, as though they were traveling across the fields of time. "I can't change. You comprehend me?"

Harriet nodded, but she didn't really understand. What was Mama trying to say?

"If Sophie won't wed Brookes—I cannot recover. I am too ashamed."

"But why, Mama? Isn't it enough we are together, and love each other?"

"I am too ashamed—of what I was." She put the glass down on the bedside table as if it weighed a few stone. "I worked to support my family. As an actress."

Harriet nodded, waiting for her to continue.

"Married your father even though I was an actress. His family blames me for our ruin."

Harriet laid the Bible on the bed and took her mother's hands in her own. "It wasn't your fault, Mama. Don't blame yourself, and don't accept theirs. We all spent the money. Don't forget Papa's library."

Mama shook her head. "I spent on everything. Blackmailers, too."

Harriet's mouth dropped open in surprise. "Blackmailers? Why?"

"Because—we kept my acting secret—only his family knew for sure. Stage name." She paused for a moment, gathering the strength to continue. "Blackmailers threatened to tell the *ton* my true identity."

Harriet sat back, a shockwave of disbelief coursing through her body, like floodwaters breaking over a dam. Her family had been blackmailed, systematically, for years. And that was a large part of why they were living in poverty now. She looked down at the faded counterpane, catching her breath. The past no longer mattered. She had to focus on the present and plan for the future.

"Without a powerful man protecting us," her mother continued slowly, each word an effort, "Blackmailers will return. Brookes was my last hope."

Harriet smiled wanly and patted her mother's hand. "There's nothing left to take, Mama. And my book will provide us with the modest living we need. Please. Please listen to what I am saying."

Her mother turned away, staring at the wall. "Young ladies shouldn't work for money. My daughters are the daughters of Sir Hugh Handley. No matter…what I was."

Harriet suppressed a sob, her heart welling with love and tenderness for her mother. She had never understood Mama's driving need for money and status. Indeed, she had counted both as great flaws in her character. But now her mother's broken words confirmed Harriet's intuition. Her mother was simply trying to muddle through life, hounded by fear and self-loathing.

Talking so much had worn Mama out. She closed her eyes and fell silent. Harriet lay down beside her mother on the bed and patted her hair silky, greying hair until Mama fell asleep.

When her mother's breathing became soft and measured, Harriet rose stiffly from the bed, trying not to shake it and risk waking her up. She pressed a kiss to Mama's forehead. *I love you, Mama,* she thought, not daring to say the words aloud.

On the bedside table, laudanum rested too near the edge. The bottle was fresh, at least according to Rose, but nearly two-thirds of the contents were already gone. Afraid the glass might fall over and break, Harriet scooted it closer to the bed. She poured fresh water from the decanter into Mama's drinking glass. Then she straightened the bed-clothes and tiptoed out of the room.

# Chapter Twenty-Six

Harriet stirred in bed, stretching stiff and sore limbs from riding in the carriage for long days on end. The first rays of daylight filtered in through the curtains. Beside her, Sophie slept, her breathing deep and silent. A metallic rattle from downstairs signaled that Rose was awake and already making breakfast. How lovely to keep resting, but home meant a return to duty, and allowing Rose to do all the work was most unfair. She rose and began dressing.

Rose's footsteps sounded on the stairs, and then her voice echoed in the little hallway. "My lady? My lady, please wake up!"

At the cry of alarm, Harriet tossed her half-braided hair over her shoulder and ran into Mama's room. Rose leaned over the bed, frightened tears streaming down her face. "Harriet, she won't stir. She's already cold."

"I don't believe it." Harriet strode over to her mother and laid a palm on her face. She drew back in horror. Mama's skin was cool, too cool to the touch. She grabbed a handheld mirror from the dressing table and placed it under Mama's nostrils, waiting for the telltale fog announcing life. The glass remained clear. Harriet dropped it onto the bed and took a step back.

Mama was dead.

Rose sank onto the bed, sobbing. Harriet stood, her back pressed against the wall for support. What had happened? The laudanum bottle lay tipped over on its side on the bedside table. Not a drop clung to the amber glass.

Her knees gave out, and she slid down the wall and onto the floor, her head bowed.

Sophie ran into the room, still in her nightgown. "Whatever has happened?" she gasped.

"Mama is dead," Harriet replied in a voice unlike her own. Indeed, she could not tell if Sophie heard her.

"Mama is dead?" Sophie screamed, and flung herself on the bed beside Rose. "Oh, it is my fault. I was too cruel. I should have married Brookes."

Harriet covered her ears with her hands. Sobbing would not help. Hysterics would only worsen matters. She must keep her head and assume control of the situation.

Harriet knew that Mama had been too careless with the laudanum. She had always taken just a little more, and then a bit more. As she wasted further away, she must have taken just that extra too much. Mama hadn't been suicidal. But she had been too dependent on a potent medicine to solve her troubles.

There was no time to grieve. She must care for Mama in death with dignity. She stood, her legs trembling so that her knees knocked together. "Rose, I think it would be best if we said the twenty-third Psalm."

Rose nodded, blowing her nose. "The Lord is my shepherd, I shall not want…" she began, her voice thick with tears.

Harriet and Sophie joined in, their shaky voices blending together. After they finished, silence held the room for a moment, punctuated by Sophie's weeping. Then Harriet moved into action. The family had so much to do. "Rose, run to the village and tell Dr. Wallace what happened. He will know what to do. I can prepare Mama for burial but he may wish us to have an undertaker do so. If he insists on an undertaker, stress to him we can only afford the plainest of funerals."

Rose looked at her, the pain she felt reflected in her bloodshot eyes. "With what money, dearie?"

"I sold Papa's books in Bath. I was going to use the money to pay my publisher. But this is more important. The sum was not much, so we must use it as carefully as possible. Sophie—" Harriet placed a gentle hand on her sister's shaking shoulder. "You must dye all of our clothes for mourning. We have a few dresses left from after Papa's death, but everything we own must be black again. The large washtub will do—you can fit several of our gowns in it at one time." She hesitated, and then continued in a lower tone. "And Sophie, you must make a shroud for Mama. Perhaps we can fashion one from her bedsheets."

Sophie bit back a sob and nodded.

"I will take the horse and ride to the church at Crich. I will ask Reverend Kirk if he will consider coming here to perform a simple ceremony for Mama. It would be a great balm to all of our souls to have him here, I think."

The two women nodded, raising tear-streaked faces to Harriet for guidance. She racked her brain, trying to think of any other task that must be performed. The Handleys would not help them; in fact, they would only rejoice at Mama's demise. If only there was someone she could turn to, who could share the burden. But he remained in Bath. And he didn't love her. Even so—Harriet recalled Aunt Katherine, warm and secure and independent. Surely Auntie would help.

"I am going to write a letter to Mrs. Crossley, who has offered to help us often. Our hour of need is upon us." She looked at Rose, and determination stiffened her spine. "Rose, after you have fetched Dr. Wallace, take the letter up to Brookes Park with instructions to send it to Bath. Her servants are returning to fetch them back home anyway. Perhaps one of them can ride ahead with the message."

Rose nodded. "That sounds like a sensible plan."

"Sophie, you must dress and start the washpot boiling. It does no good to cry. Mama is at peace. What happened is not your fault, not in the least. I beg of you, stay occupied today and do not give in to hysterics. We must be strong." She pulled Sophie up from the bed and looked her square in the eye. "We have too much to do."

"All right. Hattie—would you cover Mama? I cannot bear to." Sophie fled the room, her face buried in her hands.

Harriet and Rose stretched the bedsheet over Mama's body. Then they tiptoed out of the bedchamber and closed the door with a quiet click.

"Rose, I will compose my letter and then ride over to Crich. I will leave my dispatch on the mantel in the parlor. Be sure to take it as soon as you can."

"Right away, dearie."

In the parlor, Harriet grabbed the first sheet of foolscap she found. She had no more of the black-bordered stationery left from Papa's funeral—they used it for shopping lists and general housekeeping notes over the years. This would have to do. She opened the inkwell, but her hands shook so badly she had a difficult time dipping the pen. Taking a deep breath to compose herself, she wrote her plea to Aunt Katherine.

*Dear Aunt Katherine—*

Desire to pour out all of her troubles overwhelmed Harriet, forcing her to put her pen down. As though the sheet of paper were Aunt Katherine's shoulder, she longed to rest all of her burdens there. But she could not. She must keep her message brief and practical. Very well. What was necessary to convey to Auntie—and to John? She hastily scribbled the news, and halted, biting her lip. She must tell the truth, no matter how humiliating:

*I know not what the future will bring. As yet I have not settled Mama's affairs, so I am unsure of our means of living. I must prepare myself and my sister that we may have to seek employment. I would like to have your advice on this matter upon your return.*

*Please inform the captain that I must spend the money I have raised on Mama's funeral. If he has not contacted the publisher yet, please ask him to refrain from doing so until I have secured proper funding again.*

*I must go; there are many preparations to be made. I must thank you in advance for your help and consideration.*

Harriet sanded the pages and folded the letter, placing it on the mantel. Now she must make the journey to Crich and back. She wound her way through the hushed cottage. Amazing how her mother's death already touched the confines of the little house. She paused on the back step. "I am off to the church, Sophie. I should be there and back by dark."

Sophie looked up from the fire she built and nodded. "Hattie, I will stay outside if I may. I do not wish to be alone in the house with Mama's body."

"Of course." Harriet embraced her tightly. "Dr. Wallace and Rose will be here soon. Be brave, my dear." With a final pat on her sister's shoulder, Harriet strode over to the barn.

The family lost all of their carriages, with the exception of a light gig, which Harriet and Sophie once drove around their father's estate for fun. Now the gig functioned as their primary mode of transportation. Harriet hitched Esther, their aging but faithful nag, to the tiny conveyance. Esther had a ewe-neck, considered of poor enough conformation none of the duns wanted her, so Harriet managed to keep her for their use.

She climbed into the gig easily and gently flicked the

reins across Esther's swayed back. A moderate pace would be best. She didn't want to press Esther too much.

The stone steeple of St. Mary's loomed in the distance, and nervousness gripped Harriet like a vise. She spent the hours-long ride trying to come up with solutions to their money woes. A post as a governess would be a sensible course of action, and she might earn the money to publish her book again. Though she plotted and planned for the future, she hesitated to prepare herself to speak of her mother's death to Reverend Kirk. Could she bring herself to form the words? She might burst into tears, and that would never do. She couldn't cry. She had to be strong—the foundation of her family.

She pulled the gig around in front of a small stone house squatting beside the church. This must be Reverend Kirk's residence. She alit, tying Esther to the hitching post in the deserted churchyard. Perhaps the reverend left on a call, and no one would be home to help her. She paused. She hoped only to come here and hurry home. She hadn't counted on waiting.

A stout housekeeper ushered Harriet into a pretty but plain sitting room. A bouquet of daisies burst forth from a yellow porcelain vase on his oaken desk, lending a cheery air. Harriet sank onto a wooden chair with a worn needlepoint cushion, her composure returning. At the sound of footsteps outside the door, she rose again. Seeing the reverend's kindly face, her composure fled and she burst into tears.

Reverend Kirk allowed her to cry, saying nothing, merely patting her arm while grief consumed her. Harriet's weeping abated at length, and she wiped her nose with her sodden handkerchief. He handed his over to her, and she gratefully pressed the crisp linen to her face. She inhaled deeply, willing herself to calm down. Her eyes burned from the sudden flood.

"Miss Handley." He spoke in a gentle voice. "What has happened that grieves you so?"

"My mother died this morning. Reverend Kirk, I would like for you to officiate at her funeral service. Only my family shall be there—three of us in all. But your presence would mean a great deal to us."

"Of course I will, my child. You live in Tansley, do you not? When is the funeral to be?"

"The quicker the better. We are readying her body for burial today. Although I would rather bury Mama beside Papa, I think it would be better to inter her at the cottage. There are circumstances that make her quick burial necessary." A sudden sob fought its way up her throat. She bit it back, forcing herself to remain controlled. The farce was over. She couldn't lie to this sympathetic man of the cloth.

"What are these circumstances?" His voice grew calm and gentle, helping to steady Harriet's nerves.

Harriet closed her eyes, praying for strength. "I—I believe my mother accidentally took too much laudanum. She was ill and in pain for some time, suffering from nervous hysteria. She must have miscalculated the dose last night." The truth poured out in a torrent. She opened her eyes, unsure of the reverend's reaction. Would he refuse to perform the service?

He sat back in his chair with a gentle air. "My child, as a man of faith, I can assure you that Jesus is the savior of all mankind. He has forgiven our sins, even the transgressions of the past. Your mother's soul will find peace with His forgiveness."

"Thank you, Reverend, for your help, and for allowing me to grieve. I have to remain strong in front of everyone else."

"Not at all, my dear. If a swift funeral is best, I can be there as soon as you need. Perhaps tomorrow morning?"

She accepted the fresh spring water with shaking fingers. "Is that too soon for decorum?"

"No, especially not among us country folk. I think an immediate funeral would be best for your small family. No intense mourning rituals, but a simple service followed by internment."

She nodded and opened her reticule. "I cannot afford to pay very much—"

He waved his hands. "No need for payment, Miss Handley. I am only too happy to help."

Tears welled in Harriet's eyes again.

"No, no, my dear, don't cry," he interjected. "Consider it my tribute to your late mother."

A profound wave of gratitude rolled over Harriet, and she managed a watery smile. "Thank you, Reverend Kirk."

# Chapter Twenty-Seven

Brookes heard the rider before spotting him, as gravel scattered and pinged against the water fountain in the courtyard. "Give me a minute, Charlie," he remarked to Cantrill. He strode out of the barn, where they had been examining his latest acquisition, a mighty black stallion named Samson. Cantrill followed a few paces behind.

"Ho, there, what have you?" Brookes called, before halting in recognition. 'Twas one of his own stable lads from Brookes Park. Brookes hurried his pace, furrowing his brow. "Daniel? What are you doing here? Is something wrong at the Park?"

Daniel shook his head and dismounted, panting. "No, Captain. Trouble at Tansley Cottage, where the Handleys reside. Their servant brought this over for Mrs. Crossley about three and a half days ago. I rode as fast as I could."

Brookes snatched the letter away and patted Daniel on the back. "Go into the kitchens and have dinner and a rest. You are worn out. I will take this to my aunt. Stoames?" He strode over toward the barn, calling out, "Stoames, come and see to his horse."

Stoames poked his head out of the barn, glancing quizzically from the horse to the rider. "Trouble at home," Brookes explained, gesturing with one shoulder at Daniel. "See his horse has a good rubdown, you hear?"

"Of course, Captain." Stoames rushed over to claim the reins, his boots crunching on the gravel.

Charlie Cantrill held out his hand. "I'll be going then. Sounds like an emergency. If you leave in a rush, try to send word before you depart, old fellow."

Brookes shook his hand firmly. "I will, Charlie. Thank you."

He crossed the courtyard as quickly as possible on his wooden leg. He remembered the old days when taking the stairs two at a time gave him no difficulty. Not so anymore. He resisted the urge to open the letter himself, but his hands shook with the desire to know what happened. Was Harriet hurt? She'd made it home, hadn't she? Surely Daniel would have told him if the carriage overturned or if Harriet was harmed on the journey. He glanced down at the envelope, recognizing the graceful swirls and loops of Harriet's handwriting. No matter what turmoil occurred, Harriet was able to send word herself, but this knowledge still did not calm his roiled nerves.

He burst into the library, where Aunt Katherine sat at the desk, answering her correspondence. She glanced up, startled at his entry. "Whatever is the matter, John?"

"A letter from Tansley, sent by special messenger. Open it at once, Aunt, and read what it says aloud." He tossed the letter onto the desk and began pacing the room.

She broke the seal and unfolded the letter, perusing it silently.

"Read it aloud, Aunt," he barked. "Is she all right?"

She glanced up from the letter, her lips pursed. "Harriet is all right, but her mother is not. She died, quite unexpectedly, according to the letter." She extended the letter to him, and he snatched it from her grasp.

He read through the few lines over and over, trying

to absorb their meaning. Harriet wasn't telling the whole truth. Harriet was always honest. The hesitancy in her letter caused a flicker of apprehension to course through his being.

"Well, we must leave Bath at once, but I think tomorrow is the soonest it can be managed." Aunt Katherine sanded the letter she had been writing and recapped the inkwell. "I will begin packing my trunks immediately. We can leave in the morning if you wish. If they've sent a runner up ahead to deliver this news, we shall hire a yellow bounder and meet my berlin halfway between here and Derbyshire."

"No." His mind jumped ahead to Aunt Katherine's leisurely pace of travel. How could he bear to wait? "I will leave immediately. I can begin riding now."

"John, calm yourself. There is nothing you can do at this point. Lady Handley is dead, and will likely be buried by the time we can reach Tansley. There is no sense in taxing your leg, and your horse, by riding out in this state of mind."

He began pacing the room again. "I cannot wait. I must have some occupation. If I am riding toward Tansley, I am at least accomplishing something."

Aunt Katherine pierced his soul with one of her searching looks. "Why are you so agitated? Why do you want to reach her so quickly?"

He blurted out the first thoughts that came to his mind. "I am afraid she will leave. I am afraid she will become a governess and leave Tansley before I can see her." His gut churned, and he turned away so Aunt Katherine could not read anything further in his expression.

"Why would that matter? Surely she and her sister must have some means of survival. Harriet's plan to earn a living by becoming a governess sounds very sensible to me." The elaborately casual tone of her voice ignited his anger.

"No. I don't want Harriet to have to go away from home to earn a living."

"How, then, is she to survive?" Aunt Katherine peered at him, as though regarding him through a quizzing glass.

"By marrying me, of course. I must see her at once, without delay."

A broad smile illuminated Aunt Katherine's aristocratic features. "John, my dear, there is no need to worry. Harriet is not going to leave and find employment immediately. That is why she is asking my help. She is awaiting my arrival before she can go through with her plan."

He rubbed his palm over his forehead. "Are you sure?"

"Certain, my boy. Now, what of your worry that she will find marriage to you 'indecent'? After all, it's what you so vociferously believed a few days ago." She inclined her head and regarded him keenly.

"I don't know." He shook his head. "All I can do is return to Brookes Park, and ask for an explanation. If she does find me so, I shall endeavor to change her mind."

She nodded, finally satisfied. "John, if you want to ride ahead, I won't stop you. I will prepare a carriage and leave early tomorrow, traveling faster than I usually do—but I still may not be quick enough for you." She rose from the desk and walked over to Brookes, taking his hand. "Harriet is a dear girl—a true friend to me—and I will be happy to welcome her to the family."

He pressed her hand gently. "Thank you, Aunt Katherine."

She smiled. "Now, would you like for me to retrieve these books you have locked away in your desk? It seems to me they would make an excellent engagement gift."

Brookes tilted his head to one side. "How did you know Harriet's books were down there?"

Aunt Katherine laughed. "My boy, I know everything."

Harriet and Sophie sat in the parlor, still drained of all emotion even though Mama's funeral had taken place a week before. With the upheaval of the ceremony behind them, now Harriet insisted they must begin planning the future. She looked over at Sophie, who sat quietly in her chair, her hands idle. She avoided sewing after stitching her mother's shroud, and spent most of the week in a distracted, pensive state.

"Sophie, we must think of what to do next," Harriet prodded gently.

"Yes. Yes, of course. What shall we do?" Sophie turned to Harriet, staring at her as though from a great distance.

"The cottage was paid for outright by Papa's family." Harriet waved a letter from the Handley family at Sophie. She discovered the missive while cleaning out Mama's bedchamber. "It was the only help they gave us. We receive no pension from the Handleys now that she has died. We can stay in the house, and we've money enough to last several months, but we will have to find employment somewhere soon. Rose has been staying on with us forever, but she may wish to leave and find employment that pays well. Perhaps we will all need to part soon." Harriet tossed the letter aside and bit her thumbnail with a distracted air.

"Stop biting your nails," Sophie scolded absently.

Harriet folded her hands in her lap. "Or we could sell the house."

"Why would we do that?" Harriet looked up as a flicker of confusion passed over Sophie's tired and wan face.

"For money. If we can't find occupations in the village, then we will have to move."

Sophie shifted in her chair. "I don't want for us to part, Harriet."

"I don't either, Sophie darling, but what can we do? Tansley is so small. There are precious few opportunities here."

Sophie stared down at her hands. "I could take in sewing."

Harriet snapped her head up. Was Sophie offering to take

on work? Harriet searched her sister's face, hoping for some clue behind this transformation. "I suppose you could."

"And if your book sells, then we might have more money," Sophie continued.

"True, but I would have to pay for the printing, and I only have ten pounds left. When I wrote to Mrs. Crossley, I asked for her help in securing a position as a governess. I could earn the money to get my book printed, assuming someone will publish it. Perhaps I could work away from home for a year or two, and save up enough so that we could be together."

"Oh, no." Sophie's eyes filled with tears. "I already lost Mama through my own selfishness. Please Harriet, no matter what happens, we must stay together. Being apart, even for a year, is too much to bear."

"Hmm. Perhaps we could find placement in a wealthy home. I could be a governess and you could be the personal seamstress to a noble family. I could inquire with Mrs. Crossley when she returns. She might know of someone who could help."

"What about Rose?" Anxiety welled in Sophie's blue eyes.

"I don't know. I can't ask Rose to stay with us. Not if we can't pay her. She's done so much for our family already. I wonder if Captain Brookes could add her to his staff at the Park, or if Mrs. Crossley would hire her on?"

"I have brought on so much misery through my own selfish actions." Sophie's voice trembled. "Harriet, had I known any of this would happen, I would have acted very differently. I assure you."

"Oh, Sophie." Harriet rose from her chair and embraced her sister. "None of us could have anticipated any of this. And I don't think your motives were selfish. Did I not encourage you to dissuade the captain?"

Sophie patted Harriet's arm. "I think I shall go for a walk, if I may, Harriet."

"Of course." Misgivings began squeezing Harriet like a vise, but shook them off. A walk, away from the confines of the cottage, would be good for Sophie. A stroll might remedy some of her sadness and fatigue. "Be home in time for supper."

Sophie nodded, and retrieved her bonnet from the hook in the hallway.

Harriet stuck her head out of the parlor doorway and smiled, allowing her caution to show through her expression. "Do be careful. And remember, everything will work out fine."

Brookes had suffered in the saddle for three and a half days of heavy riding, his muscles growing increasingly tired and sore. Still, he dressed with elaborate care. After luncheon, he decided to call on Harriet at Tansley Cottage. He must make his intentions known, no matter what she might say. Stoames strolled into the room, bearing a familiar leather box.

"Mother's jewels?" Brookes smiled, and opened it with great care. He extracted the sapphire ring from its depths. The jewel sparkled in the midafternoon sunlight. He carefully closed the ring back in its box, tucking it in his pocket. Then he turned to his old friend. "Do I have your approval, then?"

"Godspeed, sir. She is a bonny lass." Stoames replied with his usual salute.

Brookes returned the salute, his palms beginning to sweat.

He pounded down the front steps, his boots ringing out over the still country air, where Talos stood, saddled and waiting in the courtyard. Weeks in the stable and the paddock while Brookes traveled to Bath made the beast fresh and restive. Yet Brookes had no desire for a canter, which might cause him to arrive at the cottage sweaty and winded. They set off at a leisurely pace over the rolling hills which formed a circle around the valley where Tansley Cottage stood.

He rounded the corner near the millpond and stopped. A bizarre feeling of *déjà vu* swept over him. A lone woman stood on the crest of the hill. Her face turned in the opposite direction, her bonnet concealed her profile. He remembered the first day he'd met Harriet, and his mouth went dry. Was she here? Had she come toward Brookes Park to meet him?

The woman turned her head and stared at him. He recognized those blond curls. In fact, he dreamed of them many nights when he was away on the peninsula.

Sophie Handley.

She walked toward him, her shoulders drooping, her face cast down. For a brief instant, he thought about riding to her, meeting her halfway. But he discarded the notion. Let her come to him. Let her do the explaining. The girl had much to explain, after all. He drew up the reins and Talos, sensing his mood, stopped dancing in impatience. Instead, he lowered his head and chomped prosaically on the moor grass.

"Captain Brookes."

"Miss Handley." He sighed. "You have my condolences for your mother's recent passing." Why were they being so formal? No matter, it suited his mood. They called each other much more endearing names in the heat of correspondence for many years. He searched her face for answers, noting the dark circles under her eyes and the drawn look around her mouth.

"Thank you, your sympathy is most kind." She broke off, tears crowding her eyes. "I…I owe you an apology, Captain."

"Do you, Miss Handley?" He stayed on his horse, enjoying the feeling of looking down on her. He wanted to convey the sense of urgency he felt. He held no desire to talk to Sophie, when Harriet might be at home right then, writing letters of application to become a governess.

"Yes. I am sorry I ever told you I wouldn't marry you."

## Chapter Twenty-Eight

"You are?" Brookes's heart plummeted to his boots. She wasn't about to throw herself at him, was she? He shifted uneasily in the saddle. The movement caused Talos to stop munching the moor grass and toss his head.

"Yes, I am. You see, my actions have been selfish and unkind. I have caused great harm to those I love by rejecting your suit. More than you'll ever know." Her eyes filled with tears, and she withdrew her handkerchief from her sleeve.

The tears were genuine. He had seen Sophie cry often enough in the past to get her own way. The rawness of her voice signaled a profound hurt.

"And I am sure I wounded your pride, if not your heart," she continued, looking up at him. "You are a good man, and a brave solider, and you deserved much better than what I was prepared to give."

He cleared his throat. A frisson of discomfort shivered down his spine at her words. What was she driving at? For wont of something more elegant to say, he replied stiffly, "You are forgiven."

"Thank you." She glanced away, and blew her nose. "Would you convey something to your aunt for me? I know I shouldn't even ask any favors, but I fear I must prevail upon you for your help."

"Of course." Aunt Katherine? What message could Sophie possibly have for his aunt?

"Harriet is going to ask her help to find positions for us. She wants to be a governess, and I can become a seamstress. But I can't bear to be apart from Hattie. The breakup of our family is most distressing, and I must be with my sister." Her voice trembled and she clasped her hands together imploringly. "Please ask your aunt to help us find a situation where we can stay together. Perhaps in a nobleman's home, where they might employ a private seamstress and a governess."

Brookes sighed. Time to end this charade. He dismounted with care and stood before Sophie.

"I am riding over to Tansley Cottage right now to beg your sister's hand in marriage."

Sophie blanched. "Hattie? Do you love Hattie?"

"Yes. I love your sister. I have for quite some time. But I didn't feel it was right to pursue her, when we had essentially been—" He cast about for the right word to describe their relationship.

"Betrothed?" Sophie supplied.

"Yes, exactly. When I returned, and we never formally broke off our understanding, I could not very well court Harriet. But I've loved her since we began working on the book together." He glanced at her from under lowered brows. How would she take the news?

A smile like sunshine broke across Sophie's face. "Oh, I am so happy. Harriet deserves someone like you, Captain."

"You aren't angry?" Ever cautious, he chose to remain still and judge the terrain.

"Not at all. I am overjoyed for both of you." She tucked her handkerchief back into her sleeve.

Her exuberance puzzled him. Did she know something

he didn't? After all, she had written the letter rejecting him—a letter quoting Harriet that a marriage to him was indecent. Boldness flowed through him, and he asked the question that had gnawed at his insides for weeks.

"Why did Harriet think marriage to me indecent?" He still found the words difficult to say. They stuck in his throat a bit, but he stayed strong.

Her brows drew together in confusion. "What? What are you talking about?"

"In the letter you wrote me in Bath, you said that Harriet called marriage to me indecent." His tone remained measured and even. He obscured the hurt that still ate away his being.

"I did? No. I meant something different. Harriet had advised me that marrying anyone I didn't love was indecent." She shook her head. "Harriet never said that marrying you would be so. Only marriage where there is no love."

Hope bloomed in his chest for the first time in weeks. "Are you certain?"

"Yes, of course. Harriet has never had anything but the highest praise for you, Captain."

"Thank you, Sophie." He swung into the saddle, eagerness nearly making him forget his manners. Talos pranced restlessly. "I will go to the cottage now, if I may."

She beamed up at him. "Yes, do. I left her there only minutes ago. Ride ahead and I will follow at a leisurely pace so you may have time to speak to her."

With joy and hope coursing through his veins, Brookes put his boots to Talos's flanks. He could not reach Tansley Cottage quickly enough. He left Sophie on the hill, waving her handkerchief to wish him Godspeed.

Harriet puzzled over the letter she found in Mama's room. The handwriting on the missive was unfamiliar, but its contents were about Papa's death and Mama's living expenses. She pored over the letter, trying to figure out its deeper meaning.

*Madame, you realize that your marriage to Hugh was most distressing to my family, and we refuse to recognize it as legitimate. We will, however, provide you with the deed to a small cottage in a nearby village and the sum of twenty-five pounds per year. We do this out of charity, not out of a sense of obligation. The money will cease to arrive if you discuss your relationship publicly with Hugh in your new village.*

Harriet stopped reading, her mouth dropping open in shock. She never thought to ask how Mama paid their few expenses. She assumed there had been some money left from Mama's stage career, or perhaps her mother had managed to tuck a bit away somewhere. Now she understood. The Handleys paid her mother the same amount they paid any common farm laborer, to keep her quiet.

She folded up the letter and cast it aside. They had a roof over their heads, but very little besides that. By spring she would need to find a position for sure. She glanced out the window. Autumn's chill already bit the air, and this was only early September. This promised a harsh winter in more ways than one.

An urgent pounding on the door shook the desk at which she sat. She jumped, alarm sending her pulse racing. The harsh words from the Handleys still ran through her mind, and she expected to see the duns, or perhaps an irate member of her father's clan, when she opened the door. She stood, frozen, unsure of whether or not she should answer.

The pounding continued, echoing through the small house. Her heart beat a nervous tattoo and her palms began perspiring. She forced her steps to the entry hall, but could not gather the strength to open the door and confront whatever awaited her on the other side.

The door flew open, causing the mourning hatchment

to swing wildly. Harriet gasped. John Brookes stood before her, his expression anxious.

"Harriet, why didn't you open the door? I've knocked several times."

"I—uh—I thought you might be someone else."

"Were you expecting anyone?" He strode into the entry and hung his hat on the wall.

"No. I was reading an old letter, and your sudden knock startled me." It dawned on Harriet that John arrived early from Bath. "Did you get my message?"

"Yes, and I am very sorry to hear about your mother. Please accept my sincerest condolences." He took a step closer and Harriet shrunk back.

"Thank you." Why was he here? Surely he wasn't looking for Sophie. Perhaps he had heard from Samuel Eagleton?

"Are you here because you've had news from the publisher?" A note of hope crept into her voice. If her book was on its way to publication, their money woes might be nearing an end.

"No." He motioned to the parlor. "Could we sit down and talk?"

"Of course. Where are my manners? I am so sorry, John. I am so easily distracted since Mama's death." She led the way into the little parlor and patted the back of the same wobbly chair he had occupied during his first visit to the cottage.

He gently grabbed her wrist. "Sit down, please, Harriet."

He sank down on the settee beside her. She could feel his warmth and resisted the urge to lean into him. Trying to keep her emotions in check, she stared down at her lap.

"Harriet, please, look at me. I've wanted to say something to you for so long. Now is perhaps the worst time to say it, considering your mother's passing, but I can wait no longer." His tone grew husky and dark.

A blush suffused Harriet's cheeks as she raised her eyes

to his. His gaze held such tenderness that it was all she could do not to look away. "What is it, John?"

"I must ask you—no, beg you—to marry me. I have loved you since my return from Waterloo, and my esteem for you only deepened as we worked together on your manuscript. I am sorry. I am a brute to be proposing to you so quickly after your mother's death. But I can't wait any longer. You must know how I feel."

She tried to rise, but he kept her still, pulling her onto his lap. Tears sprang to her eyes at the tenderness of his touch.

"Why are you crying?" He whispered the words.

"You would not ask me to marry you if you knew the truth of my situation." With trembling fingers, she clasped his hand and pulled it away from her waist.

He refused to loosen his grip or let go of her hand. "Try me." His voice issued a gentle challenge.

"Mama took too much laudanum. That's how she died." She dared not meet his eyes.

He sighed. "I suspected as much. Harriet, laudanum is a highly addictive medication. It is not difficult at all to get so accustomed to it that you can mistake how much you've ingested. As I recuperated from my wound, I was given laudanum. I know only too well its potency."

She drew in a shaky breath. "There is more. You know Mama was an actress?"

He nodded. "You told me so yourself. Why does that matter?"

"It matters a great deal to the Handleys. Papa's family. They gave Mama Tansley Cottage and twenty-five pounds per annum, to stay quiet. They will offer you no dowry on my behalf."

"I expected no dowry at all, Harriet. Why should that matter? And now that I know the horrible truth about your family, and I don't care about any of these problems, would you consent to be my wife?"

She shook her head, wiping her face on a handkerchief he retrieved from his pocket. "You should know that part of the reason for our financial ruin was because Mama was being blackmailed. Someone knew about her past career and threatened to expose her to the *ton*. Mama paid them an exorbitant amount of money over the years, which, coupled with my parents' extravagant lifestyle, destroyed my family." A shudder ran through her body. "I only learned this…on my mother's deathbed."

John squeezed her tightly, helping to suppress the shiver than ran through her. Harriet glanced up, seeking out the reassurance of his gray-green eyes. In their depths, she recognized only reassurance and love. He kissed the top of her hair. His touch gave her the strength to continue.

"If I marry you, John, I can only offer myself. And that makes me feel very poor indeed."

"And having you here with me makes me feel very rich indeed." He sighed, his warm breath tickling the nape of her neck. "You have given me so much, Harriet darling. If only you knew everything you've done for me. Will you marry me, Harriet?"

She traced the scar that zigzagged on his chin, her finger catching on the stubble. "Yes. Yes, I will, John."

"My darling…" He bent down and kissed her with the pent-up longing that possessed both of them for too many lonely weeks. But a moment or two later, she placed her hands on his chest, silently asking him to stop so she could catch her breath.

"We can't set a date yet," Harriet reminded him, and held out the dyed skirt of her dress. "It's not right to be engaged so quickly after Mama's passing."

"We'll wait six months, but not a day longer. The day you come out of mourning, you will be wearing your wedding gown." He reached out and grasped her left hand. "But surely there is no harm in wearing this, until then?"

He reached into his pocket and pulled out a sapphire ring, which winked alluringly in the dim parlor light.

Harriet gave a soft gasp and tried to jerk her hand away. "Oh, no," she breathed. "It's too beautiful, too fine…"

He tightened his hold and slipped the jewel onto her ring finger. "That is precisely why you deserve it. It was my mother's, and now I want you to have it."

"Thank you, John. It's the most exquisite ring I have ever seen. I shall endeavor to deserve it," she whispered.

"Oh, it's not merely a ring. There is a matching necklace and set of bracelets but I left them at the Park, in case I was accosted by a highwayman on the way over." He chuckled. "You deserve all of that, and more."

"I wouldn't know what to do with so many jewels."

"Well, you have the rest of your life to find out. But Harriet, I've made a dreadful hash of asking your hand in marriage. I haven't courted you at all."

"That doesn't matter, does it? I feel like we were courting each other while we wrote the book together. The book was my declaration of love for you, and it is one reason why I must find a publisher."

"My darling," he murmured, moving closer. Harriet put up another warning hand.

He smiled tightly in frustration. "Perhaps the book was a kind of courtship ritual, but we could not admit it to each other then. Nor could we be open about our affection." He sighed, leaning back against the cushions. "I think ours is fated to be an unorthodox match. I've gone about it the wrong way around. Engagement first, then courtship. But since we must wait so long before we wed, I will spend the next six months wooing you, my dear."

The front door opened and they sprang apart.

"Hattie, are you home? Hello?" Sophie's voice rang out.

"In the parlor, Sophie. Captain Brookes is here." Despite her best efforts, Harriet's voice betrayed a nervous tremble.

"Yes, I know," Sophie responded warmly, and crossed the threshold. "May I call him Brother?"

Harriet nodded, tears in her eyes.

"How wonderful!" Sophie cried. She folded Harriet into her loving embrace, laughing and weeping at the same time.

"Let me see the ring! Ooh, lovely!" Sophie grasped her sister's hand, turning it to make the sapphire sparkle in the light. "Oh, Hattie, it suits you beautifully." She turned to Brookes. "John, I am happy for you, too. You cannot find a better woman than my sister."

He nodded. "'For her price is far above rubies,'" he quoted, gazing at Harriet with love shining through his eyes.

"Or, in this case, sapphires," Sophia chirped merrily, and the little parlor rang with their laughter.

# Chapter Twenty-Nine

❦

"Well, where is my nephew, and is he engaged?" Aunt Katherine's imperious tones rang out across the vestibule of Brookes Park. Smiling, John rose from his desk in the library and came out to meet her, his arms outstretched.

"No embraces for you until I find out what has happened, and if you will be taking a bride soon," she snapped, a mischievous twinkle in her eyes. "Tell me, John, are you betrothed?"

"Yes, some three days' now," he replied, folding her in his embrace. "You see? Had I traveled at your sluggish pace, I would just now be broaching the matter."

"Oh, tut, I am an old woman and I have earned my luxuries." She pulled free of his embrace. "Did you give her your darling mother's jewels?"

"Only the ring. She has no wish to claim the rest yet." He helped her remove her pelisse and handed it to Bunting, who came striding into the vestibule.

"Ah, Bunting, I have a great wish for some scalding hot tea." Aunt Katherine smiled. "Bring it into the library directly."

"Of course, Madame." He bowed, and Brookes led Aunt Katherine toward the library.

"Now, I must have my dear Harriet over to discuss the finer points of the wedding. Has she started making her trousseau? Have you seen to reading the banns?"

He ruffled his hand through his hair. Aunt Katherine always had an exasperating effect on his nerves, even when he happily anticipated her visits. "I don't know, Aunt."

"What have you been doing these three days, my boy?"

He grinned sheepishly, feeling rather like a boy caught stealing a piece of cake. "Wooing."

"Oh, dear. You are incorrigible, John." She waved a hand listlessly through the air.

"No, nothing indecent Auntie, upon my honor. But Harriet and I have enjoyed so little time together that we have been spending as much time as possible in each other's company. Yesterday I took her for a tour of the estate and the mill. She had never seen the extent of Brookes Park before."

"Well, I need her here with me today. We must plan for the wedding. She probably hasn't a stitch of trousseau, and I am sure no money to purchase it with." She sank down onto the settee and rummaged in her reticule, pulling out a wad of bank notes. "This is to be my gift to Harriet for the wedding. This should buy her an ample amount of the necessities and the niceties, too."

He quirked his mouth in a grin. "It's a lovely thought, Aunt, but she'll never accept it. She's too proud."

"We'll see about that, my boy. I am wondrously persuasive. It was I who purchased that lovely blue bombazine for her in Bath. You know, the evening she looked so lovely you couldn't stop staring at her."

Brookes did remember, and smiled at the recollection.

Aunt Katherine jerked him back to the present by continuing her list of orders. "Now, you must see to the reading of the banns. When is the wedding to be?"

"In February of next year, when her mourning is done."

"Well, we have some time but I want you to see the reverend this morning and make the necessary arrangements. I don't believe in procrastinating when there is work to be done. I am assuming the wedding will be at the chapel in Crich?"

He shrugged. "I haven't given it much thought."

She clapped her hands sharply. "Wake up, Nephew! This is your responsibility. You will go and arrange for the reading of the banns with Reverend Kirk. And I will discuss the plans for her trousseau with Harriet and her sister, Sophie. She's handy with a needle."

A knock sounded on the door, and Bunting entered, bearing a silver tray which gave forth the enticing scent of fresh tea. "Ah, Bunting, would you please send word around to Tansley Cottage? I want both of the Handley girls to come here this afternoon, if they are able."

"Of course, Madame." He bowed and closed the door.

She rubbed her hands together briskly and busied herself pouring the tea. "Some tea before you leave, Nephew?"

He shook his head, a little embarrassed he hadn't given much thought to the practicalities of the wedding ceremony. Swept away by the thought of romancing his lovely fiancée, he fell behind on his usual methodical plan of action. "I'll hitch up the gig and drive over to Crich right away."

"There's a good boy." She stood up, cupping his head in her hands. "John, you are my only living relative, and you have been like a son to me all these years." She paused, her keen blue eyes misting over with tears. "I am so pleased you found a woman like Harriet, someone to love, honor and cherish you for the rest of your life. Be good to her, John. She is a good woman."

He reached over and planted a kiss on her wrinkled forehead. "Aunt Katherine, you are like a second mother to me. I hope I make you proud."

"I am sure you will." She pushed him away and smiled, her tears drying. "Now, run on to Crich. And give my regards to Reverend Kirk. A kinder and more empathetic man of the cloth you will never find."

Talos didn't enjoy being hitched to the gig, but Brookes's leg had been bothering him more than he cared to admit, and such a long ride daunted him a bit. After he finished this task, he promised himself a bath. Going to the hot spring would calm his pains, the perfect way to end an arduous, but productive, day. Every time he took the waters, his strength increased and the phantom pains abated. He pulled the reins in gently and Talos tossed his head. Perhaps he should consider taking the waters a few times a week, at least until he married. He wanted to be in fine form for the happiest day of his life.

The steeple of St. Mary's rose sharply out of the hills, and he reined Talos in, gazing at it in wonder. The spire pierced the sky like a mighty arrow. In six months' time, he would be here, hearing the bells peal merrily, on the day he took Harriet to be his wife.

He flicked the reins, and they were off, closing the distance until he pulled into the churchyard. A little stone house, quaint and tidy, sat in the shadow of the large stone chapel. This must be Reverend Kirk's residence. He alit from the gig and tied Talos to the hitching post. As he strode up the winding gravel path, an elderly man in a black shirt and coat waved. He was leaving through a side door of the chapel. Brookes squinted, vaguely recognizing the man from the blessing ceremony.

"I am looking for Reverend Kirk," Brookes called, extending his hand.

"You've found him," Reverend Kirk replied, and clasped Brookes's hand in a firm grip. "How can I help you, my son?"

"I am Captain John Brookes, and my aunt Katherine Crossley sends you her best wishes."

"Mrs. Crossley?" The old man smiled. "Yes, I remember her. In fact, I remember your whole family. You didn't come to services very often, because of the distance, but when you did I was always happy to see you."

Brookes shook his head. "I'm afraid I don't remember much. My parents died when I was a young man of thirteen, and my eldest brother inherited the estate and raised us both."

"Ah, yes, Henry. He was a good deal older than you, I recall."

"Yes, by five years." Brookes had grown used to Henry's absence, but the hushed and holy atmosphere of Crich brought his death sharply back to mind.

"Are you here to speak to me about Henry?" Reverend Kirk looked at Brookes, his brow furrowed in confusion.

"No, I am here because I am engaged, and I must see to the reading of the banns."

"Of course, my boy!" Reverend Kirk slapped him heartily on the shoulder. "Congratulations are in order. To whom are you engaged?"

"Miss Harriet Handley, of Tansley Cottage."

Reverend Kirk dropped his hand and his smile widened in approval. "Harriet Handley? She is a fine young lady, Captain, you are lucky to have her." His smile faded and he looked at Brookes searchingly. "I was very sorry to hear about her poor mother."

Brookes nodded. "Lady Handley suffered much pain in her life."

Reverend Kirk sighed. "Well, come inside, we'll confer here in the chapel, if that is all right with you. My housekeeper is cleaning the house from top to bottom in preparation for the autumn and winter months, and everything is in uproar."

Brookes chuckled, and inclined his head in agreement. They passed through the wooden side door into the main chapel. The midafternoon sunlight glowed through the stained glass windows, illuminating the sanctuary in a kaleidoscope of jewel tones. The reverend motioned to a pew, and Brookes sank onto its velvet cushion gratefully.

"Now, my son, we don't usually read the banns until three Sundays before the ceremony. When's the wedding to be?"

"In February, when Harriet is out of mourning for her mother."

Reverend Kirk nodded. "Well, then we have an abundance of time. I will be sure to see to it for you, my son. Would the first Sunday in February work for a wedding ceremony?"

Brookes toyed with the seam on the velvet cushion, to hide his mounting discomfort. Something was welling up inside his very soul, and he couldn't understand what it meant. "First Sunday in February?" he echoed. "Yes, that should be fine." He looked around the empty chapel, trying to come to grips with whatever was disturbing him.

"Is there something else, my son?" Reverend Kirk lifted an eyebrow and looked at Brookes.

"No. Yes. I don't know." Brookes sighed heavily. A sudden urge to confess overwhelmed him. "May I speak frankly?"

"Yes, of course you may." Reverend Kirk sat down beside him on the pew and turned to face him.

"Until I met Harriet, I had no faith in God. I had grown up, you must recall, with my parents teaching me a little about the Lord, but when they died—and Henry and I were lads raising ourselves—faith passed out of my life." He paused, finding it difficult to put his emotions into words.

Reverend Kirk merely listened, his countenance open and friendly.

"I almost died at Waterloo. When I tried to pray, I could not even form the words in my mind. I lost my faith, and my leg, that horrible night. I did not even think I could regain my hope in God until Harriet opened my heart to Him." He exhaled slowly. The knot in his chest loosened. The words flowed more easily, like the waters into the hot spring at Brookes Park.

"I have a friend, a brother in arms, named Charles Cantrill. Charlie and Harriet have both tried to show me the way since my return. I am beginning to believe. But now that I am marrying Harriet, I feel unworthy of her unless I start my faith in God anew. Tell me, Reverend, what must I do to properly start my walk in faith?"

Reverend Kirk shook his head and smiled. "Every day is a walk in faith. Your actions on a daily basis determine your relationship with the Lord. There is no need to perform any action to start your walk anew."

"But I feel the need of some formal ritual, or rite, or sacrament—"

Reverend Kirk held up his hand. "You feel that way because you are used to regimentation. That is a soldier's lot in life. But there is no need of formal rituals, my son. If you wish, I will be happy to pray with you. Or I will leave you in peace here in the sanctuary so you can pray alone. Whatever you wish." He gave Brookes a kindly pat on the shoulder, but Brookes had one more question.

"Until Harriet came into my life, I would have these nightmares. I couldn't sleep. I actually feared slumber, because with it came these horrible night terrors. But once I began reliving my experiences, and talking to Harriet about what happened, they ceased. Why?"

"I cannot be certain, Captain, but I would imagine they ceased because in sharing the horror of what you suffered, you did not feel alone anymore. In telling Harriet of your experiences, you drained the pain and the terror from your conscious being. She has truly been your helpmate, or so it sounds to me."

"She has." His heart glowed.

Reverend Kirk rose from the pew and looked down at Brookes, his face reflecting the strength and wisdom of a true man of faith. "Shall I stay with you?"

Brookes thought for a moment. "I wish to be alone, I think."

"Very well, I will leave you here in peace. Stay as long as you wish. And if I don't see you before then, I shall look forward to officiating at your wedding in February. Please convey my best wishes to your fiancée." Reverend Kirk then exited the sanctuary through the side door, leaving Brookes by himself in the hushed and holy space.

He drew a deep breath and bowed his head. All he could do was thank God over and over for the many blessings in his life—for his survival at Waterloo; for Stoames, who rescued him; for Aunt Katherine, who loved him; for Sophie, who rejected him; for Charlie Cantrill, who helped him; but most of all, for Harriet, who saved him. Harriet saved him.

Driving home in the late afternoon, Brookes watched the sun's rays touch the vista with a golden hue. The chill of autumn was already in the air. He felt the cool air touch his face, but he was still too warm in heart for it to matter. He was a changed man, and the profound gratitude suffusing him would keep him cozy through the bitter winter ahead.

Upon reaching the Park, he tossed the reins to Daniel, who came running to meet him. He strode up the stairs and into the house as quickly as he could. Harriet was there, he could sense her presence. He must see her at once. Throwing open the library door, he spied Harriet, Sophie and Aunt Katherine huddled together on the settee, staring at fashion plates. In unison, they glanced up at him, their faces registering shock from his hasty arrival. But he only cared about one. He drew Harriet to him, crushing her in an embrace, leaving her breathless.

"John! Really!" Aunt Katherine swatted at his arm with one of the plates. "Do control yourself."

Brooked pulled away from Harriet but kept her pressed tightly to his chest, almost afraid she would disappear. "Indulge me, Aunt. I am bestowing my gratitude on the woman who saved my life."

## Chapter Thirty

Brookes sorted through the correspondence which Bunting laid on his desk that morning on a silver salver. He leaned back in his chair and flicked through the envelopes, hoping to find a letter from Cantrill. Since their return from Bath, he and Cantill enjoyed a lively correspondence, and Brookes always looked forward to the other man's letters with healthy anticipation.

He paused. The handwriting on this envelope was unfamiliar. He plucked it out of the stack and peered at it closely. He broke the seal, scanning the contents, his heart skipping a beat. It was from Samuel Eagleton, Harriet's publisher.

*Dear Sir:*

*We are most pleased to accept the manuscript you submitted, entitled* Call to Arms: A Soldier's Memory of Waterloo. *Please inform Miss Handley that we will publish the manuscript and distribute it if she bears the cost of printing, which should cost twenty pounds.*

*If this is agreeable to Miss Handley, please send word by letter and include the price of the printing costs. At that time we will schedule the rewriting and proofing process.*

*Yours sincerely,*
*Samuel Eagleton and Co.*

Brookes dropped the letter on the desk and ran his hand over his brow. Harriet's dream had come true. Her book was going to be published. The book that she had written for him, her declaration of love, as she called it. He glanced down at the lower left-hand corner of his desk, which held the books he purchased back from Whitstone's. He intended to save them as a gift for their wedding day, which was still three months away.

Brookes absently ran a thumbnail over his lower lip. Harriet promised to visit later in the afternoon for tea with Aunt Katherine and to work on her trousseau. Maybe she would be so elated, he could sneak a little kiss.

Stoames entered the library, whistling cheerfully. "Captain, I am done with polishing your boots, and thought I would work out in the stables the rest of the day if you don't require anything else."

"Of course, Stoames." He cleared his throat. "If you can catch Miss Harriet before my aunt claims her this afternoon, I should very much like to speak with her."

Stoames nodded. "Anything wrong?"

"No, quite the contrary. I have excellent news for her. The publisher wrote today, and he has accepted her book. Don't let on anything, I want to surprise her."

Stoames grinned. "I won't tell a soul. That is wonderful news. And to tell the truth, Captain, I am eager to see it in print. I think she will not only spin a good yarn, but it's good to know it will be a truthful and honest tale, too."

Brookes pressed his lips together and nodded. "I agree, Stoames. That's one of the reasons I am so proud of Harriet. Her book is honest, but it's also a gripping story at the same time."

"I cannot wait to see how happy she will be." Stoames paused in the threshold and turned back toward Brookes. "As soon as she arrives, I will make sure she comes straightaway to you."

\* \* \*

Harriet steeled herself, taking a deep breath and squaring her shoulders as she walked into the courtyard at Brookes Park. Her afternoon planning sessions with Aunt Katherine were so demanding. If only the old woman possessed a little less energy, perhaps then Harriet could keep the pace she set. Aunt Katherine was placing great importance on Harriet's trousseau. Harriet had planned to continue wearing her old cotton gowns until sometime after the wedding. But Aunt Katherine assured her that it simply wasn't done, and pressed the money for an elegant trousseau on Harriet as a wedding gift. Only after much debate with Rose and Sophie did Harriet finally capitulate and accept Aunt Katherine's present.

Harriet passed the fountain and grasped her skirts as she began to walk up the steps. She had no wedding gift to give her husband, either. John paid for every part of their wedding himself, and she could offer him nothing in return. Even *A Call to Arms* remained unpublished.

Besides the material obligations, there were the little favors she asked of the kindly old woman and John to consider as well. Aunt Katherine was working to secure a position as a seamstress for Sophie among her many gentry friends in Bath. And Rose was joining the staff at Brookes Park upon Harriet's marriage. Well—John himself offered that last favor, and which she had accepted with alacrity, and a few grateful kisses.

She paused, looking up at the handsome facade of Brookes Park. The crushing weight of indebtedness threatened to overwhelm her. Would she ever measure up to its quiet dignity? Aunt Katherine made being John's wife seem so…difficult, so expensive. If only she could have come to Brookes as a Handley should, with a proper dowry. Not that she minded being poor, of course. But John paid for everything, and she had only herself to offer in return.

The crunch of boots on gravel made her look up, expecting to see her beloved. But the boots in question belonged to Stoames, who strode across the courtyard, waving a hand in her direction.

"Miss Harriet, the captain wishes to see you right away. I think you'll find him in the library."

"Is anything the matter, Stoames?"

"No, Miss Harriet. He wants a private word before his aunt claims you." Stoames grinned.

Harriet quirked her mouth in a rueful half smile and nodded. "I will see the captain directly. Thank you, Stoames."

Why was John asking to see her? Was Aunt Katherine spending too much of his money? Was the household staff at the Park too full, and he couldn't take on Rose after all? She knocked on the closed library door, bracing herself for the worst.

"Come in." John's voice didn't sound stern or alarmed. Harriet breathed a sigh of relief. Perhaps everything would be all right after all.

She entered, shutting the door behind her without making a sound. Aunt Katherine had sharp hearing, after all. "Whatever is the matter, John?"

Brookes cleared his throat. "A letter for you." He stretched a sheet of foolscap toward her.

She scanned over its contents once, then once more. In blank disbelief, she looked up at John, trying to read his expression. "They accepted it?" she questioned, and heard the uncertainty evident in her voice.

"Yes, my darling. If you like their terms, I will write to them today." He grinned, love shining in his eyes. "What do you think?"

Harriet dropped her gaze to the page again, but the letters swam together in a single line. "I think—yes." Then her heart plummeted to her boots as one particular line stood out from the rest. "Twenty pounds? I don't have that much left. I had to pay for Mama's burial, and our expenses, and I am down to precious little. Do you think they would wait until I found a way to earn the money again?"

Brookes laughed. "Don't be silly, darling. I'll pay for the printing costs. Do not worry about them. I am only too happy to do so, to see your declaration of love for me in print."

Waves of heat rose in Harriet's cheeks. Another crushing weight added to the growing pile of debts on her shoulders. "Oh, John. This is dreadful. My only wedding gift to you—paid out of your own pocket."

The ground underneath Brookes shifted. He thought he knew the terrain, but here he was, sinking into the mire, as surely as Caesar had sunk into the muddy field at Waterloo. He grasped for a sure footing. "Harriet, what's wrong? Why are you upset?"

Harriet rose unsteadily from her chair, pacing the Oriental rug, wearing a little trail into its heavy nap. "You are paying for everything, John, and I have nothing to give in return. I feel so ashamed."

He shook his head, a frown creasing his brow. "Harriet, what are you talking about? What's amiss?"

"I am indebted to your family for everything. Trousseau, servants, placement for my sister." Her voice caught on a sob but she continued her pacing. "And now the publication of my book. Honestly, I shall never repay it all, and it drives me to distraction."

Her declaration caused him to draw a sharp breath. He eyed her warily. How best to untangle this mess, without ending up with a broken engagement?

He began by picking his way out of the mire, point by point.

"Harriet, it matters not to me if you have a fancy trousseau. Indeed, we will be spending most of our days here at the Park. You aren't marrying into society by marrying me. I am a soldier, a farmer and the owner of a mill. I seriously doubt there will be many soirees in our lives. If Auntie has impressed upon you otherwise, I will speak to her."

Harriet stopped pacing, and turned to face him. At this slight encouragement, he continued.

"I need Rose here. We are in short supply of excellent servants, and I value her services. And I honor her commitment to you girls. She was like a second mother to you, and I want her to have a secure position. It's true, I am encouraging my aunt to help Sophie find employment. I think we both feel a dose of independence would be good for your sister, am I right?"

"Yes," she whispered, her head remained bowed.

"I don't know what you mean when you speak of a wedding gift. I had expected nothing from you. I need no trinket to celebrate our wedding. It is the greatest honor of my life, Harriet, and I don't require anything more than to hear you say, 'I will.'" He walked over to the settee and sat down, patting the cushion beside him. "Come, sit." He expected her to remain standing, and his heart pounded gratefully when she sat down beside him.

"I want the book to be published because I believe in you. You are a good writer—the only one I trusted with my story. You did all the work, Harriet—writing for hours upon hours when anyone else would have given up. I cannot—I will not—let that dedication go simply for a few pounds. Whether you married me or not, I would still pay for the publication, because you are a true authoress. You deserve to be published."

She looked at him, tears welling in her eyes anew. After a moment, she spoke. "Thank you, John."

"Don't cry," he admonished, tracing a finger across her cheek. "We've had too many tears these past few months."

She gave a little smile and brushed the back of her hand across her eyes.

"Now, what's mine is yours and what's yours is mine. There is no division of property between us, do you understand? From now on, everything is ours, together."

Harriet gave a shaky sigh. "I feel badly because I am bringing you so little, John. All I have is myself. That is why I became so distressed." She blushed deeply and hid her face on his shoulder.

He shook his head and drew her into his arms. "You've given me more than you will ever know, Harriet. In fact, I feel poor because all I can offer you is material wealth. You have given me so much. Not only have you loved me, maimed as I am, you have given me a reason to keep on living. Most precious of all, you have restored my faith. You saved me from despair and ruin. I shudder to think what I would be without you."

They held each other in the dim afternoon light, Brookes's heart swelling with love and gratitude. From upstairs, an elderly and imperious voice rang down. "Bunting? Bunting! Has Miss Harriet arrived yet?"

Harriet drew away from Brookes with a shaky laugh. "Will you make good on your promise to speak to Aunt Katherine?"

He nodded. "I will speak to her immediately and ask her to scale everything back to a more moderate degree. And you? Do you want me to inform your publisher that he can go forth with the publication of *A Call to Arms?*"

She nodded, laughing. "Yes. We have a deal."

# Chapter Thirty-One

Harriet stood in the sacristy of the church, waiting for her cue to march down the aisle and stand beside Brookes. Stealing a nervous glance in the looking glass, she tucked a stray strand of hair back into place under her bonnet. She ran a hand over her gown, smoothing it down. Sophie had outdone herself. The gown was everything Harriet desired. The bodice was cut low enough to frame the sapphire necklace that Brookes had given her the night before, but still modest enough that Harriet felt alluring, never exposed. The sapphires glowed in the multicolored light cast by the stained glass windows.

Harriet stepped back a pace and tugged at her gloves. Thank goodness for them—they disguised her sweaty palms. Though she was prepared—even anxious—to take her place beside Brookes as his wife, the enormity of the step was a little overwhelming.

Sophie poked her head around the corner. "We're ready to begin. Oh, Hattie, you are beautiful." She scurried toward Harriet and gave her an impulsive kiss on the cheek. "May you be this happy always."

Harriet returned the embrace. "Thank you, darling."

"Come, they are waiting." Sophie led Harriet out of the sacristy and into the sanctuary.

The small chapel was almost empty, but that's the way she and Brookes wanted it. Harriet notified the Handley clan of her mother's passing, and informed them they could keep the twenty-five pounds per annum they had been sending to Mama. But she did not invite the family to her wedding. Forgiveness would come later, when she had time to heal from her mother's death.

Only Charlie Cantrill, Aunt Katherine, Rose and Stoames were bidden to attend. They clustered together at a pew in the front of the church. Sophie, who preceded Harriet with measured steps, sank into the pew beside Rose and beamed up at her sister. Harriet's heart glowed. This little handful of people meant more to her than all the riches in England.

Harriet glanced up at Brookes, who chose to wear his soldier's dress uniform for the occasion. The sight of him took Harriet's breath away. Her hand trembled a little in his grasp. He was so handsome and brave and...imposing. Was that the right word? She thought she had worked out Brookes's character as she wrote the book. But her work had only started. She would be discovering Brookes anew for the rest of her life, and the prospect warmed her to the tips of her toes.

She turned her attention to Reverend Kirk, who beamed tenderly at her, as a father might to his own daughter.

"Dearly beloved," he intoned, and Harriet smiled up at Brookes. He grinned in return.

Brookes caught his breath when Harriet turned her lovely face toward his. Joy and hope were reflected in her countenance, and he longed to see that expression on her face the rest of their days. He attempted to focus on the words of the service, but the sparkle of his mother's sapphires around

Harriet's neck mesmerized him. They were as natural on her as flowers in a field.

"It was ordained for the mutual society, help and comfort, that the one ought to have of the other, both in prosperity and adversity..." Reverend Kirk continued. The words snapped Brookes back to attention. He conveyed that same message to Harriet during their disagreement about her book three months ago. He slanted his gaze down at her, and found her staring at him with love shining in her eyes. The certainty that Harriet was marrying him, and would be there beside him for the rest of his days, hit him full force. He no longer feared falling asleep, or waking in a cold sweat, for Harriet was next to him, and would be for the rest of his life.

He realized with a start that Reverend Kirk had paused. Brookes grasped Harriet's right hand in his own. "I, John, take thee, Harriet, to be my wedded wife, to have and to hold from this day forward..." The old-fashioned words were difficult to say when nervous, but he had practiced them over and over for months. He hoped he sounded steady and assured.

He loosened his hold on Harriet, and she grasped his right hand in hers, repeating the vow. Her quiet but clear voice and her steady hand never betrayed a nervous tremble. They loosened hands again, and Brookes withdrew the simple gold band from his vest pocket. He selected the circlet especially for Harriet, no heirloom hand-me-downs this time. He desired to give his wife something entirely her own.

He watched as Harriet removed her glove. Then he grasped her left hand, slipping the ring on her third finger. Brookes refused to let go of Harriet's hand when he finished the vow. He endowed her with all his worldly possessions, true. But Harriet had given him more. So much more, he often grew frustrated at his inadequacy.

They stood together so, facing Reverend Kirk while he finished the simple, old-fashioned ceremony, the hush of the sanctuary falling like a benediction around them.

Harriet held Brookes's hand as they crossed the church-yard to Reverend Kirk's manse. The reverend had offered to host a breakfast so the little wedding party would not endure the four miles to Brookes Park unfed. She shivered a little and Brookes drew her closer. They would journey back to the Park after the wedding. They'd chosen to delay their honeymoon trip until the spring, anticipating warmer weather, and Harriet still applauded the decision. With relief, she crossed the threshold of the little parsonage and smiled at the cozy warmth enveloping her like a woolen blanket.

"Can we have a moment alone?" John tilted his head toward the closed parlor door.

"Whatever are you thinking?" Heat flushed her cheeks. Honestly, John could be incorrigible at times.

"Nothing improper, I assure you, Mrs. Brookes. But there's something I want you to see." Taking her hand, he drew her into the parlor and shut the door.

He grabbed a worn leather satchel from the settee. "For you."

Puzzled, Harriet undid the leather lacings. As she opened the bag, she caught a whiff of a familiar scent—musty, slightly sweet, a smell reminiscent of home. Sinking onto the settee, she drew forth one book after the other, books as familiar to her as members of her own family. With a trembling hand, she smoothed the covers, worn from years of use and abuse. Tears misted her eyes. "Papa's books?"

Brookes sat beside her, grasping her hands in his. "Harriet, please don't be upset." His words tumbled out in a rush. "You had so much loss in your life. You had nothing left of your father but your memories. I hated for those books to go away and never return. I bought them back so you could keep them and treasure them forever, in the same way you have treasured your memories. I am sorry if I hurt you in doing so, though."

"Oh, John." She traced his scarred cheek with her fingertips. "I'm not upset with you at all. What a lovely gesture. And now, it's almost like I have Papa here with me, on this happy day. I cannot thank you enough."

John leaned over, and she closed her eyes in anticipation for his kiss.

"Where on earth are the bride and groom?" Aunt Katherine's voice broke through the closed door, and they both leaned back on the settee, laughing. "We cannot start breakfast without them."

"Here we are, Auntie." Harriet rose and opened the door. She beckoned for John to follow. "I shall thank you properly, Captain Brookes, later."

"I look forward to it with great anticipation, Mrs. Brookes."

"Oh, my dear, don't mind me. I can't help but cry at weddings," Aunt Katherine warbled, waving her handkerchief at Harriet. "But I will see you both in the spring, perhaps after your London visit?"

"Of course. But Aunt Katherine, you don't have to leave Brookes Park yet. Brookes and I are only delaying our wedding trip for warmer weather. Sometimes John's leg is troubled by the rain and the cold, and he wants to stay closer to home. We would love to have you stay a little longer." Harriet laid a gentle hand on Aunt Katherine's shoulder.

"My dear, it wouldn't be right at all for me to intrude on your first day at Brookes Park. It's only a week or so to Bath and I will be happily ensconced in my cozy apartment. But I will miss you, my dear. Take care of John for me." She smiled at Harriet and gave her a light peck on the cheek.

"I'll be off, then. Charlie Cantrill is riding with me back to Bath, and I hate to keep him waiting. I get scolded enough for being a slow traveler anyway."

Harriet tucked her arm into the crook of the old woman's elbow and saw her to the doorway of the vicarage. "Goodbye, Aunt Katherine. I'll say a prayer for your safe travel."

"Goodbye, my dear." Aunt Katherine blew her nose in her handkerchief and ventured out into the churchyard, where Charlie Cantrill waited in the barouche. Harriet stood, tears blurring her vision, as Brookes handed his aunt into the carriage.

"We'll be going, too, dearie." Rose slipped into place beside Harriet, with Sophie in tow. "We'll be at the cottage if you need anything. Sophie is going to work on sewing her Bath wardrobe." They each pressed a kiss on Harriet's cheek in turn.

"Goodbye, Hattie." Sophie embraced Harriet in her turn. "Remember, take that gown off and hang it up when you get home—the light fabric is easily ruined if you should accidentally spill tea on it or anything."

Harriet rolled her eyes. How like Sophie to remember something like that, and consider it most important on a day like today. She gazed down at the dress. It *was* lovely, though, and she had Sophie to thank for it. "I'll see to it at once," she smiled, and gave Sophie a sharp peck on the cheek.

When Sophie and Rose left the manse, Harriet realized that she was alone with John. Stoames left to fetch the carriage around, and the Reverend returned to the church to ready himself for evening services. She trembled a little. Was she worthy of him? He had done so much for her—did she deserve his love? She would spend the rest of her life trying to maintain his love and trust.

"Harriet, are you all right?" Brookes crossed the room to stand beside her at the window.

"Yes, I think I am a little nervous. And this gray weather is so chilly." She dared not meet his gaze.

"Harriet," he replied, his voice gently caressing, "let's go home."

She peered out into the churchyard. Stoames drove the horses around to the mounting block. "Yes, let's."

He handed Harriet into the carriage and climbed in beside her. He grabbed her hand and held it as they swayed slowly over the hills back toward Brookes Park. Tired but immensely satisfied, Harriet rested her head on his broad shoulder. She drank deeply of the chill winter air, and her shaking stopped. Resting beside him, his strength filled her, and she feared nothing the rest of her life might hold.

Harriet recalled their first meeting, when she wondered if he would understand her need for security. And here she was, safe and secure as a jewel in a vault. Protected, loved, and cherished. True, she shared her faith with him, and yes, he showered her with material goods. But he also gave her something much deeper—the security she sought in vain since that dreadful day the duns invaded Handley Hall.

A perfect peace settled between them while they rolled over the hilly terrain toward home. Harriet sighed and admired her strikingly attractive husband. "John Brookes, I love you. I have loved you since the first day I saw you out riding by the millpond."

He cupped her face with his gloved hand. "Harriet Brookes, my darling. I shall love and treasure you forever."

He claimed her lips in a deep kiss, promising nothing but warmth, love and security for the rest of her days.

\* \* \* \* \*

Dear Reader

First, let me say what an honor it is to be writing for Love Inspired Historical during their fifteenth anniversary year! As you know, this is an amazing publishing house that has brought us hundreds of inspiring and intriguing tales over the years. I am so blessed to be counted as one of their authors.

As I write this to you, it's 104 degrees outside, and has been for a few weeks. Summer in Texas makes me long for the chilly wet weather that the inhabitants of Tansley Village, in Derbyshire, experienced in 1816. Known as the year without a summer, temperatures fell 1.3 degrees Fahrenheit around the world. That sounds really good right now—minus the ensuing food shortage, of course. Fortunately, the Handleys of Tansley Cottage don't see much of this deprivation, for they don't have much to live on anyway.

Harriet Handley is determined to make sure that she, her sister, Sophie, their mother and their kindly servant, Rose, survive, no matter how desperate their circumstances. It's simply not in Harriet's nature to sit around and idly wait for rescue. So she decides to take matters into her own hands, and that means embarking on a career as an authoress during a time when the words *career* and *woman* don't exactly go hand-in-hand. Of course, to start her career, she needs the help of Sophie's intended, Captain John Brookes. His memoirs of the Battle of Waterloo will form the foundation of Harriet's book—but only if the captain will open up to her.

Harriet renews the captain's faith in God. And the two of them find love, as so many of us do, unexpectedly and without warning. Together they embark on a life filled with God's grace and abundant love. Now, it only remains for

Harriet's flighty sister, Sophie, to find that same radiant promise…

I enjoy hearing from all my readers, so please feel free to send me an email at Lily@lilygeorge.com. I hope you enjoy reading *Captain of Her Heart* as much as I enjoyed writing it.

Blessings,
Lily George

## Questions for Discussion

1. Harriet Handley feels that the only way out of poverty is to become an authoress. Why does she consider this her only option? Is financial security important to you? Do you agree with her choice?

2. Captain John Brookes is immediately attracted to Harriet, but feels honor bound to her sister, Sophie. Why does he feel he must continue to court one sister, when he loves another? Have you ever felt caught in a situation in which you felt bound to honor your word, though circumstances changed? What did you do?

3. John lost his faith during the horrible Battle of Waterloo. Why did he lose faith? Why does he refuse to talk about faith with Harriet? Do you find it difficult to discuss your faith with others?

4. Harriet has managed to keep her faith, even after losing her home and all of their possessions. Have you ever faced a difficult situation in which your faith carried you through? How did your faith keep you strong during your darkest hour?

5. Lady Handley clings to her past life so tightly that she is depressed, or "suffering from melancholy." The doctor prescribes laudanum to ease her sorrow—but what would you have done? Was there any other way to lift her depression?

6. Sophie finds that John is too different from the man she knew when he went away to war. What reasons

does she give Harriet for her change in affection? Why does she take so long to let John know of this change?

7. Why won't the Handley family help Harriet and Sophie? Do you think that it's right that Harriet cannot bring herself to forgive their actions just yet?

8. Why does John finally tell Harriet the truth of what happened at Waterloo? Why does this confession bring them closer together?

9. Reverend Kirk helps Harriet and John during very difficult moments of their lives. Have you ever had a pastor or spiritual guide who helped shape or even transform your faith in God?

10. Why does Aunt Katherine take an instant liking to Harriet? Detail the many ways she tried to meddle and bring John and Harriet closer together.

11. Harriet sells her father's books to pay for the publication costs of her book. Do you think this is a wise decision? What would you have done, if you were in her shoes?

12. Harriet feels an overwhelming sense of obligation to John. Why does she feel such a wide inequality in their relationship? Do you agree with John that their property is no longer divided? Have you ever been in a situation where you felt an overwhelming sense of obligation? How did you deal with it?

# A FATHER'S SINS
Hannah Alexander

# Chapter One

In thirty-four years of living, Dr. Karah Lee Fletcher had seldom known true fear until the past few months.

She hadn't felt fear when her parents divorced, only a deep sadness. She hadn't felt much fear after her mother died of cancer and she was on her own in med school. During residency, she had been accused of having the strength and stamina of a California sequoia—even her hair was as red as the interior of those majestic trees.

But tonight, as she unlocked the front door of the Hideaway Clinic, she felt neither strong nor fearless. Fear, in fact, had become a habit with her lately.

She made one final check up and down the shadowy, empty street for the patient who had made the emergency call to meet her here. No one. When she'd spoken to him over the telephone, his wheezing had been apparent. Had he run into trouble on his way here? She had urged him to tell her where he was calling from, but he'd insisted on meeting her at the clinic.

The silence was broken only by the splash of water down on the shore of Table Rock Lake, and the call of a loon, lonely in the darkness.

She entered the quiet building, scolding herself for her

skittishness. What was wrong with her tonight? The tiny village of Hideaway had only been dangerous one time. Typically, it had more small-town charm than nearby Branson, since the tourist crowds were not so large. Hideaway was safe. More important, she knew nothing would happen to her unless God allowed it.

But she'd seen Him allow a lot of things.

Bad memories died hard, and her brush with death barely four months ago in this very clinic had left her spooked. She hated that. She particularly missed Taylor Jackson's company at times like this.

"Stop it," she muttered as she rushed through the clinic, turning on all the lights. Taylor had made a strategic mistake recently. He'd asked her to marry him.

He was better off without her, but she'd had a lot of trouble believing these past two weeks that she could happily live without him. Nevertheless, when she calculated the number of marriages in her family that had failed, the prospect of marriage continued to frighten her. Breaking up with him just gave her one less fear with which to contend.

She was picking up the telephone to call a nurse to the clinic when the front door gave its familiar squeak. She froze with the receiver in her hand. Why hadn't she called before coming down here? *Karah Lee, you need to start thinking ahead.* She turned, and caught her breath.

The tall, broad-shouldered man that entered had a neck, cheeks and forehead splotchy with a bad case of hives. His lips were swollen. But the swelling and redness didn't mask the face of the man who'd seemed to be everywhere she was in the past couple of days. She'd seen him on the boat dock across the street two days ago. Several times she'd seen him in the dining room of the Lakeside Bed and Breakfast, almost as if he'd been watching for her to arrive.

Twice he'd managed to sit in the table next to hers, and he always seemed to be watching a little too closely. Earlier this evening he'd even tried to start a conversation with her. And now he was here?

She heard the wheezing as he stepped up to the reception window, and she felt badly for being so suspicious. He was truly in trouble. It wasn't a setup. Why would she expect it to be?

The man was possibly an inch or so taller than her six-foot frame, with dark gray eyes and hair as black as a rain-drenched night. He didn't seem to be a threat in his present condition, though the slight swelling around his eyes made him look a little sinister.

"I take it you're the Jerrod Houston who called?"

He nodded, shooting a glance at her, then looking away as if he was shy, or very self-conscious about his appearance.

"Come on back. I'll put you in exam room two. You sound as if you could use some treatment." She gestured for him to step through the open doorway between the waiting room and the clinic proper. She had left the door open when she entered.

For a moment, he hesitated, looking at her again, almost as if he was in a daze. She watched him, irritated by the frisson of alarm that skittered down her spine.

"Are you okay?" she asked.

He nodded again.

She took the stethoscope from around her neck. "Then let's get you checked out." She led the way back, hearing not only the wheeze, but stridor, which was a respiratory whistle that meant his breathing was definitely not good. A person couldn't fake that, could he?

Why hadn't she called for backup before coming to the clinic? It was protocol. But tonight this man had sounded rough over the phone, and she'd run out of the cottage with no more than a quick word to Fawn, her foster daughter.

She'd thought about calling Taylor, but had decided against it. Too painful this soon after the breakup. Stupid move!

"Have you had trouble before with anaphylaxis?" she asked.

Jerrod nodded. "Allergic to peanuts." Though his voice over the phone—and earlier in the dining room—had been a medium baritone, it was now a thin reed of sound.

"Do you ever carry an epi pen with you?"

"I've already used it."

That meant he was worse than she'd thought. Epinephrine wore off pretty quickly. She sized him up. He was a young guy; he could take another shot. "I'll need to do an assessment on you, but let's get you feeling better first." She reached for the epi syringe. "Are you allergic to anything besides peanuts? Drugs of any kind?"

He shook his head, obviously eager to get on with treatment. "I haven't eaten any peanuts. Don't know what happened."

"I saw you eating black walnut waffles in the dining room. If you're allergic to peanuts, it's possible you've developed an allergy to other nuts."

He blinked in surprise. "Black walnut waffles?"

"Bertie Meyer's famous for them. You must not be from around here."

He shook his head. "I just saw the waffles on the buffet, and they looked good. Friday night's a strange time for a breakfast buffet."

"Bertie's breakfast fare is famous, and a few months ago she gave in to public demand to keep the breakfast flowing all day on Friday, Saturday and Sunday. In town for a visit?"

He shook his head. "Unfinished business."

She grabbed an ampoule of epinephrine, 1-1000 strength, popped off the top to reveal the rubber stopper. After withdrawing all the fluid from the vial, she glanced at her patient again. "Is there someone traveling with you who can keep an eye on you tonight?"

"No."

She switched needles on the syringe, then gave him a subcutaneous injection in his upper left arm. "Let's hope you're feeling some better in the next few moments," she assured him. He didn't appear to be in anaphylactic shock. Yet.

She put him on high-flow oxygen, then listened to his breathing, automatically studying his features. As before, she had the strange impression of familiarity, and yet she couldn't remember seeing him up until a couple of days ago.

The wheeze continued. She pressed the bell of her stethoscope over his neck and picked up the stridor more clearly. He was moving air, but still not as well as she would like.

He stared up at her, and again she felt uncomfortable. Often, a patient with breathing problems remained focused on the medical provider, desperate for rescue. *Stop being so skittish, Karah Lee. The poor guy just wants to breathe.*

Of course, she was overly sensitive lately. Her father was coming to town Sunday night to make a speech Monday morning and charm the people into voting for the tax levy that would enable this clinic to have a hospital designation.

He would, of course, be as critical of her as he always was. If the great State Senator Kemper MacDonald's constituents had to endure the edge of his tongue as often as his own younger daughter did, would they continue to vote for him?

"Stick out your tongue," she said. He did as he was told. It was slightly swollen, but not bad. "Tingly?"

He nodded.

"That's typical, but we won't take chances." She checked his blood pressure, then heart rate—which was slightly increased due to the stress of his condition and his epi. "Now for the IV solumedrol," she said, reaching across to the computer terminal in the exam room to take it out of hibernation.

After establishing an IV in Jerrod's arm and placing him on a heart monitor, complete with blood pressure cuff and pulse oximetry unit, she punched her password into the computer and started a new file.

While waiting for it to pull up her screen, she excused herself and went into the reception room to call Jill, the clinic's head nurse. Jerrod would need to be kept at least for a couple of hours, or until he was completely out of danger. Karah Lee wanted company. And it was protocol.

A movement drew her attention toward the plate glass entry door, and she saw the outline of a human shadow in the darkness, just past her own reflection. Her blood ran cold. Who was out there?

# Chapter Two

Taylor Jackson controlled his irritation with difficulty as he watched Karah Lee through the plate glass door. How many times had he told her to call for backup when she had an evening emergency?

And yet, how many times had she snapped at him to stop nagging her? With Karah Lee, he had found that impossible, because she constantly took risks. His irritation with those risks had caused too many conflicts, and that was one reason they hadn't seen each other—at least socially—for over two weeks. Actually, it had been two weeks, one day, thirteen hours and twenty or so minutes. And it had felt like a couple of years.

Chagrined by the look of fear he saw on her face, he reached for the door and pulled it open, silently thanking God for his little spy. Fawn Morrison, Karah Lee's precocious, seventeen-year-old foster daughter, had taken personal responsibility for the love life of her guardian. Taylor knew a good thing when he saw it, and he shamelessly allowed the teenager to run interference for him, especially since Karah Lee had been firm about avoiding him.

When he stepped inside, recognition and relief chased

each other across Karah Lee's expression...and a hint of some other emotion. Sadness? Tension?

"Taylor, what are you doing here?"

Yep, tension. Even irritation. He had to suppress a satisfied smile. If she didn't still love him, would she be so ill at ease with him? He resisted the urge to reach out and comb his fingers through those luxuriant red waves of wayward hair.

"Just saw the lights on and thought I'd check things out." He knew she hadn't recovered from the attack last summer. He also knew she was aggravatingly independent, and that this new aspect of her character—vulnerability—annoyed her. "Need some help?"

She hesitated, glancing toward the phone.

He could read her thoughts. "Why call Jill and disturb her evening when you've already got backup right here on the premises? Let me help out. Where's the patient? What's going on?"

"He's in exam two." She glanced in the direction of the exam room, and Taylor caught the slight frown. Something about the patient disturbed her. "Bad allergy."

"What do you need me to do?"

"I've already taken care of the necessities, and it doesn't look as if he's getting worse at this time."

"So he isn't anaphylactic?"

"It could become that way. I want to keep him for a couple of hours."

"Then I'll hang around."

She hesitated, nibbling distractedly on her full, luscious lower lip. Amazing. Karah Lee Fletcher at a loss for words. It was a memorable moment. Later, when they'd been married for forty years, he'd remind her about how diligently she had fought to avoid matrimony.

*Please, God, let us be together in forty years.*

As he followed her to the exam room he could barely

keep his gaze from flitting to her every few seconds. He felt like a starving man who had gone too long without the hope of food. It only proved to him how accustomed he had grown to the thought of permanence with Karah Lee Fletcher.

He loved her indomitable will, and yet she was very much a woman, complete with a tender, breakable heart. If only she could realize that he did not intend to break that heart. And that fighting didn't mean impending loss. How could he convince her they could work it out?

He watched her as she spoke softly to the patient. Something about the tenor of her voice, however, alerted him. This man was making her nervous. Why?

"Jerrod Houston," she said, "meet Ranger Taylor Jackson. He's also a paramedic, and he helps out here at the clinic when he isn't fighting fires or making rescues." Her light-hearted small talk seemed to fall flat.

Jerrod nodded, his heavy lids drooping with obvious lethargy. Karah Lee most likely had given him a hefty injection of Benadryl. It seemed apparent, however, that even though the man was fighting the grogginess, his attention was focused intently on Karah Lee.

What was up with this guy?

By the time Karah Lee entered the patient's scanty history into the computer, he had begun to snore. She noted his breathing sounded much better.

Taylor continued to hover over her like a protective watchdog, even though it must have been obvious to him that Jerrod wouldn't be a threat to anyone in the near future.

"Mind telling me what it is about him that's bothering you?" he asked.

She entered the final bit of information in the computer. Any other time she wouldn't have hesitated to tell him. "Everything's fine, Taylor."

She could almost feel the faint strum of his irritation. Big, strong Taylor had to be able to fix every situation or he wasn't happy.

"If you don't mind, I'd like to hang around for the next couple of hours," he said.

She nodded. She didn't mind at all. Ever since a hired hit man had nearly killed her and Fawn in this very clinic, Taylor had been very protective of them. It made her feel cared for.

Still, there were doubts. Always, there were doubts. Every man wanted to be a hero, and Taylor was definitely that. But there came a time when the glamour wore off and a man was left with the plain, day-after-day experience of living with a woman. Wives weren't nearly as exciting as helpless damsels in distress. Love always cooled, and often turned to dislike. Then the fighting began. Karah Lee and Taylor had already reached that stage. What hope did they have of a good future?

She knew all about that, because her own parents had fought for years. Dad had, in fact, reminded her of that very thing when she last spoke with him on the phone. Hadn't her own sister proven that even the best of relationships didn't last? Like father, like daughter, Shona was in the painful throes of separation, as well. And that had been a marriage Karah Lee thought would last forever.

"Are you sure you can stay?" she asked. "I mean, you might get called out."

The love in those gray hazel eyes nearly melted her heart. In that strong, freckled face, she saw a man who was ethical, dependable and tender.

"I was off duty ten minutes ago," he said.

"That's perfect." She scooted her chair back and stood. "No need for both of us to hang around, and Fawn needs help with homework. We've already got the blood pressure cuff on his arm and the pulse ox on his finger."

"Can't Fawn bring her homework—"

"Take a reading every fifteen minutes. You know my number, and you know I'm just down the road. Call me if you need me." She left him standing in the middle of the exam room, relieved to get out of the clinic.

## Chapter Three

On Saturday morning, bright sunshine failed to lift Taylor's spirits as he entered Hideaway Clinic. Karah Lee had returned last night in time to make a follow-up appointment with their patient and release him. Then she'd smiled sweetly at Taylor, thanked him for staying and dismissed him, as well.

Just like that. Frustration didn't begin to describe the way Taylor felt, and he wanted to catch her before any patients arrived. They needed to talk. He shouldn't have been so quick to leave last night.

Blaze Farmer sat at the reception desk, frowning at the computer. "Morning," he called, obviously distracted.

Taylor returned the greeting. "Anything wrong?"

The seventeen-year-old high school senior looked up, his ebony face filled with confusion. "I tried to download a medical text onto the computer this morning and it wouldn't allow me on."

"Why not?"

"It said there was an illegal entry, but that's crazy. Either this computer's lying to me, or Karah Lee's been putting in a lot of hours here at night and she messed it up again."

"We had an emergency last night. Karah Lee and I took care of it. Maybe she didn't shut it down properly."

"We don't shut down the computers at night, we put them into hibernation." Blaze shook his head. "This shows Karah Lee's entries from the terminal in exam room two yesterday evening, but did she come back this morning at four o'clock for some reason? Did we have two emergencies in one night?"

Taylor glanced at his watch. "Whose password was entered?"

"Karah Lee's. Jill said she didn't get any calls last night. You were the only other person on call. Karah Lee knows after-hours calls require a support staff backup."

"Were any patient files pulled up?" Taylor asked.

"Nope, but this is weird. Karah Lee's personnel file was accessed." Blaze's eyes widened. "You don't think she's trying to update her info for some reason, do you? You know, to look for another job?"

The suggestion jolted Taylor momentarily. Would Karah Lee be so determined to avoid him that she would look for a position elsewhere? "She's contracted to work here until next June."

Blaze gave an expressive shrug. "Can't contracts be broken? I mean, if Karah Lee just wanted to check out her file, why sneak into the clinic in the middle of the night to do it? I don't know why you two are feuding, but you'd better patch it up fast, or we might lose us a good doctor."

Karah Lee balanced her cup of coffee on top of a bakery box and reached for the front door of the clinic. It came open before she could touch the handle.

Taylor Jackson, looking tired and grim, stood holding the door for her to enter.

"Thanks. You're up and around early this morning." She

took note of the set of his jaw and the look in his eyes. "Is something wrong?"

"That's what we need to find out." He took the items from her hands and carried them to the reception desk, where Blaze manned the computer. Before she could follow and rescue her coffee and a chocolate éclair from the box of pastries—Blaze shared her taste in breakfast food and drink—Taylor had returned to steer her back outside with a gentle hand on her elbow. "We need to talk."

"Why? What's going on? Is everyone okay? Has something—"

"Everyone's fine, don't worry. This is between you and me."

*Oh.* "Taylor, can't it wait? I have patients in twenty minutes, and I haven't had breakfast, and I'm not in the mood for another fight."

"No fighting, I promise, but this is important. You didn't call for backup last night when you should have, and I think that's because of this…friction between us lately."

"I know, I'm sorry. I should have called, but you know how I hate to disturb someone at home when I can handle the situation by myself."

With his hand still warm on her arm, he guided her across the nearly deserted street toward a gazebo that overlooked the lake. Early morning sunlight glittered like diamonds across the surface of the water. "I was on call, and you didn't want to call me. And then when I did show up, you wouldn't even stay in the clinic with me for a couple of hours."

Karah Lee could hear in his voice that her action had hurt him. "I wasn't lying about Fawn's homework. She's trying so hard to catch up and graduate, and she needs me. I can't let her down."

He tilted his head sideways, considering her for a long moment. "That's the only reason you left?"

She turned and strolled toward the water's edge, bypassing a pastel blue and white gazebo—one of several that dotted this broad lawn between the town square and the lakeshore. This was one of her favorite places to come and think about things. Right now, she could barely focus on walking, much less thinking. That was what Taylor did to her.

He caught up with her. "Karah Lee, I'm sorry. I have no right to make any demands on you. We haven't made any promises. I'm not going to force anything."

"I thought you said we wouldn't fight."

"This isn't a fight, it's a discussion. The problem we're having isn't just about us, it's about your father. That man did a number on you. He isn't representative of all men."

"Don't try to tell me again that marriage is all sweetness and light." She reached the water's edge and looked up at him. The morning sunlight glinted highlights across his bronze auburn hair, and etched more deeply the lines of fatigue around his eyes.

"I've never tried to tell you that," he said quietly. "But I know how satisfying and good a real marriage is. I've seen my parents happily married for many decades. We could have that kind of marriage."

She heard the sadness in his voice. His first wife had left him after the death of their only child. Karah Lee knew Taylor would never have been the one to leave. He was a hopeless romantic who believed marriage was forever. He needed to join the real world.

A car pulled into a parking spot in front of the clinic. Soon the patients would start arriving. "I have to get to work," she said gently.

"First will you tell me if you're looking for another job?"

"Why on earth would you ask that?"

"Blaze noticed you returned to the clinic very early this morning and accessed your personnel file."

"I left last night about two minutes after you did, and I never returned until you met me at the door and took my coffee and box of pastries—half of which Blaze has probably eaten, by the way. That kid eats more than everyone else in the clinic combined."

"The computer doesn't lie."

"Well, the computer is wrong this time. Cheyenne would roast me over an open fire if I even tried to look for another job. Besides, I have my own copy of my resume—I don't need to break into the clinic files for that."

"Then we need to check out a few things."

## Chapter Four

Taylor sat at the staff table in the break room facing a dejected teenager and a hungry doctor. Blaze had made a habit every evening before closing to double-check the front and back entrances of the clinic. Ever since fugitive Fawn Morrison had spent the night undetected in the clinic in June, Blaze had grown serious about clinic security.

"I can't believe I could've left a door unlocked," Blaze said.

"Don't be silly." Karah Lee sipped her coffee, which she had rescued just in time from Blaze's hands. "I'm the one who locked up last night after our patient was discharged."

"Did you check the back door?" Blaze sank his teeth into the chocolate éclair Taylor knew Karah Lee had hoped to save for herself. The kid caught her expression and his dark, thick eyebrows rose with a question. He nudged a cruller in her direction.

She picked it up with a grimace. "I had no reason to."

"You made an appointment last night with Jerrod. He's due in at ten?" Taylor asked her. "We may need to ask him a question or two."

"He wasn't in any shape to go snooping last night," she

said. "We can't just go accusing patients of breaking and entering."

Taylor nodded. The man had done nothing while he was here except sleep, and he'd done it loudly enough for Taylor to hear it all the way from here in the staff break room.

"Everybody knows the senator's coming to town Monday to encourage a good vote," Blaze said. "Maybe something's up with that. A few people don't want the hospital here."

"So why check out Karah Lee's file? Few people know Kemper is Karah Lee's father." Taylor understood that Karah Lee desperately needed to separate herself from her father's overbearing shadow. When she came to Hideaway this past summer, she purposely kept her father's name quiet. A state senator could garner a lot of attention, and this particular state senator tended to be outspoken and controversial.

He was a rogue. A popular rogue with the citizens of Missouri at the moment, but one from whom Karah Lee preferred to distance herself. She had deep scars from past history.

"There's no evidence of a break-in," Blaze said. "The doors and windows were locked when I arrived. Unless the intruder had a key, it would be impossible to lock a door or window behind him."

"I'll call the sheriff," Taylor said. "We'll check it out."

The nurse opened the door and stuck her head in. "First patient's ready, Karah Lee."

Karah Lee was taking a rare break with a second cup of coffee at her desk when the nurse, Jill Cooper, slipped through the door and closed it behind her, holding a chart in her hand. "You say the name of your patient last night was Jerrod Houston?"

Karah Lee set her cup down and pushed back from the desk. "Is he here for his appointment?"

Jill placed the chart in front of her. "Young guy, maybe late twenties, early thirties, good-looking, black hair?"

"Yes." Karah Lee felt a renewed spurt of anxiety. "What's wrong?"

Jill leaned closer and lowered her voice. "Did he show you any kind of ID? Insurance card or anything?"

"He was a cash patient."

"I don't think his name's Jerrod Houston."

This can't be happening. The whole thing was getting more and more spooky.

"Why would he lie about his name?" Especially after stalking her for two days?

Jill slid into a chair across from Karah Lee. "Unless my eyes are deceiving me, that guy went to school right here in Hideaway. He was a few grades behind my kid sister. He always followed her around like a puppy dog—like half the boys in school. He was quiet, even morose. He flushed bright red whenever she talked to him."

"If you don't remember his name, why don't you think he's using the right one?" Karah Lee asked.

"Houston is a memorable name. Maybe I'll give Noelle a call when things slow down a little and see if she can tell me anything."

Karah Lee picked up the chart.

"You want me to accompany you?" Jill asked.

Karah Lee hesitated. Yes, she did. What was this man up to? "I'll be fine, Jill. I'm sure there's a logical explanation."

Taylor knelt on the ground outside the back door of the clinic beside Fawn Morrison, checking for footprints, fingerprints, tool marks on the lock or signs of forced entry on one of the windows.

The clinic wasn't the most secure place in town, even after the June debacle. The general consensus had been that no alarm system could have kept that armed hit man from forcing his way into the building. So far, though, there'd been no sign of illegal entry.

"When you spent the night here last summer," Taylor asked Fawn, "you slipped in this door before they locked up that night, right?"

"That's right. Karah Lee's still avoiding you, isn't she?"

"Let's focus on the issue at hand, okay? How did you escape Blaze's notice that night when he locked up?"

"I hid in the hot water closet in the bathroom, but he checks that now." The girl gave Taylor an impudent grin. "Karah Lee doesn't like me talking about you, either."

When Karah Lee agreed to be Fawn's guardian this past summer, she couldn't have realized what she was getting into. Not only had Fawn been a sixteen-year-old runaway from an impossible home life, but she had become a fugitive when she witnessed a murder in Branson. Sick and frightened, she had ended up here at the clinic. If not for Karah Lee, she would be dead now. Karah Lee was the only person Taylor could think of who was headstrong enough to handle this independent child, but they had formed a strong bond.

"She needs more time," he said at last, glancing up toward the second story windows. Could someone have found a place to hide when the clinic was open, then done their snooping after it closed?

The sheriff had fingerprinted all the computer terminals. It could be a while before they had any results.

"She loves you, you know," Fawn said softly. "She's been bummed ever since you broke up."

"I didn't do the breaking up," he muttered.

"She's got issues with marriage. Now she won't even let me go out on a date with this cute guy from church. I mean, she acts as if I'm going to elope or something."

"I'm sure you told her what you thought about that," Taylor said.

"I told her not to take her disappointing love life out on

me. Just because she's too scared to make a commitment doesn't mean—"

"Ouch! Don't you think that's a little rough?"

Fawn grimaced at him. "I don't know why I try so hard for you. If you and Karah Lee get married, that'll make you my foster father. Then it'll be two against one."

"That'll even the odds a little."

She was silent for a few moments, then said, "So you wouldn't mind putting up with me if you marry Karah Lee? You won't make me leave?" She tried to sound casual about the question, but Taylor heard the vulnerability beneath the words, and he saw the carefully averted gaze as she waited for an answer.

Time to be serious. "You know I lost my son, don't you?"

She nodded, looking up at him, her blue eyes narrowed against the sunlight that had edged over the top of the building.

"Well, I would've liked more kids. I have this theory that once you've had children, there's always space in your heart for more. At least that's the way I feel."

She studied his expression for a few seconds, eyes still narrowed. "You're saying I'm a child?"

He grinned. "What I'm saying is that you would always be a welcome part of my family."

Something in her expression relaxed. She leaned forward and kissed him on the cheek. "Thanks, Dad. Now if you'll just convince Mom what a happy family we could be."

He remembered something Karah Lee had said a few weeks ago. When she and Shona were growing up, they never seemed to have a happy family because someone was always fighting. If he and Karah Lee married, would they have a happy family?

# Chapter Five

Jerrod Houston was settled on the exam bed in two when Karah Lee forced an expression of calm assurance on her face and entered with his chart. His lightly tanned face was no longer splotchy. He was a good-looking man, with a strong jawline, high cheekbones and dark gray eyes beneath well-arched, dark brows.

Who was he, really? She should have called Taylor to meet her here last night. The guy could be a serial killer, for all she knew. Killers had found this tiny lakeside town before.

"Sorry about last night," Jerrod said. His voice was full and mellow, no sign of wheezing or hoarseness.

"For being sick?" She set his chart onto the desk, stalling for time, willing her heart to stop its racing. "Don't apologize for keeping us in business. How are you feeling today?"

He shrugged. "It took a loud alarm clock to get me here."

"That isn't unusual. Allergies can do that, and so can some of the medication I gave you last night." She studied his features more closely. Of course, she didn't know the man, but he wasn't making a lot of eye contact this morning. Shy? Or did he have a hidden agenda?

Why had she rejected Jill's offer to accompany her in here? And why was she suddenly so frightened by him?

Despite her fear, he still looked familiar. Was it possible she'd seen him somewhere before?

"I heard an interesting rumor today." She paused and swallowed. Did she really want to get into this? "You know how rumors are in small towns, don't you?"

He blinked, then nodded. His eyes narrowed slightly, and she heard a momentary pause in his breathing.

"You've…lived in a small town before?" she asked.

"Sure have."

*Leave it alone, Karah Lee. Let someone else handle it.* But she had never been one to back away from a confrontation, and she wasn't going to go all skittish now. "This one, maybe?"

He looked up at her. "Does it matter where I grew up, Dr. Fletcher?"

She flinched at the sudden chill in his expression. *Don't show the fear.* "Karah Lee," she said, wondering if he could hear the tremor in her voice. "We're pretty casual around here."

He held her gaze for a tense moment. She was on the verge of leaving the room when he said quietly, "I wouldn't know. We didn't have a clinic in town when I was growing up here. Old Doc Glass had an office upstairs, but I didn't see much of him."

"So you did live here?"

"I don't anymore," he said. "And where I grew up has nothing to do with my allergy attack."

She suddenly remembered his comment last night about unfinished business. What kind of business could he be talking about? Why did she get the impression that it might concern her? The look in his eyes when he looked at her? Or maybe the fact that he seemed to have shown up wherever she was the past couple of days.

"It doesn't matter to me whether or not you grew up here." She tried to keep her voice casual. "But I get curious when someone tells me his name, and I find out later that isn't it." *There you go, Karah Lee Fletcher. Jump in with both feet. Kemper MacDonald isn't the only rogue in this family.*

"I didn't lie to anyone." Impatience sharpened his words. "My name's Jerrod Houston now, okay?"

Every instinct told her to get out of the exam room now and let law enforcement check him out. But her instincts were a little skewed lately. She resented the fear that seemed to attack her at every awkward situation, every off-key word or comment. She refused to allow her fears to shape her life or her actions.

She completed her exam, which revealed no residual complications from last night's emergency.

"I hear the great state senator's coming to town," Jerrod said as she sat down at the terminal to update his online chart.

"That's what they say." She kept her voice casual.

"And I hear you're related to him."

She typed for a moment, made several mistakes, had to go back and correct them. "It's a small town. You're likely to hear all sorts of rumors flying around."

"Would that one be true?" It sounded like an accusation.

She pivoted on her stool. "Don't tell me you're a reporter out for a story on the senator's visit. If that's why you've been popping up wherever I've been the past couple of days—"

"Did I whip out a recorder and interview you last night?"

"No, and you're not going to do it now, either."

"So you are his daughter? And yet, you don't share the same last name. That might make a person curious." There was a touch of sarcasm in his voice as he mimicked her earlier comment.

"But there's a difference," she snapped. "I've never approached you, sought you out or tried to strike up a conversation with you in a restaurant." She completed his chart, logged off and stood to escort him from the room. "You're in good shape. I'll just have to advise you to avoid nuts of any kind until you're tested by an allergist. I don't think a follow-up appointment will be necessary, but I am going to write you a prescription for an epi pen. Call the clinic if you find you're in trouble again."

She left the room, handed the chart to Blaze and went to her office, relieved to be out of the man's presence.

Karah Lee looked frazzled that afternoon when she stepped out of the clinic. She stopped when she saw Taylor standing on the sidewalk, waiting for her, and holding up a peace offering—a chocolate éclair from the bakery. He'd known she couldn't resist.

Her expression revealed the process of her thoughts. At first was the joyful smile that lit her golden amber eyes the way they must have lit at Christmas when she was a kid. Then came the obvious silent reminder, *Oh, yeah, we're not seeing each other anymore.*

"If this is a bribe, it's working," she said, taking the éclair he held out to her.

"Better believe it. Where are you headed?"

"I'm going home to check on Fawn. She still needs a lot of help on a major homework project this weekend."

"I'll walk with you. Anything on Jerrod?"

"Like what?" There was an unusual sharpness in her voice.

"Oh, I don't know, maybe a real name, where he lives, what he's doing back in Hideaway."

Her steps slowed. She frowned up at him. "You sure get around."

"I've asked a few questions here and there. Jill put me in

touch with her kid sister, Noelle, and she told me Jerrod's real name in school was Jerry Clark, so Jerry would be short for Jerrod."

"Any idea why the change of name?"

"Could be the fact that his father, Lester Clark, went to prison for murder when they lived here."

With a swiftly indrawn breath, Karah Lee stopped. "Murder?"

"Now do you understand why I don't like you meeting patients alone at the clinic at night?"

Her face paled. "Taylor, I think this man specifically singled me out. I've seen him too many times in the past couple of days for it to be coincidence. I was just beginning to convince myself he was a reporter out for a story, because he asked about Dad's upcoming trip down here."

Taylor hesitated to tell her the rest—she was already spooked. But the sheriff would need to know what transpired between Karah Lee and Jerrod.

"What is it?" she asked softly. "I know that look. What aren't you telling me?"

He met her gaze. "Tom ran 'Wants and Warrants' on Jerrod and his alias. There were none noted. But he did find one interesting tidbit of information. Jerrod got a permit for a new handgun two weeks ago."

"Oh…" She reached for his arm the way a child would reach for her father, for protection. "Last night I asked what he was doing in town. He said he had some unfinished business. What if Dad had something to do with Jerrod's father's conviction? Or what if Jerrod thinks he does?"

"I don't like this," Taylor said. "I know you don't want to be controlled by your father's actions in any way, but you need protection, at least until Kemper leaves Hideaway."

She frowned, shaking her head. "I don't need a bodyguard, if that's what you're talking about."

"You realize, don't you, that he's probably our best suspect for this morning's hacking, until proven otherwise."

"Tell Tom and Greg to increase the security for Dad when he arrives. The only reason Jerrod would come to me—if he's even doing that—is to get to Dad for some reason."

He walked beside her in silence, knowing she was fighting fear. But would she admit it to him? No. He was afraid for her, and he knew that she knew this. Sometimes they seemed so in tune it felt as if she could tell him what he was thinking before he knew it himself. When they weren't fighting.

Karah Lee wasn't usually the one who picked the fight, he was. He worried so much about her. And it was only getting worse. He didn't have the strength to back off. But if he wanted to keep her in his life, he would have to, wouldn't he?

*Please, Lord, keep her safe. She's in your hands. And please heal this relationship. I believe You meant for us to be together.*

# Chapter Six

It had become a habit for Karah Lee to eat at the Lakeside Bed and Breakfast after the Saturday morning rush at the clinic. Today the buffet held all the scrumptious delicacies for which Bertie's place had become famous. It included traditional breakfast fare, but their specialty was black walnut waffles with strawberry topping, Karah Lee's favorite food in the world.

She was just picking up a plate when someone spoke behind her. "I thought I'd find you here."

She stiffened, feeling a shock of fear run through her. Jerrod stood behind her, studying the food instead of looking at her.

Was he carrying that gun Taylor said he'd purchased? *Keep it calm, Karah Lee.*

"Have you had more allergy symptoms?"

"I'm fine."

"Stay away from the waffles unless you have a death wish." She pushed her tray forward, hoping he would take the hint and leave her alone. She placed two waffles on her plate, then drizzled them with fresh strawberry syrup.

Within seconds, she saw him approach her again from the corner of her eye.

"They didn't have this place when I lived here, but then we never had the money to eat out much when I was growing up."

She picked up her tray and searched for a table. There was only one empty, and she made her way toward it. She had barely settled with her food when she looked up to see Jerrod coming toward her.

"Look, I'm sorry I was rude to you in the clinic," he said. "I'm a little touchy about some things, but you seem to be, too. I can explain."

She hesitated, and though the dining room was crowded, she felt physically vulnerable. Still, if he had something to say to her, better to do it here than when she was alone.

She nodded toward the chair across from her. "Have a seat, then, if you'll promise me you're not a reporter looking for an interview about Kemper." Or something worse.

"I'm no reporter." He settled awkwardly across from her.

"Why don't you tell me what you're really doing in Hideaway?" she asked. "Obviously, your mother felt the need to leave town after your father was convicted of murder."

"You've been talking to your ranger friend?"

"He makes it his business to keep me safe. And while you're explaining, you might tell me about the gun you purchased recently." Amazingly, she lost her appetite after the first bite of waffle.

"My girlfriend got mugged a month ago when she was walking out of the mall at night. I wanted her to have protection. You can have the police go through all my things if you want. I don't carry a gun."

At this point she wasn't ready to believe anything he said. "Fine. Tell me your story."

While Karah Lee sipped coffee and poked at her food, Jerrod quietly told Karah Lee about the tyrant of a man who was given to fits of rage, whom everyone in town hated, and who terrorized Jerrod and his mother. The man went to prison for murder when Jerrod was fifteen.

"Why did your mother stay with him?" Karah Lee asked.

"Why does anyone stay in an abusive relationship? She was more afraid of being on her own with a hard-to-handle kid than she was of him. She divorced him and remarried not long after his sentencing."

"And then?" Karah Lee prompted, aware that this man could tell a convincing story. Was it just that? A story?

"And then I spent some time at a boys ranch across the lake."

The boys ranch was a place where incorrigible kids were sent for breaking the law. How incorrigible had Jerrod been? "Were you there long?"

"Only about six months. I had a pretty bad temper as a teenager."

And how was his temper now? "'Why are you back in Hideaway?"

He met her gaze. "I remember seeing you here all those years ago."

Anxiety tightened a band around her stomach. Karah Lee and her family had loved to vacation here when she was growing up, before her parents divorced.

"Mom pointed you out to me," he said.

"Why would she do that?"

"Because you were Kemper MacDonald's daughter. You and your sister were walking on the square with your father. You had all that curly, bright red hair. Hard to forget that hair." He paused, a long, thoughtful silence. "Your father was famous even then. My mother was an amateur photographer, and she took a lot of pictures. She kept a photographic record of your father's career."

*Time to leave, Karah Lee. This is a case of "Like mother, like son."* "Why would she do something like that?"

"I guess when a woman is married to an abusive man, she's going to look for someone else to admire."

"Don't make my father out to be a hero. He'll let you down, just like your father did."

"Oh, I'm not doing that," he said softly. "You don't remember me, do you?"

*Leave now, Karah Lee. He's unbalanced.* "Is there a reason why I should?"

"I spoke to you one day when you were in town. I think you were about twelve at the time. I was eight. You walked out of the general store, and I had been waiting for about thirty minutes for you to come out. You were with Shona and Kemper, and you smiled at me and said hello. Shona didn't even notice me, and neither did the great Kemper MacDonald."

She couldn't miss the sarcasm, the bitterness in his words, but neither could she miss the sadness of a little boy with a horrible home life, standing out on the street, waiting for someone to notice he existed. "You remember that after all this time?"

"Did you know that a picture is worth a thousand words?" He reached back, as if to pull something from the pocket of his jacket, then his gaze shifted to something behind her, and he stiffened. She turned to see Taylor coming toward them. Her rescuer was at it again, and this time she didn't mind at all.

Taylor was not typically a violent man, but when he found Jerrod seated across the table from Karah Lee, he prepared for battle.

"Hello, Jerrod. Glad I found you here. Could I have a word with you, privately?"

Jerrod blinked up at him, hesitated, then shrugged. "Sure, I guess. Karah Lee, it was good talking to you." He paused, as if wanting to say more, then got up and walked from the dining room with Taylor.

"I've heard some interesting things about you today," Taylor said as they stepped from the Victorian building and across the flagstone steps toward the street.

"So I understand." Was that a trace of defeat in the man's tone? "News travels quickly in this town."

"Lots of old-timers around here," Taylor said. "I know a few things about your past, but not much about your present. For instance, what do you do for a living?"

"I'm a mainframe system designer for a private company in Kansas." Jerrod preceded him across the street.

"Interesting," Taylor said. "Computer system designer. So you must really know your way around computers. I spoke with our deputy sheriff, who also knows a few things. He's been complaining for quite some time that our clinic computer system is so ancient we're susceptible to any good hacker who might want to find information about a patient."

"Hacking into patient files is against the law." Jerrod's steps quickened as he reached the sidewalk that encircled the town square. "I take it there's a point to this conversation."

"I noticed last night that you had a neat little gadget in your shirt pocket. At first I mistook it for an ink pen, but now that I think about it, I've decided that could well have been a tiny video camera."

Jerrod stared.

"In fact, if someone needed a password and user name of a doctor, all he'd have to do is make a doctor come in after hours for an emergency, then possibly use a small video camera to record the doctor's fingers as they strike the keys. Later, since the computer system remains on all night, our hacker can simply use his laptop in the privacy of his own hotel room to break into the system."

"That person would have to be pretty stupid to intentionally eat something he knew could kill him on the off chance he would have the opportunity to do that."

"Maybe. I'm trying to figure out why a complete stranger would want to hack into our clinic computer just to pull up Dr. Fletcher's personnel file."

Jerrod stopped in front of an antique shop on the square—Vintage Treasures—and reached for the door handle. "I'm sorry I can't help you. Maybe you should ask the friendly people of Hideaway a few more questions."

## Chapter Seven

Later that afternoon, Taylor found Karah Lee sitting on her favorite bench on the lakeshore, watching the sun as it slipped past the horizon. A blaze of red and gold rimmed the trees on the far shore and reflected from the surface of the water.

Taylor sank down beside her on the bench. "Security has now been tripled for your father's arrival, and you will also have a bodyguard when your father arrives."

Karah Lee shrugged. "Why am I not surprised? Taylor, I think Jerrod is a second-generation stalker. His mother took pictures of Dad, though I don't know to what extent. Jerrod mentioned photos of our family, and I'm wondering if he was issuing a veiled threat."

"Could his mother have been a blackmailer?"

"Possibly. If so, there's no telling what she could have caught on camera."

"I had a talk with Jerrod," Taylor said. "I think he was the one who looked up your information on the clinic computer. He didn't deny it."

"I think he was just trying to find out if I was really Kemper's daughter," she said. "How I wish I weren't."

Taylor picked up a flat stone and skipped it across the

water, shattering the smooth surface into a cauldron of sparkling color. "Not all men are like Kemper MacDonald."

"Of course they aren't. Some are worse."

He suppressed a sharp retort. "Some are better."

She sighed. "I know that, Taylor. I have no doubts about you."

"I thought both of us had managed to get beyond the bitterness of our pasts."

"It's hard to get over the past when you don't know everything about your past. My father has lied to so many people, pulled so many strings to suit his own desires that I can't help wondering what he's done to attract a blackmailer."

"Why should that affect us? We're still who we are. You know I'm not going to hurt you as your father has. And I know you are stubborn enough to make a marriage work no matter what it takes."

She sat quietly as they watched the sparkles of color smooth and deepen across the lake once more. Then she chuckled softly. "You make marriage sound like a lifelong wrestling match."

He put a hand on her shoulder and gently turned her toward him. "I love you, Karah Lee. I don't want you to forget that. I never thought I'd be as happy as I have been since I met you."

"And I have never in my life been as lonely as I am now when I'm not with you," she said dryly. "I'm not sure that's such a good development."

"It's a great development. It means we need to spend more time together, not less." He gently touched her cheek, and lowered his lips to hers. For just that moment, she gave him hope.

Karah Lee had almost reached her cottage Saturday evening when Jerrod Houston stepped from the shadows like a silent wraith. Then he spoke.

"The man who lived with my mother and me wasn't my father."

She stopped, too startled to feel fear immediately. "Jerrod, what are you—"

"And the reason I remember the day I saw you was because it was the only time my own sister ever voluntarily spoke to me."

Karah Lee's lungs failed her for a brief few seconds. "Your mother told you that?" *This can't be happening. This man needs to be locked up in a psych ward.*

"She never told your father about me," he continued, "but she never wanted me to think I belonged to that jerk she was married to."

"You can't expect me to believe you." She turned from him, suddenly desperate to escape.

He reached for her hand.

She jerked away. "What I think you've been telling me today is that you've stalked me ever since I was twelve, and that your mother stalked my father. Look, I don't know who you really are, or what you're up to, but I want you to stay away from me!"

"Please, just listen to me for a minute."

"Get away!" She scrambled to keep an arm's length between them.

"I'm not going to hurt you, Karah Lee! Please, all I ask is that you look at a couple of pictures. I've tried to find the courage to show them to you sooner, but I couldn't do it. I'm doing it now. If you don't believe me after you've seen them, then I'll never bother you again."

She glanced toward the door of the cottage. She couldn't go in there and possibly lead him to Fawn. "You promise you'll leave me alone?"

"I promise." There was no threat in his expression, only sadness that looked weathered into his face. In his hands he held a billfold, and from it he slid a photo of a beautiful, dark haired woman who appeared to be in her late twenties. "Does this person look familiar to you?"

*It's a trick, Karah Lee. People can do anything to photographs these days.* "That looks like Dad's second wife, Irene. Anyone could have taken this picture."

"Look closer," he said handing her the photo. "That woman's name was Margaret. She was my mother. She died three months ago. She always wanted me to get to know my father and sisters, and I don't have any other relatives on her side. Except for you and Shona and Kemper, I don't have any family. You can't possibly understand how that feels."

"Look, you can't just go claiming family ties because of a resemblance in a picture."

"I've seen a photo of your mother with you when you were little. Our father apparently had very specific tastes." He pulled another snapshot from the billfold and handed it to her, as well. "That's my mother and me when I was ten."

Karah Lee took it, then caught her breath. Despite the gender difference, this could be a photo of Shona as a child, with the dark hair, the dark gray eyes, even the same tilt of the eyebrows. No wonder she'd thought he looked familiar.

"I'm not the son of a murderer," Jerrod said. "I'm the illegitimate son of a philandering politician, which is almost as bad. I dare you to confront our father with that picture."

State Senator Kemper MacDonald was a tall, broad-shouldered lion of a man with a thick mane of auburn hair liberally streaked with silver. He had piercing, golden brown eyes and could usually undermine Karah Lee's confidence with a few well-chosen words.

Early Sunday evening, however, he sat in the executive suite above the Lakeside Bed and Breakfast lodge as he stared at the two photographs on the coffee table in front of him. His typically ruddy complexion paled.

"Where did you get these?" he asked.

"From him." She pointed to the little boy in the picture. "He's four years younger than me."

Kemper looked up at her sharply, his eyes narrowing.

"The worst thing about this is that I can't help wondering how many other people might approach me in the next few years claiming to be a sibling of mine," she said.

Kemper closed his eyes and slumped back in the club chair. "Where is he now?"

"I don't know if he's even still in town."

"Trust me, he didn't come all the way here just to give you a couple of pictures. He's somewhere in Hideaway, and he'll be sure to show up sometime during my speech tomorrow. In fact, I wouldn't be surprised to see his mother here, as well."

"His mother is dead."

Pain flashed briefly across Kemper's expression.

"Did you love her?"

He rubbed his face wearily, sighed, shook his head. "I barely knew the woman."

She could tell he was lying. "You slept with a woman you barely knew?"

He glared at her. "How many others has he told about this?"

"Jerrod didn't say."

"Haven't you learned by now that people come out of the woodwork when they think you have something they want? It would take more than a couple of snapshots to convince me of any paternal responsibility. Those things could be doctored."

"Haven't you seen how much he looked like Shona at that age? The family resemblance is still there, Dad. I can't believe I'm saying this, but I think he's telling the truth."

Kemper stood up and strode into the kitchenette.

Karah Lee followed him. "You haven't denied having an affair with Margaret."

He reached into the cabinet for a couple of mugs. "Coffee?"

"This isn't something you can ignore or dismiss."

He put the mugs down on the counter. "If you hadn't gone into medicine, you would have made a good prosecuting attorney."

"You haven't denied the possibility that Jerrod could be your son."

"No, Your Honor, I have not," Kemper drawled with that Missouri twang for which he was well known. "And if I'm going to keep my reputation, it would behoove me to keep my mouth shut about it."

"So you're telling me your political career is more important to you than your family."

"I didn't say that."

She collected the photographs from the coffee table and left the suite without another word.

## Chapter Eight

Karah Lee stood beside her sister, Shona Tremaine, slightly apart from the crowd Monday morning at the park. It seemed as if all of Hideaway and perhaps half of Branson had congregated to hear their father endorse Hideaway Clinic to be designated in the future as a hospital.

His voice boomed from all the strategically placed speakers, and he looked polished, as usual.

"Did you select his suit for him?" Karah Lee asked Shona under the cover of his words. "And write his speech and arrange for lodging and prompt him on the ride down?"

"Watch it," Shona said, reaching up to tame several strands of black hair that blew in the breeze. "Your claws are showing again."

"Why do you still let him dominate your life the way he does?"

"You should talk. You seldom even see him, but your resentment of him affects everything you do."

"He broke up your marriage," Karah Lee said.

Shona gave a quiet sigh, her dark gaze automatically studying the crowd with all the focus of a secret service agent. "I broke up my marriage. I made the wrong choices. I have only myself to blame."

"Have you seen Geoff lately?"

"Every night on the news channel. He's an anchorman now."

"When is the divorce final?" Karah Lee asked.

Even grimacing, with the sun in her face, Shona was a stunningly attractive woman, whose appearance concealed well her thirty-eight years. "There's been no date set. I'm tired of being reminded about the divorce. I'm not pushing it, and neither is Geoff. Let it rest. If you'd stop blaming Dad and get on with your own life—"

"I'm getting on with it." And it was true. Although Taylor didn't know it, their discussion had stayed with her. She'd sat with him on that same bench so many times, arguing and debating, sharing and praying together. She hadn't realized it so clearly until last night, but they had begun forming a strong bond months ago. A bond...

She found herself automatically searching the crowd for a glimpse of the one person she most wanted to see. "Last summer my relationship with Taylor seemed to kick into high gear when we started praying again, after years of avoiding God. To me it proved that a relationship is strongest when God is a vital part of it."

"Well, there you have it, then." Sarcasm weighted Shona's voice. "We can blame all our family problems on our godless heritage." Though their mother had been a church-going Christian, Kemper only gave lip service to God when he wanted the vote from that sector of the population. "How do you explain all the divorces that take place among Christians these days?"

"Studies show that among couples who pray together daily, only one in a thousand ends in divorce. How often did our family pray together when we were growing up?"

The crowd laughed at something their father said, and Shona was obviously relieved at the chance to change the subject again. "If your relationship kicked into high gear, then what's this problem between you now?"

"How do you know there's a problem? You just got here last night."

"Fawn told me."

"Of course. I don't think the problem between us is as big as it appears," Karah Lee said softly. They had something going for them that she hadn't considered. It was what could give them lasting strength. It was God.

Kemper roused the crowd to still another round of cheering and hearty applause, then waved at the people and stepped down from the bandstand.

Karah Lee finally caught sight of Taylor, and to her shock she saw Jerrod with him. As Kemper continued to wave at the crowd, Taylor and Jerrod approached him.

"Warning," she said to Shona. "Fireworks about to erupt."

Shona nudged her arm. "Come with me and be amazed." She led the way through the dispersing crowd toward their father.

"Are you a glutton for punishment?" Karah Lee exclaimed.

"Dad and I had a talk last night after you showed him those pictures. He's actually eager to meet his son. He wants to take responsibility for what he did."

"That wasn't what he told me."

"You don't have a lot of patience. You left before he even had a chance to think about it." She turned her attention to Jerrod as they approached the men. "So this is our long lost brother," she said, ever in control in even the most awkward of situations as she took Jerrod's hand.

As Kemper MacDonald drew his son aside, Taylor took Karah Lee by the arm. "Could we talk for a few minutes before you go to work?"

She glanced toward her father and hesitated, as if she thought she might have to intervene in a fight.

"They'll be fine," he said.

Finally, she relented and walked with him. "Somehow I get the feeling I've missed out on some interesting action."

"You could say that. To begin with, your brother finally admitted this morning to hacking into your personnel file, though he told me he did *not* intentionally eat nuts to make himself sick. He simply took advantage of the situation. Given his intentions—and the fact that he also offered to program security into the system—I don't think there's a need to press any charges. And as for him and Kemper... well, you were the one who got the ball rolling in the first place. This morning your father called and asked me to find Jerrod and arrange for a meeting after the speech."

"Did he say why?"

"Yes, and my estimation of your father has had to undergo a major overhaul."

"He's ready to admit Jerrod's his son?"

"More than ready. He told me this morning that he was ashamed of many things he's done in his life, but he's not going to apologize for Jerrod's existence. He wants to get to know his son. He had a change of heart, Karah Lee. People can do that, you know."

For a moment she was silent, then she said, "You're right. People can change their minds."

"Even someone as stubborn as a MacDonald."

"You're pushing it."

"Sorry."

Again, she walked a few more steps in silence, head bowed, studying the grass in front of them as if it were the most fascinating thing she had ever seen.

"Taylor," she said at last, "I've fought hard my whole adult life to be independent of my father's money and influence. Because of his interference in the past, I still question how much of my career I've earned on my own terms and how much input he had on my grades and my school rank."

"You are an excellent physician, caring and bright. Your father had little to do with that. He also had no input when I asked you to marry me."

She looked up at him. "Did you know that a bond of three cords is not easily broken?"

He reached for her hand. "Where did that come from?"

"When I was talking to Shona a moment ago, I remembered a verse I chose to memorize when I was a kid because it was short. Or so I thought. I think God had other ideas."

"Our bond would have three cords."

She gazed into his eyes, and he realized something had changed. He no longer saw the telltale sign of wariness in her expression. What he saw was love and trust.

"Does that mean you think we should get married?" she asked softly.

"That's what it means."

"A bond of three cords?" she asked.

He took her into his arms then, not the least bit concerned that half the town was probably paying a great deal of attention. "Exactly."

Her smile lit her whole face. He couldn't resist. He kissed that face, cheek to cheek to forehead to lips.

A bond of three. It was the perfect prescription for happiness.

*The End*

\* \* \* \* \*

*Originally Published for Harlequin.com*

# INSPIRATIONAL

Wholesome romances that touch the heart and soul.

*celebrating*
**15 YEARS**

## HISTORICAL

### COMING NEXT MONTH
### AVAILABLE MARCH 13, 2012

**THE COWBOY COMES HOME**
*Three Brides for Three Cowboys*
**Linda Ford**

**THE BRIDAL SWAP**
*Smoky Mountain Matches*
**Karen Kirst**

**ENGAGING THE EARL**
**Mandy Goff**

**HIGHLAND HEARTS**
**Eva Maria Hamilton**

# REQUEST YOUR FREE BOOKS!

## 2 FREE INSPIRATIONAL NOVELS
## PLUS 2
## FREE
## MYSTERY GIFTS

Love Inspired.
# HISTORICAL
### INSPIRATIONAL HISTORICAL ROMANCE

---

**YES!** Please send me 2 FREE Love Inspired® Historical novels and my 2 FREE
mystery gifts (gifts are worth about $10). After receiving them, if I don't wish to receive
any more books, I can return the shipping statement marked "cancel". If I don't cancel,
I will receive 4 brand-new novels every month and be billed just $4.49 per book in the
U.S. or $4.99 per book in Canada. That's a saving of at least 22% off the cover price. It's
quite a bargain! Shipping and handling is just 50¢ per book in the U.S. and 75¢ per book
in Canada.* I understand that accepting the 2 free books and gifts places me under no
obligation to buy anything. I can always return a shipment and cancel at any time. Even
if I never buy another book, the two free books and gifts are mine to keep forever.

102/302 IDN FEHF

| | |
|---|---|
| Name | (PLEASE PRINT) |
| Address | Apt. # |
| City | State/Prov. | Zip/Postal Code |

Signature (if under 18, a parent or guardian must sign)

### Mail to the **Reader Service:**
**IN U.S.A.:** P.O. Box 1867, Buffalo, NY 14240-1867
**IN CANADA:** P.O. Box 609, Fort Erie, Ontario L2A 5X3
Not valid for current subscribers to Love Inspired Historical books.

### Want to try two free books from another series?
### Call 1-800-873-8635 or visit www.ReaderService.com.

\* Terms and prices subject to change without notice. Prices do not include applicable
taxes. Sales tax applicable in N.Y. Canadian residents will be charged applicable taxes.
Offer not valid in Quebec. This offer is limited to one order per household. All orders
subject to credit approval. Credit or debit balances in a customer's account(s) may be
offset by any other outstanding balance owed by or to the customer. Please allow 4 to 6
weeks for delivery. Offer available while quantities last.

---

**Your Privacy**—The Reader Service is committed to protecting your privacy. Our
Privacy Policy is available online at www.ReaderService.com or upon request from
the Reader Service.

We make a portion of our mailing list available to reputable third parties that offer products
we believe may interest you. If you prefer that we not exchange your name with third
parties, or if you wish to clarify or modify your communication preferences, please visit us
at www.ReaderService.com/consumerchoice or write to us at Reader Service Preference
Service, P.O. Box 9062, Buffalo, NY 14269. Include your complete name and address.

---

LIH11B

*When Cat Barker ran away from the juvenile home
she was raised in, she left her first love, Jake Stone.
Now Cat needs help, and she must turn to
her daughter's secret father.*

*Read on for a sneak peek of*
*LILAC WEDDING IN DRY CREEK*
*by Janet Tronstad.*

"Who's her father?" Jake's voice was low and impatient.

Cat took a quick breath. "I thought you knew. It's you."

"Me?" Jake turned to stare at her fully. She couldn't read his face. He'd gone pale. That much she could see.

She nodded and darted a look over at Lara. "I know she doesn't look like you, but I swear I wasn't with anyone else. Not after we—"

"Of course you weren't with anyone else," Jake said indignantly. "We were so tight there would have been no time to—" He lifted his hand to rub the back of his neck. "At least, I thought we were tight. Until you ran away.

"She's really mine?" he whispered, his voice husky once again.

Cat nodded. "She doesn't know. Although she doesn't take after you—her hair and everything—she's got your way of looking out at the world. I assumed someone on the staff at the youth home must have told you about her—"

His jaw tensed further at that.

"You think I wouldn't have moved heaven and earth to find you if I'd known you'd had my baby?" Jake's eyes flashed. "I tried to trace you. They said you didn't want to be found, so I finally accepted that. But if I'd known I had a daughter, I would have forced them to tell me where you were."

"But you've been sending me money. No letters. Just the money. Why would you do that? I thought it was like child support in your mind. That you wanted to be responsible even if you didn't want to be involved with us."

Jake shook his head. "I didn't know what to say. I thought the money spoke for itself. That you would write when you were ready. And I figured you could use food and things, so…"

"Charity?" she whispered, appalled. She'd never imagined that was what the envelopes of cash were about.

Jake lowered his eyes, but he didn't deny anything.

He had always been the first one to do what was right. But that didn't equal love. She knew that better than anyone, and she didn't want Lara to grow up feeling like she was a burden on someone.

Cat reminded herself that's why she had run away from Jake all those years ago. She'd known back then that he'd marry her for duty, but it wasn't enough.

*Can Jake and Cat put the past behind them for the sake of their daughter?*

*Find out in LILAC WEDDING IN DRY CREEK by Janet Tronstad, available March 2012 from Love Inspired Books.*

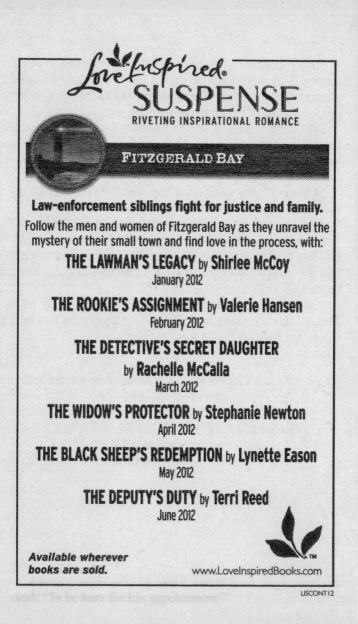

# Love Inspired
## SUSPENSE
### RIVETING INSPIRATIONAL ROMANCE

### FITZGERALD BAY

**Law-enforcement siblings fight for justice and family.**

Follow the men and women of Fitzgerald Bay as they unravel the mystery of their small town and find love in the process, with:

*Available wherever books are sold.*

www.LoveInspiredBooks.com